MURDER
THE TEY WAY

BY

MARILYN LEVINSON

Cover design by Polly Iyer
Formatted by IRONHORSE Formatting

ISBN: 1502413264
ISBN-13: 978-1502413260

For my granddaughter, Olivia Brooke Levinson:
I hope you grow up to love books as much as I do.

CHAPTER ONE

"Who's clever enough to solve a fifteenth century murder by studying a portrait in his hospital bed?" I asked in my most professorial tone.

No one answered, of course, since I was alone in my car.

"Josephine Tey's Inspector Alan Grant of Scotland Yard is who, in her unique and unforgettable novel *The Daughter of Time*."

A damn good opener for tonight's meeting of the Golden Age of Mystery book club, I decided as I exited Mondale University and headed for home. I was in a glorious mood. This morning my "Shakespeare's Comedies" *and* "Chaucer's Tales" students surprised me with their insightful observations, leaving me hopeful that literature, as we academics know it, will continue to thrive, even when read on electronic devices.

I made a quick mental review of the food supply in my refrigerator and pantry, and concluded that I needn't stop for groceries. Home these days was a modest three-bedroom ranch house in Ryesdale, Long Island. I was paying a ridiculously low rent because the house belonged to my boyfriend, Allistair West. I'd lived in a state of transition this past year, ever since my estranged second husband burned down my house and managed to incinerate himself in the process. Al wanted to take our relationship to the next level. I balked at moving in with him just as I'd balked at buying a home of my own.

1

If I were being totally honest, I'd admit the state of transition suited my comfort zone. The few times I'd opted for commitment and permanence had ended badly. Still, as my forty-ninth birthday grew near, some latent nesting instinct kept urging me to settle down.

I joined the flow of light traffic traveling east on Northern State Parkway and exited twenty minutes later. I bypassed downtown Ryesdale, which consisted of three long blocks of shops and restaurants, made a few turns, and followed Magnolia Lane almost to the dead end.

I drew to a stop in front of my neighbor's house. "Hey, Felicity," I called through the passenger's window. "Your decorations are awesome."

Felicity Roberts looked up from her crouched position. She was setting up a festive Halloween scene in her rock garden. She'd already staked in a goblin and a green-faced witch, and had placed three ghosts of white sheeting in the nearby tree. I felt a twinge of guilt for not having put so much as a pumpkin on my top step, though Halloween was a few weeks away.

"Do you think so?" A note of anxiety sounded in Felicity's little-girl's voice, making her seem much younger than her twenty-something years. "Corinne claims I make too much of Halloween. She says I'm not a kid anymore.

"But the children love my Halloween decorations," she said earnestly, as if I'd sided with her older sister. "Besides, Halloween's my favorite holiday after Christmas." She grinned. "I can't wait to dress up in my vampire costume and put in my fangs when the kids come by for Trick or Treat."

"Sounds like fun," I told her, though inwardly I wondered, and not for the first time, if Felicity was all there. She held down a part-time job at a local children's clothing store and shared the large, rambling house with her older sister, a practical, no-nonsense sort of person and vice president of a bank in a neighboring town. Both sisters belonged to the mystery book club.

"Bye. See you tonight," I called out.

It was a good thing I hadn't driven on, because Felicity chose that moment to run toward the car and lean into the open passenger window.

"Do you think every murderer leaves evidence behind?" she whispered, though no one was around to hear us.

I smiled at her earnestness and couldn't resist. In a low, conspiratorial tone, I asked. "Did you kill someone, and you're worried the police will catch you?"

"Of course not!" Felicity's blush covered her ears and her neck, making me regret having teased her.

"I finished reading *The Daughter of Time* last night, and it got me thinking," she explained, giving her little-girl laugh. "I know I'm being silly and it's only a novel, but if Inspector Grant could prove Richard the Third didn't kill his nephews five hundred years after the fact, then it seems to me any murder can be solved."

I cleared my throat and felt my professorial persona take over. "I believe everything we do leaves a trail of crumbs, so to speak, especially murder and other criminal actions. Tey didn't come up with the theory that Richard was innocent, though her novel certainly popularized it." I smiled. "I'm glad you find the subject intriguing. We'll talk about it at our meeting tonight."

Felicity hunched her shoulders. A tremor ran down her skinny frame as she stared down at the ground. "Lexie, don't be angry, but I can't make the meeting. Something's come up."

"Oh," I said, embarrassed because she was such an awful liar. "That's okay, Felicity. This isn't school. You can miss a meeting if you like."

"But Corinne's coming," she added quickly. "I know she's looking forward to seeing everyone tonight."

"Great."

I waited until Felicity returned to her Halloween decorations, then turned into my driveway. Puss, my friend Sylvia's Russian Blue tom I'd adopted after she died, greeted me with a plaintive meow meant to inspire guilt. I fed the nagging feline, then made myself a sandwich for lunch. In the spare bedroom I'd set up as my office, I flipped through my notes for this evening's presentation and realized I didn't need them. *The Daughter of Time* was one of my all-time favorite mysteries.

For once I had no papers to grade or administrative paperwork to complete for my anal department head. I was free to devote the next few hours to my Work in Progress.

I'd started writing a woman's literary novel some years ago. This past summer I deleted all 220 pages and began a mystery. But facilitating a mystery book club, even having hands-on experience solving real-life murders, hadn't improved my fiction-writing skills. I'd been stuck on chapter three since August. Still, I refused to give up! I was intelligent! I had a PhD! If all those writers out there could complete a manuscript and get it published, then I could too!

I turned on my laptop. Minutes passed while I stared at the first page of Chapter One. I changed a few words then changed them back again. The phone rang. It was Al.

"Hi, Lexie. I'm off to the airport. My limo should be here within the hour."

"I told you I'd be happy to drive you."

"It's better this way. You might run into heavy traffic coming home from Kennedy. And you have a meeting tonight."

Thoughtful Al. One of the reasons I liked him so much.

He paused. "I know it's premature—and we needn't act on it as soon as I'm home again—but I'd like you to think about our moving in together."

I swallowed. "I'll think about it, Al."

I heard the smile in his voice, when he said, "I know we'll be happy, Lexie."

His use of the future tense instead of the conditional sent a *frisson* of anxiety along every nerve in my body. I cared about Al, but after two failed marriages I was far from certain I wanted to share quarters with him or any male, for that matter.

A doorbell rang at his end, sparing me further discussion along these lines. "Time to go," he told me a minute later. "The limo driver's taken my luggage. Why do they always arrive so early?"

Now someone was ringing my doorbell. I suddenly wished Al hadn't taken on the architectural project that would keep him in England for the next two months. "I'm going to miss you," I admitted.

"Me, too, but we'll talk on Skype. We'll text and exchange emails. I'll be home before you know it."

I sent him a kiss and put down the phone. The doorbell rang more insistently. I flung open the door to find my friend, Joy—

former FBI agent and current soccer mom—jogging in place. Though the weather was cool for mid-September, Joy wore racing shorts and a sleeveless polo as though it were still July. She slipped into the house, panting and sweaty.

"What's up?" I asked. "Want a cup of coffee?"

She shook her head as she led me into the kitchen, where she continued to jog in place. "I have five minutes. Mrs. Horton leaves at two sharp. She'll give me hell if I'm home one minute late."

I burst out laughing. "A tough gal like you afraid of a little old lady?"

"You're damn straight I'm afraid—terrified she'll stop sitting for us and take up with a punctual on-time mommy. My two older kids consider her their third grandmother. Brandon stops crying when he hears her voice."

"Al just called to say good-bye. He's on his way to Kennedy."

Joy grinned. "You still have that sexy homicide detective to fool around with."

A quiver of excitement tinged with guilt shot through me.

"I've seen Brian Donovan exactly three times since I moved here—if you count the night he got called away before we even touched our main course. I don't consider him relationship material."

"Says who? Cops make damn good spouses when they set their minds to it."

I smiled, picturing her teddy-bear of a husband carrying their six-year-old on his shoulders. "Except your Mike went into security work so he could keep normal hours."

Joy nodded. "'Family first' is Mike's motto. Did you hear? There was another break in last night."

"No? What happened?"

"A couple who lives on Thornton, three blocks away, came home to find their home burgled. She kept all her jewelry in a wall safe. Everything was taken. Mike's former partner said it looks like an inside job."

I bit my lip. "It almost makes me glad I have nothing to steal."

"On a lighter note, do you have everything you need for the

5

meeting?"

"I think so."

"Including gluten-free cookies for Marge Billings?"

I pressed my hand to my cheek. "I forgot Marge has celiac disease! I'll run out to Stop & Shop. They carry the cookies she likes."

"Don't bother. I'll whip up a batch. Two batches, in fact, and keep one for us. Ruthie's supply of gluten-free desserts is running low."

I laughed as I saw Joy out. The quintessential homemaker. Who would ever guess that Joy had been a much decorated FBI agent before setting down to have her third offspring?

I sat down to reread Chapter One of my manuscript. I promised myself I'd read for content, but the editor in me took over. I wasn't happy with a phrase in the first sentence, then I decided the entire sentence had to go. I changed more phrases and deleted another sentence. I'd reached page two, when the phone rang.

"Lexie?" The voice was almost a whisper.

"Gayle! I'm glad you called," I told my baby sister, embarrassed because we hadn't spoken in months. "I was never sure you received the card I sent with my new address and phone number."

"I did. Lexie...."

She paused so long, I was about to ask what was wrong when her words spilled out in a torrent. "Can I come stay with you for a while?"

"Of course," I said automatically, though my stomach twitched with anxiety. "What's wrong? You sound upset."

"I'm in Ohio. I should get to you some time after nine."

"You're driving here?"

"Uh huh. I left Utah two days ago."

And you're first calling me now? My typical go-with-the-flow sister. I swallowed back my annoyance and asked, "Do you know how to get to my house?"

"I plotted it out on Map Quest. Lexie, don't tell anyone I'm coming."

A chill ran down my body. "Who would I tell?"

"I mean, *anyone.* Promise me, Lexie."

"I promise, Gayle, but why would anyone call me about you?"

Instead of answering, she disconnected. When I called back, there was no response, not even a robotic voice instructing me to leave a message.

I drove to the supermarket and bought what I remembered were Gayle's favorite foods: bagels and cream cheese, tuna fish salad, stuffed grape leaves and chocolate-covered nuts. How she used to devour chocolate-covered nuts! And all the while I mulled over what was driving her from the home she loved so much—a four-room cabin her friends had helped her build seven years ago in rural Utah.

Gayle was forty-two, six years younger than me, and would have been at home among the Flower Children of the Sixties. She'd left college in her freshman year to wander around Europe on God knows what money. She'd ended up living in an ashram in India. When she returned to the U.S., she moved to California then to Utah, living a communal life with friends until she built her own home. She made jewelry with semi-precious stones, and these last few years had gotten into pottery. She'd had various lovers over the years, but no one she'd stayed with for more than two years. She was my sister, but we'd seen each other half a dozen times in the past twenty-five years.

Home again, I put away the groceries and tried to call Gayle. No answer. I told myself there was no use fretting. I'd find out what was happening when she arrived tonight sometime during my meeting. The thought left me even more unsettled. I returned to my manuscript and spent the rest of the afternoon tweaking Chapter One.

It was nearly five o'clock when I closed my laptop, forced to admit that I didn't much like my sleuth. She was too cerebral, too hesitant to act. I sighed. Maybe tackling a novel was too big a job to start with. Maybe I should write short stories instead, at least until I my writing skills improved.

I made a cheese omelet for dinner, then dragged three dining room chairs into the living room and placed them between the sofa and two armchairs, forming a circle around the rectangular cocktail table. We'd be seven without Felicity, a small but lively group of people more than willing to voice their opinions.

I turned on lamps and set out the snacks. Now the room looked almost homey. Al and his wife had bought the house fifteen years ago, and he'd been renting it out ever since. Except for the two paintings I'd hung on the wall, the living room was devoid of character. I decided not to pull the curtains on the picture window looking out on the cement patio. No one could see us, since tall hedges separated the backyard from my neighbors behind me.

The doorbell rang at a quarter to eight. Marge and Evan, was my educated guess, and I was right. Retired dairy farmers in their mid-seventies, both were large in every sense of the word, with generous smiles and curly gray hair. They looked more like brother and sister than husband and wife.

After each had hugged me, Evan claimed one of the armchairs. Marge handed me a plate of cookies. "Gluten-free."

"Wonderful," I said. "Joy's baking another batch for you."

Marge chuckled. "How sweet. Our own Martha Stewart." She followed me into the kitchen and was spooning decaf coffee into the coffee maker a minute later.

The bell rang again, and Evan went to the door. I heard Timothy Draigon's booming bass alternating with Sadie Lu's sweet contralto as they came into the kitchen to find me. We exchanged greetings and hugs. I was fond of both Tim, a tall, jocular lawyer in his mid-forties, and Sadie, a high school guidance counselor ten years his junior. Both were divorced. They drove to book club meetings together. I couldn't decide if they were a couple or not.

Joy arrived, her face flushed and frowning. "A slight emergency," she whispered, shoving a tin of cookies at me.

"Relax! What happened?'

She pressed her lips together. "Nothing I won't get to the bottom of ASAP."

"That explains it very clearly," I tossed over my shoulder as I placed the cookies on a plate and checked on the coffee. When I joined the others in the living room, Evan was exclaiming,

"We got hit last month in broad daylight while we were at the supermarket. The no-good SOB took off with all of Marge's jewelry—her good pieces as well as her costume jewelry."

"How did he get in?" Sadie asked.

"We don't know," Marge said. "None of the locks were forced."

Tim grimaced. "No sign of a forced entry when I was burgled in the spring, also in the middle of the day. He took my stamp collection, which was worth several thousand bucks. At least my gold coins remained secure in the safe."

"It sounds like the thief had access to your homes and knew what to go after," Joy said.

Tim stared at her. "What are you implying?"

"I'm not implying anything," Joy responded in a cold tone I'd never heard her use before. "I was wondering what strangers had been inside your homes."

"We don't have a cleaning woman," Marge said. "And Evan and I never leave workmen alone in the house."

Tim thought a bit. "I have. On occasion."

"I've heard of other burglaries in the neighborhood," Marge said, her eyes wide with anxiety. "We moved to Ryesdale because it was voted one of the most peaceful towns in America." She turned to her husband. "Maybe we should have stayed in Wisconsin, like my sister begged us to."

Evan patted her hand. "Don't you worry, honey. It's only a matter of time before they find the guy and throw him in jail."

Sadie and I exchanged glances. Finding the thief was one thing, keeping him behind bars was another.

Five minutes later I opened the door to Corinne and a sad-looking Felicity. Corinne, slim and angular, her black hair cropped short, was still dressed in her banker's suit and low-heeled pumps. She tossed out a general greeting as she entered the living room. Felicity sent me an apologetic look.

"I decided to come, after all," she said meekly.

I patted her arm. "I'm glad."

The Roberts sisters headed for the two remaining dining room chairs. Tim offered to move so they could sit next to one another, but Corinne shook her head, her lips pressed in a tight seam. Was she angry at Felicity or simply in a bad mood? Probably the latter, I decided. Corinne wasn't a warm and fuzzy person, but she was always solicitous toward her younger sister, whom she treated more like a daughter than a sibling.

And what was bugging Joy? Hours earlier she'd been her

usual bouncy self.

I cleared my throat and began my spiel. "Josephine Tey is the pseudonym Elizabeth Mackintosh used when writing five of her mysteries. She was born in Inverness, Scotland, in 1896. She trained as a phys ed teacher, and taught for some years before returning home to care for her ailing widowed father. She was a private sort of person, and we know little about her personal life. Using the name Gordon Daviot, Mackintosh wrote several plays. Her biggest success was 'Richard of Bordeaux,' whose leading actor was none other than John Gielgud."

"How fascinating!" Marge exclaimed. "It seems famous people are always crossing paths with one another."

Sure they do, I thought cynically, but her husband and Tim nodded. The four young women wore blank expressions.

I grinned at Joy. "You do know who John Gielgud is, don't you?"

She shrugged. "Sure. He played the butler in the old version of 'Arthur.'"

Tim laughed. "Gielgud was one of the most famous British actors of the last century, on screen and in the theatre."

Felicity glanced at her sister, sitting still as a statue, then looked down at her feet. Were those tears I saw in her eyes, or merely a reflection from the light? I wondered what Felicity had been planning to do tonight before Corinne badgered her to come to the meeting.

"Lexie?" Evan touched my arm, and I nearly jumped out of my seat.

"Sorry," I mumbled. I'd mull over my neighbors' moods on my own time. After all, I *was* getting paid to facilitate these meetings. I cleared my throat.

"With only a handful of mysteries to her credit, Josephine Tey has a fixed place among the more prolific Golden Age of Mystery authors. She was fascinated by psychology, and was of the opinion that facial characteristics reveal a person's character. She also took great interest in history, and believed many so-called historical facts are no more than legends passed along from generation to generation."

"Like Oliver Stone movies," Tim murmured.

I grinned at him. "Exactly. Tey's interest in facial expressions and historical accuracy play important roles in her novel, *The Daughter of Time*. From his hospital bed, Inspector Alan Grant gathers solid historical facts to prove that Richard the Third never murdered his young nephews as most people claim he did."

"I found it a most unusual type of mystery novel," Marge commented.

"I couldn't put it down," her husband said.

Tim and Sadie nodded in agreement. But Joy and the Roberts sisters remained lost in their own thoughts. Gloomy ones, judging by their frowns.

Suddenly, Joy bolted from her seat. She ran to the picture window and stared out into the night. "Did you see that?"

"See what?" Evan asked.

"The face in the window! Someone's out there."

"How can you see anything?" Sadie asked. "It's dark outside and we've lights on."

Joy didn't bother to answer as she unlocked the door to the patio and bounded out into the night. The rest of us gathered at the window, but could see nothing. For a moment, no one spoke. Then the murmuring began.

"She seemed edgy when she came in," Sadie said kindly, in what was probably her Guidance Counselor voice. "No doubt the new baby's exhausting her."

"I doubt it," Marge said. "Brandon's almost a year old now and sleeping through the night."

Corinne turned from the window to frown at us. "I can't make anything out, but Joy must have. She was an agent, for God's sake! She's been trained to notice things we don't."

"Oh, no!" Felicity exclaimed.

We stared at her. She'd turned pale. Her shoulders heaved with emotion.

"May-maybe it's that thief who's been breaking into houses," she said. "Maybe he's planning to rob you next, Lexie."

Corinne put her arm around Felicity and stroked her hair. In a gentle voice I'd never heard her use before, she said, "Don't be frightened, sweetie. Joy was an FBI agent. She'll protect us."

Minutes later Joy returned, gasping for breath. "I chased the guy across three lawns and lost him."

The doorbell rang, startling us all. I went to answer it.

"Check the peephole first," Tim advised.

I did, then swung the door open to admit my sister.

I was shocked by the lines in Gayle's face that hadn't been there the last time I saw her at some relative's wedding. Her long brown hair hung limp and unkempt. I reminded myself she'd been driving the better part of two days.

"Hello, Lexie."

She sank into my arms. I hugged her tight. She felt brittle. Fragile.

"You must be starving, "I told her.

"I ate on the way." She reached down to grab the duffle bag at her feet. "I'm thoroughly exhausted. Do you think I could just rest, maybe go to sleep?"

"Of course."

"Oh!" Gayle exclaimed, sounding more anguished than surprised at the sight of seven people staring at her.

"We were holding a meeting of our mystery book club," I explained.

She cupped her hand to my ear and whispered, "You never told me all these people would be here."

I swallowed back my exasperation. Gayle was sweet-tempered, but under pressure she had a tendency to blame others for imagined faults.

"I never had the chance to," I pointed out as Joy approached, some of her good cheer back in place.

"Hello, Gayle! I'm delighted to meet Lexie's sister. I'm Joy Lincoln."

Gayle stared at the outstretched hand, then shook it. "Hi." She managed to work up a half smile.

The others took this as a signal to get into the act and introduce themselves. I worried their attention would agitate Gayle further, but their friendliness calmed her.

"I'm sorry to have disturbed your meeting," she said, then turned to me. "Can I go to sleep now?"

"Of course." I started for the bedrooms, when Marge said, "You didn't disturb our meeting in the least. Joy caught someone spying on us. She chased him across several backyards."

"And lost him," Joy added, shaking her head in disgust.

Gayle bit her lip. "I almost hit him when he ran into the street—if it's the same guy."

"Five-eleven? One hundred and eighty pounds?" Joy reeled off. "Wearing a black woolen hat?"

Gayle nodded.

"We should call the police," Evan said.

"Why bother?" Tim asked. "There's nothing they can do. Or will do."

"They should have it on record that an intruder trespassed in Lexie's backyard."

"Yes," Marge agreed.

"I'm going home!" Felicity sounded on the verge of tears.

I glanced around the room. No one was in the proper state of mind to talk about books. I decided to call it a night.

"I'm sorry for the way things turned out. You're welcome to come back here Saturday morning. We'll finish our discussion of *The Daughter of Time* and talk about *Brat Farrar*. Does that suit everyone?"

The book club members all nodded.

"Wonderful!" I exhaled a breath of relief. I wasn't sure how I'd have resolved matters if one of them couldn't make it. "And meanwhile, I've plenty of refreshments. You're welcome to stay and have coffee and cake."

Only the Billingses, Tim, and Sadie took up my offer. I saw the others out, and told Joy we'd talk tomorrow.

"Good, because I need to run something by you."

"Okay." I paused then said, "I wonder what that peeping Tom was after."

"I don't know," she said, giving me a peck on the cheek, "but something tells me we haven't seen the last of that guy."

13

CHAPTER TWO

"Lexie, wake up!"

I burrowed under my quilt to escape from the maddening person in my dream.

The maddening person shook my shoulder hard. "You have to get up!"

I blinked my way into consciousness. In the dim light, I saw Gayle hovering over me, her eyes wide with fear.

"What's wrong?"

"There's a man in your backyard!"

I sighed as I slipped out of bed and into the early morning chill. Seven o'clock, my clock said. My alarm was set to go off in an hour since I didn't have to be at the university till eleven, but I had to calm my sister before she had an all-out heart attack. I didn't want a strange man in my backyard, especially with that peeper from last night. But neither was I especially worried. Ryesdale residents often gave themselves permission to cross their neighbors' yards. Joy, who lived two houses from me in the opposite direction of the Roberts sisters, did it often enough when she stopped by for a visit. And I had faith in the alarm system Al had installed when I'd moved in.

I peered out the window. "He's gone."

Gayle pointed to the extreme left. "He's lying face down on the lawn. Just beyond the patio."

"Oh!"

She gripped my arm so tightly, I knew there'd be marks. "Do you think he's dead?"

Now I was worried. "I've no idea."

I raced into the kitchen, my sister behind me close as a shadow. I peered out the picture window. The man lay face down on the lawn. He hadn't moved.

I spun around to stare at Gayle. "How did you know he was out there?"

She stared down at the floor. "I woke up hungry, so I made tea and toast. He was there when I looked outside the kitchen window."

"What time was this?"

Gayle shrugged. "I'm not sure. Only minutes before I woke you up."

I opened the kitchen door and stepped into the cold, damp air. I crossed the cement patio to kneel beside him. My heart hammered so loud, I was sure Gayle, who had followed me outside, could hear it. I placed my fingers on his neck. No pulse. He was dead, all right, though I saw no head wound or bullet holes in his windbreaker jacket. Whoever had killed him had done it face-to-face.

Peering closer, I saw blood had trickled from under the torso and onto the ground. A black cap lay a few feet away. I started to hyperventilate. This was the man Joy had chased last night! There was something familiar about him and his cap, but no name came to mind.

Who had killed him?

Why was he here?

I rose unsteadily to my feet and stumbled backward into Gayle.

"Is he dead?" she asked, helping me regain my footing.

"Yes."

I stood there panting, too shaken to walk. Finally, I crossed the patio on rubbery legs. When I got to the door, I realized Gayle was still beside the body. I turned in time to see her reach out as if she meant to turn him over.

"Don't touch him!" I shouted.

For a minute I thought she was going to ignore my order, then she followed me inside.

I lifted the phone to dial 911. Gayle grabbed my hand. "Don't call anyone!"

"I have to call the police." When she refused to relinquish her hold, I stepped back. Suddenly, I was afraid of my baby sister.

Gayle's face crumpled. "Don't look at me like that. I didn't kill that man. I don't even know who he is."

"Then why don't you want me to call the police?"

"Call them after I'm gone," she shouted over her shoulder as she ran to the front door.

I chased after her. "Where are you going? A man was murdered. The cops will want to take your statement."

Gayle burst into tears. "I can't talk to the police. I can't!"

She allowed me to lead her back into the kitchen, where I sat her down on a chair and brought her a glass of water. She gulped it down, then started crying harder. Something was terribly wrong, something to do with the dead man outside.

"What's going on? Why did you drive across the country as if the devil were chasing you?"

Her sobbing grew louder. She gasped for breath, then started to cough.

I wrapped my arms around her. "Sweetie, what is it? You're here, safe inside my house."

"That man out there. He...he..." She was hiccupping so badly, she couldn't finish her sentence.

I swallowed the fear rising in my throat. "You recognized him?"

"I don't think so. But he followed me here. He must have!" She covered her face in her hands.

"From Utah?"

A banshee wail filled the room. "Of course! That's where it began."

I handed her a fistful of tissues.

"Gayle, you came here so I could help you, because it's safe."

"But it isn't safe. That man—"

"That man, whoever he is, didn't hurt you."

She whimpered, making small mewling sounds. "Shawn will send someone else. I know he will."

"Who's Shawn?" I rubbed her back in small circles the way she liked when she was little. Her muscles felt as taut as the strings on a tennis racket.

"Shawn Estes. He's a cop." Gayle raised her tear-stained face to me. "That's why you can't tell them I'm here. He'll find out. He'll—"

"Sshh. Everything will be all right," I crooned, though I hadn't the foggiest idea what she was talking about. What was important right now was calming her down so she could tell me what she was running from.

"Do you know Shawn well?"

She shook her head. "He was Chet's friend." She snorted. "Some friend he turned out to be!"

I paused, then asked, "You want to tell me what happened?"

Gayle inhaled deeply. Her body was still rigid, but she was beginning to relax.

"When I started making jewelry, I often bought supplies in Chet's store. He was always helpful and made useful suggestions. When we ran into each other at the local bar or the coffee shop, we'd chat. About nothing specific, but I always felt good after a talk with Chet."

She gave a little smile. "He finally asked me out. A month later, we were spending nights at each other's place. We were falling in love, Lexie."

"Chet sounds like a really good guy," I said.

"He was. And now he's dead." Gayle's eyes darted up at the clock. She shot to her feet. "I have to go."

"How did he die?" I asked softly.

She sat down and sank into herself. "Shawn killed him."

"Oh."

"I heard them arguing." She looked directly at me for the first time since she'd awakened me half an hour ago. "It was about six-thirty Monday night. I was outside Chet's house, my arms full of groceries because I was going to make us a nice steak dinner. Chet said he wasn't going to do something any longer, and Shawn said yes, he was, if he knew what was good for him. I think they were talking about their poker games, but I'm not sure. I think—" she hesitated, "there was something fishy about those games."

"Why do you say that?"

Gayle bit her lip. "The games were never regular, like every

Friday night, and they held them in different places. Never the same place or in someone's house. And Chet was different just before a game. Excitable. Like someone had given him a shot of something."

"Do you think they were scamming marks, and Chet wanted to stop?"

Gayle nodded. "That's exactly what I think." She grimaced as she remembered. "I put my ear to the door, but nothing was happening. I went around the side of the house to peer in through a window, when Chet cried out in pain. I wanted to run inside and take care of him, but I was afraid to. If Shawn had hurt him, then he'd hurt me, too."

"You did the right thing," I murmured.

My sister's breath grew ragged. "Finally, Shawn raced out of the house. I stayed out of sight until he drove off on his truck, then hurried inside. Chet lay crumpled on the floor. His hand covered his stomach where blood had poured from. But he wasn't moving. His eyes were wide open. He looked terrified."

"As you must have been."

"He was dead, Lexie! I dropped the bag of food and ran back to my car. I stopped by my house to pack a bag, grab my charge cards, and started driving east. I must have driven seventy, eighty miles when my cellphone rang. It was Shawn." She swallowed.

"He knew you'd been to Chet's because he saw the bag of groceries," I said.

"Probably." Gayle let out a laugh that was anything but funny. "By then he'd been called to investigate Chet's homicide in his 'official capacity.' He said I should come back to town, that I'd be treated well. He'd help me hire the best lawyer. For a minute I didn't know what he was talking about. Then I realized he was speaking as though *I* was murder suspect number one. I forgot to be afraid and did the stupidest thing."

She pressed her lips together. "I told him I knew he'd killed Chet. Shawn laughed. He said since I wasn't coming back on my own volition, he'd be sending out someone to take care of me."

"So naturally you thought Shawn sent the dead man after you."

Gayle nodded. "To kill me."

My baby sister was terrified. I had to protect her.

"Gayle, we'll go to the police! They have safe houses. And we'll hire the best defense lawyer."

Gayle gripped my arms and shook me. "You can't protect me, Lexie. No one can! Not from the likes of Shawn Estes."

This time I made no attempt to stop her from leaving the kitchen. My first impulse was to call Brian to ask for his help. The trouble was the murder had been committed in Utah where Shawn was a police officer. He had jurisdiction there. He could have Gayle sent back to Utah where he'd kill her to keep her quiet. She was right. I wanted to help, but could offer no protection.

I went to the closet in my office where I'd installed a tiny safe. I removed the five hundred dollars I kept there for emergencies and shoved it in a number ten envelope. Gayle was already in the hall, her duffle bag in hand.

"Take this." I handed her the money. "It's all I have, but if you wait, I'll run to the bank and get more."

Gayle peered into the envelope. "Thanks, Lexie. This will be fine."

"You mustn't use your credit card."

"I won't. I had cash in the house. I'll be okay."

She threw her arms around me. We held each other in a fierce grip. Finally, I let her go.

"Do you know where you're headed?"

"Maybe. But I'm not telling you."

I gave her a bittersweet smile. "In case someone asks me. Like the cops."

"Right. When you call to tell them about him," she gestured with her head toward the backyard, "please leave me out of it, if you can."

I nodded. "Of course."

"I'll call you soon," she told me without my having to ask.

"Don't use your cell phone."

"Of course not. Soon as I leave here, I'm destroying it and buying a disposable phone."

I watched her drive off, then called the police.

They arrived in a matter of minutes—one unmarked car and two squad cars. My heart thumped as I watched Detective Brian

Donovan step out of the unmarked car. I was happy to see him and worried at the same time. Conflicting thoughts and emotions sparred inside me. *Keep Gayle out of it*, was my mantra for the day. Then there was the matter of the dead man lying in my backyard, whoever he was.

"Hello, Lexie."

I nodded, too flustered to meet Brian's pale blue eyes. Sexy eyes. Sexy body. Lust streaked with guilt because I found him hotter than Al. Al, who wanted a permanent relationship, while Brian wanted...

I hadn't the foggiest idea what Brian wanted.

"Lexie?"

I jumped when he touched my arm.

"Sorry. "

"When did you notice the body in your backyard?"

"Shortly after I woke up, around seven-thirty." *A small lie*, I told myself.

"Did you go outside?"

"Yes."

"Touch the body?"

I nodded. "I felt his carotid artery. No pulse."

The men followed Brian through the kitchen door and across the patio. They moved like robots, I decided, stifling a giggle. *Bad Lexie!* I scolded myself, then realized my nerves were stretched as far as they could go. I turned on the faucet and put up a large pot of coffee.

A few minutes later, Brian returned to the kitchen. He sat down at the table and pulled out his notepad.

"Know who he is?"

"I couldn't see his face, but he doesn't look like anyone I know." I handed him a mug of coffee and poured one for myself.

Brian added two spoons of sugar and stirred. We sipped in silence. Then he asked, "Are you sure you don't recognize him?"

I heard a roaring in my ears. I ignored the warning and took the bull by the horns. "You mean because he's lying dead in my backyard?"

"For starters."

I shrugged. "I wonder if he's the same guy who was out there last night, spying on our book club meeting."

Brian looked up from his notepad and grinned. "So you're still leading mystery book clubs."

"Yes. A member saw his face in the window and chased after him."

He raised his eyebrows. "You're kidding. Someone took off after him in the dark?"

"That's right. Joy Lincoln's in top shape. She's a former FBI agent."

Brian did a lousy job of masking his surprise, which gave me a stab of pleasure.

"She chased him across several backyards and described him to us afterward." In time, I stopped myself from adding that my sister's car had almost struck him.

"So you're telling me this guy was playing peeping Tom here last night. Someone saw him and ran him off. He came back hours later and got himself killed. What was he after?"

Brian was doing a good job of scaring me. Maybe the dead man *was* after me. Or planning to kill my sister.

"I don't know what he was after!" It came out stronger than I'd meant it to.

Brian frowned. "Since you live here, it makes sense that he wanted something from you."

"Maybe he's the one burgling houses around here."

Brian nodded. "Maybe he is and maybe he isn't. You're hiding something, Lexie. I'm disappointed. You know you can talk to me."

My face grew warm. I wanted to tell him everything Gayle had told me, but it wasn't my story. "Believe me, Brian, I don't know that man's name. Maybe he wanted to see one of the book club members. Or…"

"Or?" Brian pounced on my hesitation.

"Or nothing."

A uniformed officer came to the door. He conferred with Brian in whispers.

"I'll be back," Brian said. "Please write down the name and address of everyone who was here last night."

Everyone? "Of course," I said and reached for a pen and pad.

Outside, yellow tape blocked off the area of the backyard where the body still lay—as though anyone would want to go there! Well, maybe some curious kids would, once word got out. I straightened up the kitchen and left the names of the mystery book club members on the kitchen table. I was considering leaving Brian a note to say I'd gone to shower and get dressed, when he stepped back into the kitchen.

"Thanks," he said, pocketing the list of names.

"Sure."

"Will you be home this afternoon?"

"I suppose."

"Good. We'll talk again soon."

Was that a threat? His voice held no affection, but when I opened the front door he put his hand on my arm.

"I've been so damn busy, I'm only realizing now that I've missed you."

"Should you be handling this case?"

Brian gave me one of his heart-stopping grins. "Why not? You don't know the vic, right?"

I saw him out, then headed for the bathroom. I was dressed and putting on makeup when I glanced out the window as they were removing the body. Car doors slammed. A minute later they were gone.

I was halfway to the university when it dawned on me: the kitchen door *had* been unlocked when I went to look at the body. Gayle had lied. She *had* gone outside before waking me up.

A shiver ran through me. I failed to stifle the question that filled my head. *Had Gayle killed the man before he had a chance to murder her?*

CHAPTER THREE

I drove slowly to the university, churning over everything Gayle had done and told me since she'd turned up unexpectedly. I loved my sister and feared for her life, but part of me wondered if her story about Shawn killing her boyfriend was true.

Gayle had been an imaginative child. She had an imaginary playmate named Hans, and insisted that Mom fix a plate of food for Hans at every meal or she wouldn't eat. She stuck to it, too, which led to our throwing out lots of food in those years. Hans attended kindergarten with Gayle, until she decided she didn't want to share her valentine cards with him. As suddenly as he'd appeared, Hans disappeared. She never mentioned him again; it was a though he'd never existed.

In middle school and high school, she had a few dorky friends with whom she played Dungeons and Dragons and other web-based electronic games. Gayle's grades were average, though she'd scored high enough on her SAT boards to get her into the college of her choice in Colorado. She called me late one night during finals of her freshman year, sounding frantic and out of breath. This guy she'd been dating was stalking her. I told her to calm down so she could tell me about it. Instead, she grew more agitated and angry at me for not taking her side. She hung up and refused to answer the phone when I called her back.

I called my parents to inform them of Gayle's state of mind. My mother called the university the following morning. The dean promised to look into it, and called back later that day. Gayle had refused to talk to her, but her roommate, Linda, had plenty to say. She and her boyfriend were considering filing a complaint against Gayle. It seemed my sister had developed a crush on the guy and had taken to following him around wherever he went.

When my parents called Gayle to say they'd be coming to pick her up, they were told that Gayle had packed up and left school. She called them days later to say she was in England. She made it clear that she didn't want them to call her, that she didn't need their money, and that she was finally leading the life she'd always wanted. She spent the next few years traipsing around Europe. She'd call me or our parents every few months to let us know she was all right. I worried about Gayle, but I was a single mother. Working and raising Jesse while getting my PhD took up every waking moment. I loved my sister and wished her well, but I knew nothing of her life.

I pulled into the parking spot closest to Prentiss Hall where I taught my classes, and reached for my briefcase. In broad sunlight on this crisp October morning, I told myself that even if everything she'd told me was true, Gayle had no reason to fear this Shawn while she was on Long Island. The police here could protect her. Brian would, I knew.

It was a relief to immerse myself in administrative paper shuffling and students' problems. Even hearing about one girl's parents' divorce and another's sick grandmother was better than dwelling on the awfulness I'd left behind. It all flooded back the moment I stepped into my car to drive home.

Where was my sister now? Had she killed that man? Was he working for Shawn? If he wasn't, what was he doing in my backyard?

I mulled over these questions again and again, which got me nowhere. I was a mental mess by the time I turned down Magnolia Lane. When I saw no sign of a police car or the crime team, I released the lungful of air I hadn't realized I'd been holding. I'd go bonkers if I stayed alone in my house, rehashing my concerns. I left the car in the driveway and walked across my neighbor's lawn to ring Joy's bell.

She looked frazzled when she opened the door, a finger to her lips. And she was still in her bathrobe. "Brandon's sleeping. He was up all night teething."

"And you were up with him," I said.

"Natch," she said sourly. "Who else?"

"Mike?" I offered.

"Mike," Joy said, and laughed. It wasn't a happy sound.

Puzzled, I followed her into the living room strewn with toys. Joy plunked down on the sofa and closed her eyes. "Brandon finally fell asleep at dawn. The commotion at your house woke him up."

"Sorry about that."

"Not your fault." After a minute, she said, "How weird is it that the peeping Tom from last night ends up dead in your backyard?"

"The weirdest," I agreed.

"I'm starving," Joy said, but made no move to get up.

"Did you eat lunch?"

She shook her head. "Nor breakfast, if I remember correctly."

With a pang, I remembered how distracted and upset she'd been last evening. Something was dreadfully out of kilter. "What's wrong, Joy?"

That awful laugh again. "You mean, what happened yesterday between the two times I saw you?"

"Yes."

"I found out Mike, the bastard, is having an affair."

I pressed fingers to my lips to keep from laughing. Mike Lincoln was the last man on earth who would cheat on his wife.

Joy opened her eyes to gaze balefully at me. "I knew you wouldn't believe me, but I have proof. And proof is indisputable."

I swallowed, not at all happy to hear this. "What kind of proof are you talking about? Don't tell me you came home and found Mike in bed with someone? Not with Mrs. Horton here."

"Of course not! It happened when I was baking the gluten-free cookies. I'd fed the kids, and Mike was giving Brandon his bath. I went upstairs to check on things, when I heard him on the phone with my innocent baby son in his arms!"

Joy, the tough and the brave, looked like she was about to burst into tears.

"What was he saying?"

"For one thing, he called this woman 'sweetie'."

"He calls me that sometimes," I pointed out.

"Yeah, but he was holding the phone cupped in his hand which meant he was talking to someone he shouldn't be talking to."

She had a point. I was a great believer in body language.

"What else did you hear?"

Joy blew her nose. "He was setting up a date and reminded this 'sweetie' to make sure I didn't get wind of it."

I sat down beside her and put an arm around her shoulders. "The rotten bastard. What are you going to do?"

She shrugged. "Make him pay. But I haven't decided how."

We sat there quietly until I nudged her.

"Come in the kitchen. I'll make us some coffee and sandwiches. Where are the kids?"

"Zack's at soccer practice and Ruthie's at dancing school. Thank God it wasn't my day to carpool."

I found some cheese and sliced turkey in the fridge and got to work. Joy devoured her sandwich and I made her another. When she pushed back from the table, she looked more like herself.

"Brian Donovan stopped by this morning."

My pulse quickened. "Because you chased the dead man last night?"

"He plans to talk to everyone who was at your house last night. I was too zonked out to speak coherently so I said I'd come down to the station tonight to make a statement."

A tremor ran up my spine. I opened my mouth to ask Joy not to mention Gayle, then decided it was too much to ask. Besides, one of the others had probably mentioned her by now. I stood to put my empty dish in the sink. "I have to go. I've tons of things to see to."

Joy walked me to the front door. She seemed more relaxed when she hugged me good-bye. "Thanks for stopping by. I feel much, much better."

"Don't do anything rash," I told her. "Maybe Mike was talking to his sister."

She gave me a lopsided grin. "Sure he was. By the way, your sister's sweet. How upset was she to find someone had been murdered in your backyard during her visit?"

My heart thumped so fiercely, I was afraid Joy could hear it.

"Gayle missed the big event. She took off early this morning."

"Really? I thought she was planning to stay with you a few days."

"She decided to first visit friends, and spend time with me after," I made up as I went along.

Joy saw through my lie, but thank God she interpreted it her own way.

"Don't tell me you guys quarreled already."

I shrugged. "Gayle and I see the world very differently."

Which was true enough.

CHAPTER FOUR

"They've ID'd your corpse." Brian leaned back in his chair and sipped his coffee.

"He's not my corpse!" I said.

"The vic's name is Leo Lionni. He was a soldier for a New Jersey mob, until a few years ago when he came to Long Island."

I shuddered. "A mobster! What was he doing in my backyard last night?"

"That's the million dollar question."

Brian watched me as he added, "He was known around town as Len Lyons."

The dead man's cap flashed before me, and the pieces came together. "My God, Len! I couldn't see his face, but I should have recognized the cap. I never saw him without it."

"So you did know him." Brian didn't seem surprised.

"He fixed a few things around the house that needed attending to when I first moved in."

Brian grimaced. "Lionni worked as a handyman when he wasn't doing other jobs—if you get what I mean."

"Oh." I digested that a minute. "Is he the thief who's been burglarizing houses in the neighborhood?"

"Looks that way. They searched his apartment. Found a cache of items he hadn't disposed of."

"How was he murdered?"

"Someone stabbed him in the gut."

28

I sighed with relief as I remembered that Gayle had no blood on her clothes when she'd come into my bedroom this morning. "I didn't notice a knife on the lawn."

"We still haven't found the weapon."

"Oh."

"The crime scene people found his position very odd. They said he wouldn't have fallen on his stomach, with his arms at his side."

"Of course not," I said, remembering how he'd looked this morning. "He would have been clutching his wound." I bit my lip as I wondered. "So why did the murderer rearrange him?"

"To hide his face, or hide the bloody wound from sight."

"From me?" I asked without thinking.

Those icy blue eyes bore into me. "From you or from someone else. You're sure you didn't hear anything during the night?"

I shook my head. "My windows were shut and I slept soundly." I had a sudden thought. "Did you see signs of drag marks? Maybe he was killed then brought here."

"No indication of that," Brian said. "Do any of the members of your mystery book club live close by?"

"Corinne and Felicity Roberts live next door, and Joy Lincoln lives two houses away in the other direction. Marge and Evan Billings are a few blocks from here." I pursed my lips. "But you know all that."

He flashed a smile. "Asking questions gets me different answers."

I blushed, remembering how I'd insisted I'd never set eyes on the murder victim.

"Who referred you to Len Lyons?"

I thought back. "I think it was Joy. I'd mentioned the house required a few repairs, and she gave me his name. She said she hadn't needed his services, but a few of her friends had used him and were happy with his work. The Billingses recommended Len as well." I pressed my hand to my mouth. "Oh my God! They were burgled!"

"Did Lionni act weird while he was working in your house? Did he seem to be casing the place?"

I thought back and shook my head. "No. He was polite.

Didn't speak much. And he knew what he was doing. He fixed a leaking pipe in the bathroom and saved me a visit from the plumber."

"Uh-huh," Brian said, jotting down what I'd said in his notebook. When he finished, he cocked his head and grinned at me.

"Interesting, your landlord hadn't seen to those repairs. I thought you two were on pretty close terms."

My face grew warm. "I didn't want to bother Al. He was kind enough to let me have the house for a very low rent."

"And when were you planning to tell me your sister paid you a visit last night?"

"I was going to tell you, of course, but it slipped my mind. Gayle left early this morning."

"Did she see Lyons' body out back?"

"No! That is, I'm sure she didn't since she didn't mention it." Now my face was blazing as if I were standing close to a five alarm fire.

"How did *you* happen to notice it?"

"I just did."

"When you woke up? While you were eating breakfast?"

I blinked as Brian shot questions at me faster than I could answer. "While I was eating breakfast, I suppose."

"You suppose?"

My pulse speeded up with every question. I had the weird feeling my head was about to explode.

"I mean, of course I noticed it while I was eating breakfast. I glanced out the window and there it was. So I went outside and checked it out."

"Alone?"

"Of course alone! I told you, Gayle left early."

"Without eating anything?"

"She wanted an early start to visit her friends."

"Where do they live?"

"She didn't say."

Brian's eyes bore into me. "Hard to believe. She's your sister, right?"

I drew a deep breath. "Gayle and I lead very different lives. The truth is, we don't keep in touch as often as we should. I hadn't spoken to her in months when she called, and it's about six years since last we got together. I don't know her friends so I can't help you there."

"Is she running from something or someone?"

"Of course not! What makes you ask?"

"Your answers. They're the weirdest." Brian let out a grunt of exasperation. "You tell me the two of you are practically estranged, yet she drives all the way to Long Island from Utah. She arrives at night, then takes off early the following morning to places unknown. And you're as hyper as a jumping bean." He pointed an accusing finger. "You tell me how it sounds."

I pressed my hands together to stop their trembling. "I'm telling you what happened. I'm nervous because someone killed a gangster in my backyard, and you're accusing my sister of—I don't know what!"

He reached across to stroke my arm. The unexpected gesture set my body tingling.

"Lexie, when you're ready to talk, I'm here to listen."

Brian asked me for Gayle's cell phone number. I gave it to him. If she'd done as she'd promised, her phone was in pieces miles from here.

"I haven't heard from her," I said defensively.

"I believe you. Please call me when you do."

He squeezed my shoulder and took off, leaving me terrified for my sister. The fact that Len was connected, as they say, could only mean he'd gotten word that Gayle was heading for my house and had been instructed to kill her. After all, wasn't the mob one big company with each "family" controlling a specific area? That dirty cop in Utah must have put the word out, and fast.

Only someone intervened and killed the killer. I paced up and down the living room as I thought. Who could that someone be? Len had done repair jobs for the Billingses and for Tim. He could have seen where they kept their keys, taken an impression, then returned to rob them at his convenience.

I shuddered. What if Evan or Tim put two and two together then decided to kill Len? But why in my backyard? Unless...

My questions only spawned more questions. I had to get out of the house! The sane part of me wanted, no *longed* to tell Brian what Gayle was running from, but I'd made a promise. And right now that promise took precedence over the legal system and my erratic romance with Brian Donovan.

I called my best friend, Rosie, who lived in Old Cadfield, a twenty minute drive from here.

"Can you meet me tonight?" I asked the minute she answered the phone.

"And hello to you, too." When I didn't respond, Rosie asked, "What's wrong, Lexie?"

"I'll tell you later."

"Sure you don't want to come for dinner? I'm making salmon the way you like it, and roasted vegetables."

"Sounds yummy, but I can't eat," I admitted.

"It's that bad?"

"Worse," I told her. "Can you meet me at the bar in the bowling alley on Jericho Turnpike?"

"Sure. I can get there at seven-thirty, since Hal promised to be home early."

I smiled, thinking how successful my old college boyfriend had turned out. "Give him a hug for me."

"He'll be disappointed when he finds out you've refused dinner. We haven't seen you in weeks."

"I'll stop by soon," I promised. "As soon as this storm passes."

"How about Friday night?" she pressed. "Seven o'clock?"

"Sure." I sighed, knowing when I'd been bested.

"Lovely! And tonight we'll talk and you'll get everything off your chest."

Knowing I'd soon be spilling everything out to my no-nonsense best friend helped put me in a better frame of mind. I fed Puss, nibbled on a few slices of turkey and cheese, and was just changing into a long-sleeved sweater, when the phone rang. I ran to get it, hoping it was Gayle.

"Hi, Lexie. Hope I didn't catch you at a bad time."

"Hi, Al. What time is it there?"

"Midnight." His voice sounded amazingly clear, considering that it was coming across the Atlantic Ocean. "I just got in from a meeting."

"Which went well, I gather, from your upbeat tone."

"The CEO and other officers of the company like my plans for the new building. Surprisingly smooth sailing for this project, so far."

"I can't say the same is happening here. A local hood who worked as a handyman was killed in my backyard during the night or early morning. The odd thing is, last night he was seen looking in the window at our book club meeting. I've no idea what he was after."

"Lexie, I can't believe you've gotten yourself mixed up in another murder!"

Was that a note of criticism I heard? Al knew that the murders in Old Cadfield this past summer had nothing to do with me. I opened my mouth to issue a retort when I decided he was probably worried about me.

"You must be terribly upset," he said. "Do the police think it's safe for you to stay in the house by yourself?"

"Brian didn't seem concerned. Oh!" I clapped my hand over my mouth, but it was too late.

"Brian Donovan's in charge of the case?" Al asked, an edge to his tone.

"He is a homicide detective," I reminded him. "At this point no one knows much of anything. Though from what I've gathered, the victim has burgled the homes of some of the book club members."

"Lexie, promise me you won't play detective again. Last time, you came close to being severely injured."

I hid my annoyance as best I could. "I don't intend to play at anything. And now I must cut our conversation short or I'll be late. I'm meeting Rosie. It's been ages since we've gotten together."

"Keep safe. Make sure all the windows and doors are locked. And use that alarm system I installed."

"I will," I promised, thinking how vulnerable we all were if someone wanted to kill us.

"We'll talk again soon. Love you."

"Love you, too," I said automatically, and hung up.

Did I love Al? I pondered the question as I climbed into my car. I cared for him and I was glad he cared for me, but I felt neither lust nor an overwhelming romantic yearning to be with him, both of which I'd experienced in the past and now regarded as bothersome addictions.

I wanted Al in my life, but I didn't want to marry him. I wasn't even sure I wanted to live with him. So maybe I didn't love him—yet. He was kind and level-headed, a mature man capable of taking part in a mature relationship. The kind of man I *should* be involved with at this point in my life.

I backed out of the garage. Darkness had fallen, so I edged carefully into the street to avoid hitting any walkers. A car door closed as I was about to pass the Roberts' house. A sleek black Lincoln zoomed out of their driveway, just missed ramming into me, and sped down Magnolia Lane. I slammed on the brakes and squealed to a stop, furious at the driver's arrogance. Corinne, dressed in one of her power suits, approached. I lowered the car window.

"Who the hell was that!" I demanded. "He almost crashed into me."

"I'm sorry, Lexie. My friend and I had a disagreement. He has a short fuse. I'll give him hell when I call him later."

Her apology took most of the wind out of my sails. "Just tell him to be more careful when he backs up."

"Don't worry, I will," she said, her tone flat but oddly menacing. She gestured with her chin to my backyard. "That was some hell of a sight you must have woken up to. The place was lousy with cops and techies when I left for work this morning. All they would tell me was that the victim was a male in his thirties."

"His name's Leo Lionni. He fixed a few things for me when I first moved in, but I've no idea why he was spying on us last night—unless he was planning to rob me. I heard he was in the mob."

Corinne's eyes opened wide in astonishment. "Really? Who told you that?"

"I can't remember," I lied. "So many people have called to talk about it."

She lowered her voice. "This commotion has Felicity totally strung out. She couldn't go to work today. I offered to stay home, but she insisted she'd be fine."

"I wish you would have called me. I would have looked in on

her."

The front door opened and Felicity appeared in a bathrobe, her face pale without lipstick.

"I heard a car drive up, but you never came inside," she said querulously.

Corinne rushed over to her sister. "Sorry, love. I was talking to Lexie." She waved to me and shut the door behind them.

There's something odd about those two, I thought as I drove away, though I couldn't put my finger on it. But maybe I was overly suspicious, given the events of the day. *A murder in the neighborhood leaves us feeling vulnerable.* That word again. *We're terrified of becoming the killer's next victim.*

Though my neighbors were odd, I wished I could comfort my sister as easily as Corinne had comforted Felicity. Instead, I'd handed over her cell phone number to Brian like a passive bovine. I prayed she'd destroyed it, because if Brian decided to put out an alarm for her, that Shawn Estes might see it and get to her first!

I pulled over to the side of the road and called Gayle. Nothing. A good sign, I told myself. She'd gotten rid of her phone! Still, I wanted to hear her voice. Make sure she was safe. Frustrated because I couldn't do anything more, I headed for the bowling alley.

Brian wouldn't be so intent on contacting Gayle if he had a few solid suspects right here in town. I had no idea if Leo Lionni had been spying on one of the book club members, or if he'd been casing my house and planning to rob me. Regardless, the members were my only lead, and I had to start from there.

CHAPTER FIVE

Rosie downed the last of her apple martini and set the glass down with a thump.

"Ask your pal Joy. I bet she can uncover all sorts of dirt about the other book club members. Maybe even find a hidden link between one of them and the dead man."

"Joy was at the meeting last night," I pointed out, "which makes her a suspect like everyone else. She's strong, fearless, and lives two houses from me. She could have killed Leonni, slung him over her shoulder, and dumped him on my lawn."

"True. But why would she want to kill the guy?" Rosie burped. "Sorry. I'm not used to this high powered stuff."

"Which is why I'm drinking slowly. See." I sipped my martini.

Rosie let out a snort. "So speaks the woman who, in our college days, could drink every guy under the table. Returning to our subject, Joy is your friend. She has no reason to incriminate you by leaving the body on your back lawn."

"I'm glad you think she's innocent because she's my friend," I said.

"It's common sense, dodo. From what you've told me, she has enough on her hands without setting out to murder someone first thing in the morning."

Rosie held up her left hand to tick off her fingers. "First off, she has three young kids. I can't see her leaving the house to

36

meet some gonzo at dawn. Her husband or one of the older kids might have awakened and followed her outside"

I nodded. "Maybe."

"Second of all, she's preoccupied with her husband's affair."

"The bastard," I mumbled. "And Mike seems like such a nice guy."

"If she was planning to kill anyone, he'd be her target."

"And finally," finger number three, "she's former FBI. They say anyone's capable of homicide, but FBI agents are trained to protect us. It's in their blood. And your friend Joy sounds like a good gal."

"I like to think so," I agreed. "Rosie, these are all good reasons for me to put my trust in Joy, but none is foolproof."

Rosie shrugged. "What's foolproof? Dead people are foolproof."

"Right. I'll drink to that." I drained my glass and raised my hand to catch the waitress's attention.

"I'll have another—" I began when the waitress appeared, but Rosie overrode me.

"We'd like something to eat," she told the young woman. "May we see a menu?"

I pressed my lips together so I couldn't ask why Rosie who, unlike me, had eaten dinner, was about to eat again. She'd never lose those thirty pounds she kept talking about.

"We don't have menus," the waitress said. "We serve hamburgers, cheeseburgers, turkey club and tuna salad sandwich. Only the tuna's all gone."

We both opted for a cheeseburger, medium rare, one order of fries very well done, and two colas.

"All right," I said when the waitress left, "if I ask Joy to help me check out the others, do I tell her about Gayle?"

Rosie thumped her forehead in disbelief. "Of course you tell her about Gayle! That's the purpose of all this. So she can help you. Joy's not on the Feds' payroll, and she's not a cop. But she has connections. She might be able to get you information about the bent cop that killed Gayle's boyfriend."

"And find out more about the other club members," I mused. "I know nothing about them, aside from what they've told me. For all I know, they all have lurid pasts."

Rosie grinned. "That's the spirit!"

We chatted about her daughters and my son, Jesse, until our food arrived, then we got down to some serious eating. We ordered decaf coffee, and Rosie ordered an apple pie. I must have frowned despite my attempt not to show disapproval, because Rosie said, "I know I shouldn't, but I have been getting to the gym most mornings."

"Working out in the gym is good," I replied in my best nonjudgmental tone of voice.

To her credit, she pushed away her dessert plate, the crust mostly intact. I finished my coffee refill and gazed out at the bowlers while Rosie asked for the check.

"Feel like bowling a game or two?" I asked. "I'm too restless to go home."

"Who could blame you for being on edge? Sure, I'm game."

We paid the bill then went to rent bowling shoes. As we laced them up, Rosie said, "The last time I bowled was for some charity do."

"I think the last time I went bowling was when we were still in college."

Rosie pointed at me. "Senior year. During one of your break ups with Godfrey."

I nodded, remembering. "You and Hal took me bowling, then out for pizza."

We each selected a bowling ball and carried it to our lane.

"Do we get a few practice balls?" Rosie asked.

"I sure hope so, considering how long it's been."

It felt good, tossing a heavy ball before me. At first most of our balls ended up in one gutter or the other, but as we played, our skills picked up. Our scores remained close, which infused me with a sense of excitement and the desire to win the game. But Rosie won, by seven points.

I glanced at my watch. "It's nine-thirty. Care to bowl another game?"

"Sure, but after that I have to go home. In fact, I'll call Hal, then toddle over to the ladies' room."

"I'll be here," I said.

I sat down and looked around. Most of the bowlers belonged to teams, judging from their same-colored shirts. It was a fun sport, I supposed, but not one I cared to pursue. Actually, I wasn't interested in any particular sport, though I intended to join a gym and take aerobics and yoga classes. Maybe one day, when things settled down.

My cell phone rang. It was Gayle.

"Where are you?" I demanded.

I heard an intake of air, voices in the background. "At my friend's house. But I can't stay here. I'm leaving tomorrow. Did the police tell you who that man was?"

"He's a small-time hoodlum from New Jersey."

"I knew it! Shawn sent him."

"We don't know that. Why did you—?" I stopped, afraid to hear what she'd say when I asked why she'd lied about seeing the body before she woke me up.

"Why did I what?"

"I meant to say, why don't you come back here?"

"I can't. If Shawn sent that guy, he'll send someone else to finish the job."

I let out a humorless laugh. "Come on, Gayle. This Shawn from Utah isn't all that powerful."

"You don't know him, Lexie. If he can't get someone to kill me, he'll come after me himself."

Before I could say Len's murder probably had nothing to do with her, she hung up. I pressed the call back button before I remembered her phone wouldn't take my call.

Angry at myself for not handling things better, I headed outside for a breath of fresh air. I sidestepped a group of noisy teenagers, and walked toward the parking lot.

Gayle was terrified and believed she had no place to go. Instead of badgering her, I should have asked why she had to leave her friend's place. I should have been supportive and kind, instead of logical and sarcastic. She was my baby sister. She was terrified and alone, and I'd done nothing to protect her.

The sound of two men going at it hammer and tongs jarred me from my musings. They faced off in the shadows beside a pickup truck. The younger of the two —almost seven feet tall and built like a bull—loomed over the paunchy older man, who, though no match for The Giant, stood his ground.

His midwestern accent caught my attention. "My wife and I

paid you what you asked! We expect you to keep your end of the bargain!"

"Like I said, expenses cropped up we didn't figure on. Bring me another ten grand by next week, or the deal's off."

"How do I know next week you won't ask for more? So far, you're not a man of your word."

The Giant roared with laughter. "Man of my word? Who do you think you're dealing with—the clergy? I'm the only hope you have of ever seeing that kid. Meet me here next week with the money."

They lowered their voices and I couldn't make out their final exchange. The older man stomped off to his car in the second row of parked vehicles. When the light caught his face, I covered my mouth to keep from gasping.

Evan Billings, of all people! What was he mixed up in?

I hurried inside, and felt a great sense of relief when I caught sight of Rosie. I wasn't up to bowling a second game, but I didn't want to disappoint her, so I said nothing.

"What's wrong with you?" she demanded after I'd thrown my fifth gutter ball.

I told her about Gayle's phone call and Evan Billings' conversation.

"Time to call it a night." She gathered up her belongings. I did the same, and followed her to the shoe rental room.

In the parking lot, she gave me a fierce hug. "Lexie, Lexie. Always involved in intrigue and drama. Try to get a good night's sleep."

"I will."

"Are you coming to dinner Friday night? Hal said to tell you he misses you."

"Sure" I smiled. "Tell him I miss him, too."

I backed out of my parking space, still smiling. Most people would find it odd that Hal, who'd been devastated when I'd broken up with him in college, ended up happily married to my best friend and on the best of terms with me. However, it suited the three of us just fine. I drove home worrying about my sister, and wondering why the Billingses were paying money to a thug.

To do what? I had difficulty imagining they'd break the law, much less arrange a contract killing.

Then again, I couldn't cast *any* of my book club members in the role of murderer, though one of them might have murdered Len.

At home, I was too restless to settle down. I opened the refrigerator and, though I wasn't hungry, made myself a toasted cheese sandwich. My mom used to make them for Gayle and me on rainy days and when one of us was too sick to go to school. Puss stood by my chair and meowed, not something he usually did. Though I didn't want to start a bad habit, I pulled off a tiny bit of my sandwich and gave it to him. He devoured it in record time.

The phone rang as I was undressing for bed. I picked it up and heard a click as someone hung up.

Damn! This was getting annoying. And scary. Gayle's fear was affecting me. I wondered if Shawn was at the other end of the phone, trying to find out if she was here in my house. *Would he break down the door and kill me?*

I jumped when the phone rang again. I answered after the third ring. "Yes?" I demanded, my voice sharp and staccato.

"Lexie, it's me. Mike."

I heard his mellow laugh and wanted to slap his face—for scaring me and for deceiving Joy.

"What is it?"

"I want to talk to you."

"Did you call five minutes ago?"

"Yep." He lowered his voice. "Sorry I hung up. Joy walked by. I didn't want her to hear me talking to you."

"What's this about?" I asked.

"A surprise birthday party. At The Lion's Head Inn the second Saturday night in December. Joy has a big one coming up December fifteenth."

I counted on my fingers. "She'll be thirty-five."

"Right. She tells me she's turning into an old hag, though I swear she looks as good as when we met. Still, every morning she checks her eyes for crow's feet and other signs of aging."

"What should I say?" I asked dryly.

Mike chuckled. "Come on, sweetie. You know you look great."

Sweetie! "You mean, for my age?"

"Hey, Lex, I thought we were friends. What's with the attitude?"

"Did you call someone last night and whisper into the phone?"

He thought a bit. "I called my sister. Started telling her about the surprise party, when Joy came into the room."

"Joy thinks you're having an affair."

"You're putting me on, right?"

"No."

"That's crazy, Lexie. Why would I have an affair?"

Because that's what men do, I thought, then reconsidered. Mike wasn't most men. Joy and his kids came first. "I believe you. The problem is, you have to convince Joy that you're not."

"I refuse to tell her about the party," he insisted. "It's gotta be a surprise."

"She's furious, Mike. You'd better come up with something."

"I'll work on it," he said and hung up.

CHAPTER SIX

A fierce wind was gusting when I turned down Magnolia Lane late Friday afternoon. I had an armful of papers to grade that would keep me busy most of the weekend. I'd stopped at the supermarket for Puss's food, but they were out of the only flavor he'd eat. I had to go to two pet stores before I managed to buy a carton of his turkey meals. I hoped the company wasn't planning to stop making that particular formula. If they did, I'd have a starving feline on my hands.

"Lexie!"

I slammed on the brakes, barely managing to avoid hitting Felicity as she dashed in front of my car to reach me.

I rolled down the window. "Careful, Felicity! I nearly mowed you down!" *Again*, I thought, but didn't have the heart to say aloud.

She flashed me a nervous smile. "You'd never do that."

"Not *on purpose*, but what if I couldn't stop in time?"

"Sorry." She leaned on the frame of the rolled-down window. In a frantic whisper, she asked, "Lexie, what was Leo doing in your backyard yesterday morning?"

"Leo? Oh, you mean Len."

She nodded. Even in the poor light I could make out her strained expression.

"I've no idea what he was doing there. Did you know him?"

"Yes. He came to our house to fix the furnace."

"He fixed things for me, too."

"But he liked *me!*"

For a moment I feared the poor creature was deranged. Tears filled her eyes. Regardless of what went on inside her head, her emotions were real.

Then it hit me. "Felicity, had you arranged to see Len er-Leo Wednesday night?"

The tears spilled down her cheeks. "We had a date, but Corinne said I had to go to the meeting. I didn't want her to find out about Leo and me, so I went."

"Do you think he looked in on our meeting hoping to catch your attention?"

She nodded again. "He asked me to meet him instead of going to the meeting because he had to tell me something important. I said I would." She glanced around, worried someone might hear us. "But Corinne was in one of her moods. When that happens, there's no talking to her. And I couldn't call Leo. Not with Corinne in the house."

"Why not, Felicity? Why not tell Corinne you had a date with your boyfriend?"

Felicity reared back, as if I'd dangled a snake in her face.

"Corinne says I'm too fragile to have a boyfriend. I'd be devastated if we broke up, and then..." she gulped, "and then I'd end up going back to the hospital."

"You were in the hospital?"

"Yes, but I'm fine now. Only Corinne worries. She'd be angry if she found out about Leo." She gripped my hand so hard, it hurt. "You won't tell her! Promise me you won't tell her about Leo and me."

I pulled my hand free. "Of course I won't." My voice remained calm but inside my heart was singing. Len and Felicity had a romance going. He had nothing to do with Shawn from Utah. Now Brian would have no reason to link Gayle to the murder!

My sense of relief was cut short when it occurred to me that Gayle might have killed Len because she *thought* he worked for Shawn. She could have changed her bloodied clothes before waking me and stuffed them in her duffle bag. No, that was too preposterous. I ignored the tug at my moral strings and said I had to get home.

Felicity gave me a tremulous smile. "I don't mean to be a bother, only I feel I can talk to you."

"I'm glad, Felicity. Any time." *Except now.*

I fed Puss, showered and got dressed for my dinner at Rosie and Hal's. I thought about my conversation with Felicity. Now I knew why Len had been peering in at our meeting. But it didn't explain how he ended up dead in my backyard the following morning. I hadn't realized until now that Felicity was terrified of her sister and fearful of making her angry. I could understand why Corinne wanted to protect Felicity. They were no more than two or three years apart, and must have been close their entire lives. True, Felicity was fragile, and she had awful taste in men. I wondered if, even now, she knew that her boyfriend had been a thief. But did that give her older sister the right to control her?

Which made me think about my sister. I laughed out loud, and it wasn't a pretty sound. Gayle was naïve and did one stupid thing after another. Not that I blamed her for running when she realized Shawn had murdered her boyfriend. But I'd never presume to have the right to control her life.

Had Len really cared about Felicity, or did he have an ulterior reason for getting involved with her? She was easy prey. Given her sheltered life, she had little opportunity to socialize and was probably thrilled that a nice looking man like Len was interested in her. I wasn't too surprised when she told me she'd spent time in a hospital. I assumed it was a psychiatric hospital, where they probably fed her tranquilizers until she was calm enough to leave.

But where could a relationship with Felicity get him?

Almost two hours later I was back in the car and heading for Old Cadfield, the big-bucks town where Rosie and Hal lived and where I'd spent the previous summer. Though I took pleasure devouring every bite of my pot roast, roasted potatoes, and salad, I was happy when Rosie cleared the table and the three of us got down to analyzing what was going on in my life.

Rosie shook her head in disbelief as I repeated the conversation I'd had with Felicity.

"I have a problem seeing her with a man like Len Lyons," she said.

"Are you sure she's not pulling your leg?" Hal asked. "Maybe their relationship was all in her head."

"I'm skeptical but parts of it rang true." I nodded to his offer to refill my wine glass. "She believes Len loved her and they were a couple. I'll check out her story as best I can."

Rosie grinned. "You have to tell Brian Donovan what she told you."

"Of course I will, though it doesn't explain what Len was doing in my backyard."

"Maybe he asked Felicity to meet him there—close to her house but with little chance that Corinne would see them," Hal said. "It figures, since he wanted to tell her something."

"And she killed him?" I stared at him incredulously. "Felicity's fragile and has the mind of a child."

Rosie narrowed her eyes. "Children kill."

"But she loved the guy," I protested.

My best friends exchanged knowing glances.

"Tell Brian everything she said," Rosie advised.

"Do that," Hal seconded.

"I said I would!" I snapped, annoyed by their hovering. "Then maybe he'll stop questioning me about Gayle."

"Any word from her?" Rosie asked.

"Not since the other evening," I said.

"The poor kid's on the run," Hal said. "She's too afraid to ask the police to protect her for fear they'll turn on her."

"Or charge her for two murders," I pointed out.

My hosts exchanged another glance. This one made me angry.

"My sister's a flake, but she didn't kill anyone!"

"Of course she didn't!" Rosie murmured.

She and Hal made soothing noises, but I was still miffed when I left for home after downing some of Rosie's apple pie and ice cream and two cups of coffee. My sister *didn't* murder her boyfriend or Len Lyons, and I'd prove it!

I drove home at a dangerously fast speed, my blood and thoughts churning. I was too agitated to settle down. As soon as I walked through the door, I called Joy. I hadn't called her after Rosie had convinced me to include her in my sleuthing plans the other evening. It was time I brought her up to date.

"Listen," she began before I even said hello. From her hushed tones I knew she was covering the phone with her hand. "The bimbo who Mike called the other night has her number blocked. But as soon as I get a minute, I'll call an old buddy and track it down. As for my dumb-ass husband—"

I stopped her in mid-sentence. "I desperately need your help to solve a few murders ASAP."

That caught her attention. "Two murders? I only know of one. Did someone else get bumped off while I was driving the kids to soccer practice?"

"Any chance you can get out for an hour?"

Joy gave a devilish laugh. "Certainly! Mike was planning to watch the ball game at Buddy's house. I'll tell him he has to watch the kids. Both Zack and Ruthie have a friend over. He won't like it one bit."

Despite my focus on proving my sister's innocence, I couldn't help sparing a few grams of pity for Mike. "Don't you think you're being hard on him?"

"Nope."

I made my voice sound as incredulous as I could. "You overheard half a sentence and assume he's cheating on you?"

"Yep! That and his smug, satisfied smile."

So much for Joy's training to weigh evidence carefully before going after a suspect. I sighed. "All right. I'll pick you up in ten minutes and fill you in on the way to the diner."

Joy remained silent after I told her about Gayle's boyfriend's murder. We sat in the diner's parking lot while she digested everything.

"Do you think Brian likes Gayle for Len's murder?" I finally asked.

Joy pursed her lips. "Brian Donovan goes by the book. Without any incriminating evidence, Gayle's in the clear." She sent me a side-long glance. "But you have to admit it's kind of weird how she left one murder scene and walked in on another."

"Gayle didn't kill anyone!" I said with more zeal than I felt. "And I have to prove it, or she might get sent back to Utah and straight into the hands of that dirty cop."

"A worthy enough reason," Joy said. "We'll plan our strategy over dessert."

The diner was busy. We had to wait a few minutes to be seated. Thank goodness, the booth was in the corner on the window side of the big room, a good distance from a noisy table of eight. I ordered coffee and a Danish. Joy ordered a banana split.

"A banana split!" I exclaimed when our middle-aged waitress left to fill our orders.

Joy grinned. "I'm making the most of my getaway."

The busboy plopped two glasses of water down on our table.

Joy leaned over the table to whisper. "If Gayle didn't kill Len or whatever his name is, there's a good chance one of the book club members stabbed him. We'll raise some provocative questions at the meeting tomorrow morning, then watch to see how everyone reacts."

"Oh, my God!" With everything happening, I'd all but forgotten the meeting.

She burst out laughing. "Did I catch our book club facilitator unprepared?"

"Only where the food's concerned. I'm out of coffee. I'll buy some on the way home. And bagels and cream cheese."

"Is everyone coming?" Joy asked.

"As far as I know."

"Good. All suspects will be on board."

"I'm pretty sure Len was looking into the window to get Felicity's attention. They had a date that evening, but Felicity caved when Corinne made her go to the meeting. She didn't want her sister to find out about her relationship with Len."

Joy frowned. "I bet she didn't. Corinne is one control freak. She all but tells Felicity when to go to the bathroom. On the other hand, Felicity has a screw loose. She had no business getting involved with a gonzo at least ten years older than her."

"That is, if they really were involved and the romance wasn't a figment of Felicity's imagination."

"Also a viable possibility," Joy said.

"Felicity mentioned spending time in a hospital."

"She did, about three years ago. It was around the time they bought the house. Corinne moved in alone and Felicity joined her a few months later. Corinne told anyone who asked that her sister was away on a trip. Her story sounded phony, so I checked it out. Turns out Felicity had been a patient at Herring House for several months."

"The psychiatric hospital," I mused. "I'm not surprised. She seems so fragile."

"And naïve," Joy added. "I'd worry about her if she were my sister."

I shuddered as I wondered where my own sister was right now, frightened and on her own.

"It's interesting how all the book club members knew Len Lyons," Joy said. "Maybe one of them killed him. The Billingses and Tim assume he robbed them after making repairs in their homes."

I suddenly remembered. "The other night I saw Evan talking to a goliath of a man at the bowling alley."

"What were you doing at a bowling alley?" Joy asked, amused. "I didn't know you belonged to a bowling league."

"I met my friend Rosie there," I explained. "The alley's halfway between here and her house."

"Okay," Joy said, sounding unconvinced. "I'll check out the Billingses' history, along with Sadie's, the twisted sisters', and Tim's."

I laughed. "You and I are excluded."

"Of course," Joy said gaily. "We're the detectives."

The waitress arrived with our order. I sipped my coffee.

"But I'm afraid Gayle's not excluded," Joy said.

For a moment, I didn't know what she was talking about.

"Your sister showed up at your place for a reason, Lexie. To see the whole picture, we have to find out why."

CHAPTER SEVEN

"I think it's safe to say *The Daughter of Time* is a one-of-a-kind mystery," I said, making eye contact with each of the members of the book club.

All seven of them, including the few chomping away on cream cheese-smeared bagels, nodded in agreement. Joy winked to let me know she was about to start things rolling.

Tim chuckled. "Amazing how drawing logical conclusions from old but verified reports proves Richard the Third never murdered his nephews."

"And points a finger at Henry The Seventh," Joy said. "Tey makes a good case that he ordered the murder of the two princes, then did away with everyone standing between himself and the throne."

"And got away with it scot-free," I added.

"The king had total power in those days," Sadie mused. "He killed whomever he pleased."

"Let's not forget that Henry the Seventh grabbed the throne after Edward the Fourth died in battle," Evan said.

Felicity shivered. "Murder was so common in those days. On the battlefield and at court."

"Poison was a popular means of disposal," Corinne commented. "Which was why rulers often had someone taste their food before eating it."

"And the murdering goes on," Joy said blithely. "Are you

forgetting the dead body that turned up in Lexie's backyard?"

Odd that no one had mentioned it till now. I watched them exchange glances in pairs—the Billingses, Sadie and Tim, and the Roberts sisters.

Evan was the first to speak. "No big loss," he said. "Len Lyons was a two-bit thief! Who cares that he's dead?"

Felicity moaned and pressed her hand to her chest.

To take the focus off her, I said, "Thief or not, he didn't deserve to be stabbed. I've no idea why someone killed him in my backyard. Or what drew him to our meeting Wednesday night."

"That was Len spying on us?" Sadie asked incredulously.

"You knew him?" I asked.

Sadie shrugged.

"I realized Len was the man I'd been chasing once he was ID'd as the homicide victim," Joy said.

"I hate to say it, Lexie, but he was probably checking out your house because he intended to rob you," Ted said. "Maybe that's what he was about to do the morning he was killed."

I shivered. "I never considered that possibility."

Joy glared at Tim. "At least Lexie won't have to worry about that now."

"But I'm worried there's a killer running loose in our neighborhood," I said.

Heads nodded but no one offered a comment. What a fiasco! Though what did I expect, someone jumping up and admitting he or she stabbed Len Lyons for being a worthless human being?

Sadie and Marge took advantage of the lull in conversation to use the bathroom or go in the kitchen for refills. I wasn't sure who did what because by the time they'd rejoined us, their plates piled with cookies, I'd stopped playing Miss Marple and had resumed my role of book club facilitator.

"Let's move on to *Brat Farrar*, a totally different type of story than *The Daughter of Time*." I smiled. "Would you call *Brat Farrar* a mystery or a novel that includes a mystery?"

"I'd say a novel because of its depth and psychological insights," Marge said. "We get to know the four Ashby children and their Aunt Bee. They live on an estate and raise horses in the English midlands. There's lots in the book about that."

Felicity clapped her hands. "I love Brat! He's my favorite character of all!"

"Mine, too," I agreed. I winked at her, glad she'd recovered from our earlier conversation about her deceased boyfriend. "But doesn't it bother you that Brat comes to Latchetts, pretending to be Patrick, who disappeared or died eight years ago? He's going to steal Latchetts from Simon, who's expecting to inherit the estate."

Felicity's lip quivered, and I feared she was about to burst into tears. Corinne reached over to take her hand, but Felicity pulled it away.

"Brat's a good person! Sometimes good people do bad things, though they don't mean to." Felicity ran from the room. Her sister chased after her.

"What was that all about?" Tim murmured.

For a moment I feared that another meeting was about to fall apart, when Joy grabbed the reins.

"You know how Felicity takes everything to heart. Corinne will calm her down and have her back with us in no time." She cast me a meaningful glance.

"Let's talk about Brat Farrar," I said, and went into a detailed exposition of his vagabond life until he meets up with Alec Loding. "Loding is an actor and the Ashbys' neighbor. He's impressed by how much Brat resembles Simon, Patrick's twin brother, and convinces him to impersonate Patrick. As the older twin, Brat will inherit Latchetts; in return, Brat will provide Loding with a bundle of cash."

Evan gave a little laugh. "Clearly Alec doesn't like Simon."

"Simon's not very likable," Sadie said. "His only admirer is his younger sister, Jane."

"We don't like Simon, either," Joy said. "We suspect he's killed Patrick, even though he appears to have an alibi at the time his brother disappeared. Patrick's murder is at the heart of the novel."

Was it my imagination, or did everyone suddenly jerk to attention? I cleared my throat.

"Shortly after his parents are killed in an accident, Patrick disappears. He is thirteen years old. For much of the novel, we don't know if he's dead. If he's dead, we don't know if Simon killed him or why?"

"The why is easy," Tim said. "The oldest surviving sibling inherits Latchetts."

"Kind of like Henry the Seventh killing off everyone standing between him and throne," Marge pointed out.

"Excellent point!" I beamed, pleased that the members were seeing similarities in Tey's plots.

"Simon has an alibi," Joy pointed out, "until Brat unravels it."

"No one suspects Simon because he was only thirteen at the time Patrick disappeared," Sadie said. "Most of us have difficulty acknowledging the brutal truth that children commit murder."

Felicity crept back into the room and took her seat. Marge and Sadie reached out to pat her arm. I heard the muffled sound of a toilet being flushed. Minutes later, Corinne slipped into her chair.

I continued. "As Felicity pointed out, we like Brat Farrar." I smiled at Felicity, who offered me a wan smile in return. "Loding tells Brat he's an Ashby, and Brat insists he isn't. At the end of the novel we learn, along with Brat, that he *is* an Ashby, though he grew up without a family. The more Brat learns about Patrick, the more he identifies with him and wants to be part of *this* family. At the same time he feels guilty for impersonating someone he's never met."

"He's playing a role," Joy chimed in.

I nodded. "We see evidence of Josephine Tey's theatrical background throughout the novel. Alec Loding, an actor himself, coaches Brat Farrar so that he can play the role of Patrick."

The professorial aspect of my nature pushed forward. "We see this theme occasionally in literature. The film, 'The Return of Martin Guerre,' is based on a true story that occurred in the 1600's. A man arrives in a French village, claiming to be someone who left some years earlier. In the end, we discover he's an impostor. In *Brat Farrar* we see most of the story from the impersonator's point of view. We know from the start that Brat's not who he says he is."

In full gear, I charged ahead. "Brat falls in love with the Ashby family, especially with Aunt Bee and Elinor."

Sadie laughed. "But not with Simon, who tries to kill him."

"How?" I asked.

Marge fielded that one. "Twice in incidents involving horses. Horses play an important role in this book."

We talked a bit about the showdown between Brat and Simon and about the ending.

Sadie sighed. "*Brat Farrar's* a wonderful read, even by today's standards."

I nodded. "It's a classic, with great characters, a fantastic setting, good pacing, and a satisfying conclusion."

Everyone murmured in agreement. The perfect moment to end our meeting, I thought, until I caught Joy's mischievous grin.

"Why do we love to read mysteries?" she tossed out to the group, pretending a fierce curiosity.

Tim laughed. "That's easy. We enjoy the suspense as we try to ID the guilty party. When he's unveiled at the end, we feel a sense of closure and justice fulfilled that's rarely achieved in real life."

Joy shrugged. "Or maybe we're all potential murderers and experience a vicarious thrill when we read about people getting away with it—at least for a while."

"And imagine we wouldn't get caught because we're smarter than the killer in the book," I added.

Silence. Would no one agree for fear of being branded Len's killer?

Joy charged ahead. "Any of us will kill when pushed to the edge. We're all prospective murderers. We'll kill to protect our children. To protect ourselves."

Her cheeks were rosy with emotion as she looked at each of us. "'Fess up. When did you feel the urge to murder someone but didn't give into it, of course?"

Sadie pursed her lips as she silently debated the question. Tim gave a devilish grin. Evan and Marge exchanged worried glances.

"I wanted to kill someone once!"

We all stared at Felicity.

"Be quiet!" her sister growled.

I tamped down the twinge of guilt, and urged Felicity to answer. "Whom did you want to kill, Felicity, and why?"

"Johnny! For killing Oscar, my pet ferret!"

"How awful!" I looked about for Puss, and sighed with relief when I saw him fast asleep in the corner against the baseboard

"A pet killer," Joy said with distaste. "Who could blame you?"

Corinne shot her an angry look. "The creature was sick and dying. Our father asked a family friend to put it out of its misery."

"Oscar wasn't sick!" Felicity insisted. "Don't you remember? It was because Daddy hated—"

"Felicity!"

Felicity whimpered.

"We don't air family matters in public."

I expected Felicity to burst into tears. Instead she bowed her head and murmured, "I'm sorry, Corinne, but thinking about Oscar upset me all over again."

Corinne put an arm around her sister and marched her out of the room and into the hall. "Good-bye. Thanks for everything, Lexie," she tossed over her shoulder as she slammed the door behind her.

Good job, Lexie, I told myself, convinced I'd just lost two members of the mystery book club.

CHAPTER EIGHT

"What do you make of Felicity's ferret story?" Joy asked the following Wednesday afternoon as she handed me a steaming cup of coffee.

She'd called, asking me to come over ASAP, when I was driving home from teaching my morning classes. I fed Puss, ate a few tablespoons of tuna salad standing at the sink, and hurried over. I was still glowing from last night's date with Brian. I'd called to tell him about Felicity's relationship with Len Lyons, and he asked me to meet him for dinner at our local diner. Afterward, we shared a long, lingering kiss in my car, both of us grinning like fools when we said good-night. My heart soared because I had the definite sense our feelings for each other were mutual.

"Lexie?"

"Mmm?"

"I thought I lost you on another planet."

"I'm here," I said, struggling to retrieve her question. I stirred in a dab of milk and sipped. *Heavens! The Soccer Mom made awesome coffee.*

"Felicity's story has me mystified," I said. "What kind of father asks someone to kill his daughter's pet?"

"And why was Corinne so intent on shutting her up?" Joy asked, grinning like the Cheshire Cat. "I've an idea I'm working on. Meanwhile, I've learned a few things about our fellow members you'll find interesting." She crooked her finger. "Come with me."

I followed her into the small room off the kitchen that she'd turned into an office. I noted the pile of pages beside the printer. Joy picked up the sheath of papers. "This is the info I've gathered so far."

"All that. I'm impressed. Anything of interest?"

"Uh-huh. Everything's of interest. I'll start with Sadie."

"Sadie?" I moved some books to the floor so I could sit on the chair next to a small bookcase.

"She's pretty much what she claims to be, a guidance counselor at the local high school. Though she has some DWIs from over ten years ago."

"Really! I've never seen her drink."

"Probably doesn't any longer. Sadie's divorced. No children. Three months ago she arranged for a loan to buy a bigger house."

"The one she's living in is beautiful! And certainly large enough for one person."

"Haven't you noticed? Sadie likes having the biggest and the best: perfect hair, beautiful clothes. She drives a Mercedes. Her expenses far exceed what she earns on a guidance counselor's salary."

I nodded. "I suppose. Maybe she's inherited money. Or got a great settlement when she divorced."

"Neither. Sadie's maxed out her credit cards and owes money to the bank. The loan I'm referring to was arranged by Len Lyons."

"Oh? He set her up with a loan shark?"

"Looks that way. It seems Len Lyons had his finger in quite a few pies. Tim settled a minor case for our Dearly Departed Handyman a few years ago. I'm willing to bet Tim introduced Sadie to Len."

I shuddered. "What dirt you dug up about Tim?"

"Nothing much. He's not making the big bucks you'd expect a lawyer from an ivy league law school would make. Mainly because he's rarely in his office. He likes to play poker for high stakes. Runs up debts to unnamed sources."

"To friends of Len Lyons?"

"Coincidentally, yes."

I frowned. "I can't reconcile what you're telling me about Len Lyons with a guy who was romantically involved with Felicity."

"Me, neither, but that part seems genuine. I spoke to Carol Barnes, who owns the shop where Felicity works. Carol said Len stopped by at least five times to see Felicity. He seemed enchanted by her. Once he brought her flowers. When he left, Felicity asked Carol if she could keep them in the shop because she didn't want Corinne to ask where they came from."

"The Roberts sisters sound odder and odder. But getting back to Sadie, even if she knew Len Lyons, as most of us did, that doesn't mean she killed him."

"Of course not, but her dealings with the man were illegal, and often one crime leads to another. Len probably wanted a kickback for arranging the loan. What if she didn't want to give it to him?"

I pictured petite and elegant Sadie in my mind. Could she stab a man? "It's possible," I admitted. "She's in good physical shape. I think she works out with a personal trainer. What did you find out about the Billingses?"

Joy rifled through several sheets of pages. "The story of their lives, but nothing that links them to Len Lyons."

"Care to share?" I prodded

"They've been law-biding citizens all their lives. No arrests. Pay their taxes on time. Three years ago, they sold a thriving dairy farm and moved to Long Island to live near their granddaughter and her young family."

Joy pursed her lips, a sign I was in for bad news. "The Billingses have no money problems, but they've had bad luck regarding their personal lives. Only one of their four children, a son Daniel, is alive and well."

I sighed. "Poor Marge and Evan. What happened to the others?"

"Their oldest boy died in a farming accident. A daughter's dead because of a botched liposuction procedure. Their youngest, a girl named Dahlia, went to Peru four years ago and ended up living with the rebels."

"With members of The Shining Path?" I asked incredulously.

Joy nodded. "Dahlia and one of the leaders fell in love. They had a child—a little girl. In July, the Billingses got word that Dahlia had died."

I shuddered. "How awful! What did she die of?"

"The letter didn't say. The father's probably dead, too, because the letter writer said a woman was taking care of the child, but she couldn't for much longer. Now Marge and Evan are spending every cent they have to bring the child to the United States."

I stared at Joy, both impressed and saddened that she had access to this kind of information. "How did you find all this out?"

Joy laughed and waved a hand. "Don't ask."

"The man Evan met at the bowling alley looked like a thug." I shuddered. "If that's who they're dealing with, the child's being brought here illegally."

"Probably," Joy agreed. "It doesn't sound like he's an official in our state department."

"Do you think Len Lyons arranged that connection for them?"

"I couldn't find out, and not for want to trying."

I closed my eyes and tried to process what Joy had told me about the other members of our mystery book club. Everyone had baggage, be it family tragedies, addictions, or plain bad luck.

"The most intriguing of all are Felicity and Corinne Roberts." The Cheshire Cat grin returned. "If that's their names."

I opened my eyes in astonishment. "What are they, impostors?"

"Could be."

Suddenly Corinne's veiled references, which I never understood, made sense. The many times she told Felicity to stop talking when she'd brought up something regarding their childhood. "You mean like Brat Farrar?"

Joy shrugged. "I Googled Corinne. Didn't find out much. Nothing on Facebook. She doesn't tweet. Just a few articles about her bank VP job, and that she went to college in Indiana. Which proved very interesting."

"Oh?"

"I have a friend who accesses college yearbooks for

investigators. She checked out the school's yearbooks every year Corinne supposedly went there. Guess what? No photo. No mention of a Corinne Roberts."

A chill snaked down my back. Still, I wouldn't think the worst. "That doesn't mean anything. Corinne strikes me as the type of person that hates being photographed."

"Yeah. Add that to their general weirdness."

"Maybe they're hiding from their father. He sounds like an awful person."

"He does," Joy agreed, all humor gone from her voice. "I'll get to the bottom of their story sooner than later. And I haven't had time to check out Gayle's story," she said in the same somber tone. "I'll work on that next."

"Don't bother. Gayle's done plenty of dumb things in her life, but she's no liar."

"Everyone lies, about one thing or another. Speaking of which, I'm getting nowhere tracking down Mike's bimbo."

I swallowed. "Did you ever stop to think there is no bimbo?"

"Last night he was on the phone again, talking in that excited, secretive way."

"Joy—"

"Let me finish," she snapped.

I was about to snap back, then I saw the pain in her eyes.

"He mentioned The Lion's Head Inn."

He was on the phone talking about Joy's surprise party. Obviously, the idiot still hadn't made things right!

Joy sniffed. Was that a tear I saw in her eye? "I'm dying to eat there, but Mike always insists it's too expensive. And now he's taking a bimbo to stay in one of the rooms! I'll kill him!"

I was saved from answering, because Zack and Ruthie burst into the house with the pent up energy of two kids who'd been in school all day. As though on schedule, little Brandon let out a bellow to let the world know he'd awakened from his nap.

I was glad to leave the Soccer Mom to her charges. I walked home, worrying about Gayle. Then I mulled over the dirt Joy had unearthed about the members of our book club. What a sad bunch they turned out to be! We had a gambler, a compulsive spender, a couple who'd lost children and were paying some goon to smuggle their grandchild out of Peru, and two sisters with mysterious pasts.

All I had to do was find out which one killed Len Lyons and clear my sister of his murder.

CHAPTER NINE

A white pickup truck in sad need of a scrub down sprawled across my driveway. Its arrogant angle prevented any car parked inside the garage from driving off. My heart leaped to my throat when I caught sight of the orange and white Utah plates. I was about to floor the gas pedal and drive away when a bearded bear of a man stepped down from the truck and walked towards me. He wore jeans, boots, a fringed leather jacket, and a cowboy hat, and appeared to be in his early thirties. A toothpick jutted from his mouth.

"Good afternoon, ma'am. You Alexis Driscoll?"

I nodded. "And you are?"

"Pete Rogers. I've been deputized by the Stone Ridge Police Department to bring Gayle Gruen back to Utah for questioning regarding a homicide."

I stared at him, too upset to speak.

The toothpick jumped to the other side of his mouth. "Gayle's your sister, isn't she?"

"She's not here," I told him.

"You sure?"

His insinuation that I was lying did the trick. My fear turned to anger.

"Of course I'm sure! Do you see her SUV anywhere?"

He jutted his chin toward the garage. "It could be parked in there."

I glared at him as I pulled out my cell phone. "I'm calling a good friend in the Nassau County Police Department to tell him you're harassing me."

Pete Rogers stuck out his meaty palms in a conciliatory manner. "Hey, hey! No need to get testy, Ms. Driscoll. All I want is for you to tell me where Gayle is."

"She went to visit friends and didn't leave their name."

His lips split into a broad grin. "Now that's what I call downright unfriendly. Not something you'd expect of a sister."

"We argued. She left in a hurry."

He nodded as though I'd made an insightful observation. "Gayle has a habit of running off. It leaves people kind of miffed."

Miffed! Stressed as I was, I nearly laughed aloud at his choice of words. I watched him reach inside his shirt pocket and pull out a card.

"This card has all my phone numbers. What I'd like you to do is call me when you hear from Gayle. Or if she should happen to come back here."

He cast me a sly glance, as though he were revealing a secret. "Someone stabbed her boyfriend to death. The Stone Ridge Police want to talk to her."

Stabbed! "Why? Gayle didn't do it."

Pete Rogers shrugged. "Maybe yes, maybe no. But me and my partner drove all the way from Utah to bring her back for questioning. We're not leaving till we find her."

I glanced at the skinny guy sitting in the passenger seat, whom I hadn't noticed till now.

When I turned back to Pete Rogers, he'd stepped closer so that my face practically touched his jacket. I almost retched from the smell of leather, sweat, and something foul I couldn't name. I resisted the impulse to step back, and was forced to feel his breath as he spoke down to me.

"When you hear from your sister, have her call me, no matter the time. If you hide Gayle or advise her to run, you can be arrested for aiding and abetting a fugitive."

I fisted my hands to stop their trembling and forced myself to meet his gaze. "Gayle's no fugitive!"

His guffaw suddenly frightened me more than his macho

posturing had done. "Actually, she is. One of the conditions of her suspended sentence was not leaving town without notifying the authorities."

"I've no idea what you're talking about."

He studied my face. "Ms. Driscoll, I believe you're telling me the honest truth."

He jerked open the pickup's door, and swung himself into the driver's seat. "Have yourself a nice evening, and tell Gayle to call me."

Shaken, I put my car in reverse and backed up so he could drive off. Then I reached for my cell phone and called Brian.

Half an hour later, we were ensconced in the corner booth of a darkened bar while a piano played Cole Porter tunes in the background. I'd downed one apple martini and was working on my second as I told Brian my sister's story, from her boyfriend's murder to Pete Rogers' visit. Brian listened without interrupting.

"He tried to convince me she'd killed Chet. I'm sure that's what Shawn Estes told him happened."

Brian frowned. "That guy had no business approaching you. He should have talked to us."

"But why did he call Gayle a fugitive?"

Brian sighed deeply. He put his arm around me and drew me close. "Because legally that's what she is."

I pulled away to stare at him. "What are you talking about? That deputy never said she'd been charged with homicide."

"Six months ago, Gayle and her boyfriend, Chester Fenton, were apprehended for growing marijuana."

Stunned, I sank back against the cushioned banquette. "How do you know?"

"I called the Stone Ridge Police Department and spoke to a police sergeant. She and Chet were both on probation. Gayle wasn't supposed to leave town without first contacting the authorities."

"So it's true." After a minute, I asked. "What about Shawn Estes? Was he growing marijuana too?"

"That's the odd piece here. Shawn Estes was the arresting officer."

I shook my head in disbelief. "How weird. Gayle said Chet and Shawn were friends. They'd been working a card game scam together." I turned to Brian. "Maybe Shawn was involved in the marijuana business too."

"If he ran a scam, he's dirty. It's possible they were growing weed together. He must have had something over Chet and Gayle that stopped them from telling the authorities he was involved."

"But why would he turn on Chet?" I asked.

"You said Chet wanted to stop the card game scam. Maybe he wanted to stop growing weed, too. There's no point in speculating about what happened until we find out more."

"Gayle was involved with a bunch of crooks," I said. "No wonder she ran." My sister was in more trouble than I'd imagined.

"What bothers me is that Chester Fenton was stabbed to death with a knife. The wound was very much like the one that killed Len Lyons."

I scowled at him. "You sure found out a lot about Gayle."

"I had to, Lexie. It's my job."

My head was spinning. I'd only told Brian about Gayle so he'd protect her. Now he'd probably put out a BOLO for her and she'd end up in jail. What had I done?

"Are you saying my sister killed her boyfriend then drove all the way to Long Island and knifed Len Lyons?"

"You said yourself that Gayle thought Estes sent Lyons to take care of her."

"But Gayle would never kill anyone! Besides, she had no blood on her when I saw her that morning."

"She could have changed her clothes before she woke you up." Brian's voice turned gentle. "I'm going to have the techs examine her room—in fact, the entire house. I should have ordered it last week."

I downed what was left of my drink and stood up. "Thanks, Brian. I ask you to help my sister and instead you treat her as a suspect!"

Brian signaled to the waiter to bring the check, then whipped out his phone. "I'll have the crime lab send over a few investigators now, so you won't have to sleep someplace else tonight."

"How kind of you," I said.

"Lexie, I—" Brian put his hand on mine, but I brushed it aside. He let out a deep sigh. "My mistake. I should have handed over the case when I saw the address."

*****

I made it easy for the crime scene people. I put Puss in his carrier for an overnight at the vet's, then drove to Old Cadfield to spend the night at Rosie and Hal's. They were both as sympathetic as I could hope, plying me with tea and kind words as I told them my sad story. I fell asleep in their guest room, mulling over Gayle's failure to come clean about her illegal activities when she'd told me about Chet's murder. I tried not to view this as a betrayal, but her omission ached like an unhealed wound.

She probably was afraid I'd be less than sympathetic after learning she'd been arrested for growing weed. And she was right. How could she have been so stupid? What was she doing, getting involved with people like Chet and Shawn, letting their disregard for laws and ethics rule her life? Had she been so desperate for money, she no longer cared how she made it? I'd done many crazy things in my time, but I'd never gone around committing felonies.

Which made me realize once again that I hardly knew my sister. I loved Gayle and still felt the need to protect her, but I knew next to nothing about her everyday life in Utah, her friends, or her values. Except for the fact that she hadn't killed Len Lyons.

CHAPTER TEN

Detective Paulson leaned back in his swivel chair and grimaced. He was a large man in his mid-fifties and radiated immense presence.

"We found a knife in the room your sister slept in when she stayed with you."

The small office tilted, first in one direction then in the other. Strong hands gripped my shoulders. I opened my eyes, surprised that a man of his size and girth could move so quickly. Surprised, too, by the sympathy in his eyes.

"Miss Driscoll, are you all right?"

Of course not. "I—could I have some water?"

He opened the door and barked out my request. A bottle of water arrived a minute later. I gulped it down like a dehydrated traveler after three days in the desert.

"Where's Detective Donovan?" I asked. "Why isn't he telling me this?"

My moment of sympathy was over. "Lieutenant Donovan's no longer on the case. I'm in charge of the investigation."

Tears welled up, and I blinked them back furiously. Gayle was in the worst possible trouble, and Brian hadn't had the courtesy to tell me himself!

"Where was the knife?"

"Behind the bookcase."

I forced myself to think logically. Rationally. "Maybe a

former tenant left it."

"I understand the house was painted before you moved in."

I staggered to my feet. "I want to see the knife."

"You can't. The crime lab is testing it to see if it's the weapon that was used to stab Leo Lionni."

I glared at the detective. "You can't think for a moment my sister killed that man, left the knife to incriminate herself, and took off! No one's that stupid or self-destructive. Someone planted it there!"

Detective Paulson nodded. "That may be true, and I'm not saying your sister killed Len Lyons, but you have to face facts. We found the knife in the room Gayle slept in. We need to talk to her, Lexie. And the fact that she ran off the same morning he was murdered doesn't speak in her favor."

I gnawed at my lips. "I explained to Bri—Detective Donovan why she took off."

"You also told him your sister thought Lyons had been sent by Shawn Estes to murder her."

I suddenly remembered. "I hosted a book club meeting Saturday morning. Any of the members could have hidden the knife in that room on their way to the kitchen or the bathroom! No one would have noticed. I certainly didn't."

Detective Paulson handed me a pad. "Please make a list of everyone who attended that meeting. We'll talk to them. Someone may have seen something that morning."

I did as he asked and noticed, with a pang, that he'd set up a recorder while I'd been writing.

"If you don't mind, I'd like to tape our conversation as I take you through the morning you discovered Leo Lionni's body in your backyard."

He questioned me most thoroughly, then segued into my relationship with Gayle and the reason she gave me for leaving Utah. After he had me repeat my conversation with Pete Rogers practically verbatim, he shut off the recorder.

"I think that's it for now."

I sat back, thoroughly drained. We'd been going at it for almost two hours. I left after promising to call him if I remembered anything I'd failed to include or if Gayle contacted me.

"If your sister hasn't contacted you in twenty-four hours, we'll put out a BOLO and she'll be brought in in handcuffs." The detective looked troubled when he added, "For everyone's sake, convince her to come to the precinct. If you help her do otherwise, you'll be charged with obstruction of justice."

I sat in my car, too distraught to drive. Gayle had gotten herself into one hell of a mess. Now the police in two states were after her, and I hadn't the slightest idea where she was!

I'd gone to the precinct after teaching my classes, and now I dreaded going home. I should have gone straight to the vet to rescue Puss from his cage. Instead, I drove to the nearby mall and wandered mindlessly from one department store to the next. At three o'clock I was about to stop for a sandwich when my cell phone rang. I sat on a bench outside Bloomingdale's to answer it.

"Lexie, it's me, Gayle."

"Oh."

"What's wrong? You sound exhausted. Or angry."

"You're right on both counts. Where are you?"

"In Brooklyn. Still at my friend's apartment."

"Shawn Estes sent a deputy here to bring you back to Utah. Pete Rogers? He wants you to call him."

"Pete went to your house! Did—did he hurt you, Lexie?"

"Of course not. But he said you're a criminal. You failed to mention you and Chet were charged for growing weed."

Silence. I waited it out.

"I'm sorry. I should have told you. Chet had set up everything before we even met. I swear, all I did was water the plants. Shawn was a silent partner."

"Really? Then why did he arrest you?"

"Because some other cop found out about the plants. He was suspicious about Shawn. Shawn arrested us to throw the other officer off and prove he wasn't involved. He swore he'd erase it from our records."

I laughed at her ludicrous reasoning. "Shawn's one swell guy. And you believed him?"

"Chet said we had to. I was afraid to tell the judge about Shawn's involvement."

"I find it difficult to keep up with your life of crime," I told her coldly.

"Please, Lexie! I don't know where to go. My friends told me I can only stay here another day." She lowered her voice. "And I'm running out of money."

"You have to come back here."

"I won't! Pete will come after me. He can be rough, even to women."

I shuddered at my near miss, then felt a wave of anger at my sister for having put me in harm's way.

"Gayle, there's more. The Nassau County police want to talk to you. They found a knife hidden in the room you slept in at my house. They think it's the knife that killed Len Lyons."

"I didn't put it there! I swear I didn't." Gayle began to bawl deep, heart-wrenching sobs. "I never killed anyone! I don't know how I got involved in all of this. My life is a mess."

"Don't cry, Gayle. We'll figure something out."

"Why is all this happening to me?"

Her self-pity grated on my nerves. "Because you got mixed up with the wrong people. You should have walked away from Chet the moment you knew what he was up to."

"But he was the sweetest man, Lexie. And he loved me-e-e."

I waited for her crying jag to subside. When it didn't, I said, "My advice is to come back here and talk to the police. A Detective Paulson's in charge of the case now. He seems like a decent man."

The waterworks came to an abrupt halt. "I'll think about it," Gayle said, and hung up.

I headed for the parking lot, no longer hungry. Our last sisterly conversation had awakened memories I'd managed to put on the back burner of my mind. I'd forgotten that Gayle was a whiner with a healthy sense of entitlement and the habit of blaming other people for whatever went wrong in her life. After she'd come home from Europe, she'd drifted from one place to another, always picking up and moving on because someone had done her wrong.

At first I'd call to give her pep talks and encouragement. I did my best to boost her ego and her spirits. But after watching her make the same mistakes again and again, I grew disgusted and started telling it like it was. "Think before you get involved with a guy," I'd advise. "I knew he was bad news from what you told me." Gayle didn't like hearing what I had to say. She called me a nag, uptight and worse. And so we'd drifted apart, speaking on rare occasions. When we talked she kept our conversations light and impersonal. So much time had passed, I'd forgotten how it had always been. Until now.

But Gayle wasn't a liar. She'd sworn that she hadn't killed Len Lyons and I believed her. She hadn't left that knife in the guest room any more than she'd killed Len Lyons. I didn't know if someone was trying to frame her or had hidden the knife to deflect suspicion from himself or herself. Gayle needed my help. She was my kid sister and in a terrible jam. Even though it was partly of her own making, I had to help her.

I rescued Puss from the vet's and brought him home, where he ignored me until he was too hungry to keep on snubbing me. He allowed me to pet him as he gobbled down his food, which made me smile. Suddenly I was starving. I took a frozen focaccia from the freezer, nuked it, and polished it off as I stood at the counter. The doorbell rang. Worried that it might be Pete Rogers back for a second visit, I peered through the peephole, then swung open the door for Brian.

"I should have told you I'm off the case," he said by way of a greeting.

"That would have been civil. Considerate. Decent," I said coldly.

"What do you have to drink, and I don't mean coffee?"

I poured him a jigger of scotch, which he downed in record speed. We sat down side by side on the living room sofa.

"Were you thrown off, or did you recuse yourself or whatever the department calls it?" I asked.

"A bit of both, after I told the captain of my close ties to a suspect's sister."

Close ties! I didn't know a person could feel elated and annoyed at the same time. "Will this count as a black mark against you?"

Brian shrugged. "It is what it is. Now that Gayle's a possible suspect, I'm too close to the case. When it comes to trial, I don't want to be the one to screw up the possibility of a conviction, regardless of who the murderer turns out to be. My captain agrees."

"What's Detective Paulson like?"

"He's a good man. I've worked with him on several homicides."

I drew a deep breath. "Gayle called me. She swears she didn't kill anyone, and I believe her."

Brian laughed. "You're her sister. You're supposed to believe her."

"Thanks. She's done lots of stupid things in her life, but I believe her when she says she's no killer. I told her to come back here."

"Is she coming?"

I shrugged. "I don't know. She's running out of money, so maybe she will. Oh!" I suddenly remembered. "Gayle said Shawn was a partner in the marijuana plant business. He only blew the whistle because another cop was about to."

"That makes sense," Brian said.

"It does?"

"Sure."

I hugged him. "Then you believe Gayle's innocent?"

"Hey, I didn't say that. Just get her to come back here. She doesn't want to get Paulson mad. He comes across as a sweetheart, but he can be one mean SOB."

I shuddered. "I'll do my best."

We ended up on the living room couch smooching away. The house phone rang. I disentangled my arms and legs and hurried into the kitchen to answer it.

"Hi, Lexie, it's Sadie."

"Oh, hello."

"Are you all right? You sound funny."

"Yes. I just woke up from a nap."

"Sorry. I called to see if you're free next Sunday night."

"I suppose so. Who can think that far ahead?" I murmured.

"I'll take that as a yes. It's Halloween, and I've decided to throw a costume party," Sadie said. "That is, Tim and I thought a party would be fun. We'll host it here, at my house."

"Sounds like a great idea."

"Come in costume. And bring someone, if you like."

I peered into the living room where Brian sat up rearranging his clothes. "Maybe I will."

Then her subliminal message kicked in. "I didn't know you and Tim were dating." I cringed because the expression sounded so old-fashioned. These days it referred to a couple's sexual relationship.

"We are." Sadie laughed. "We're still getting used to the big shift in our relationship. It happened the night Len Lyons spied on our book club meeting."

Something in her voice made me ask, "Did you know it was Len at the window?"

The laughter left her voice. "I saw his face and wondered if he'd come looking for me." She faltered. "I owed him money and was late paying him back."

"I see."

"I was too embarrassed to say anything at the time, but his appearing like that really got to me. Tim realized how upset I was when he drove me home. He meant to comfort me as a friend." The happiness was back in her voice. "And ended up spending the night."

"Oh. How nice," I added belatedly.

"We were shocked to find out someone killed Len the very next morning. And in your backyard, Lexie."

"Not as surprised as I was," I said wryly. "Do you still have to pay Len's estate what you owed him."

"So far I haven't heard from anyone. I hope I never do."

Could Sadie *and* Tim have killed Len? Two people doing the deed made it easier than one and might explain the body's position. *But how would they have lured him to my backyard? And why?*

I sat down next to Brian and placed a hand on his knee. "Sadie just invited me to a Halloween party next Sunday. Wanna come?"

He shrugged. "Sure. Why not?"

"The members of the book club will probably be there."

He gave me a wolfish grin. "I'm off the case, remember? Do we have to wear costumes?"

"Yep."

"I'll leave that to you, along with two rules: no tights and no fangs."

"Okay."

He kissed me long and hard. When I came up for air, I said, "Sadie told me she and Tim are going out. The morning Len Lyons was killed, they were together."

"I know."

"You do?" I drew back, stung by his smug expression.

"I interviewed them, remember? And don't give me that look. I can't share what I learn about your book club pals with you."

"I suppose," I conceded. "But Sadie owed Len money, and he robbed Tim. Maybe the two lovebirds got together and killed him."

"Maybe," Brian said skeptically.

"You don't think so."

"I don't think one way or another. We're checking out every angle, every alibi. That is, Paulson and his men are. I'm out of it."

I stroked his cheek. "I'm sorry you're off the case because of me."

"I should have passed on it immediately. In a way, it's a good thing we don't have a suspect in custody. His attorney would have a field day once he found out I knew you, maybe get the case thrown out of court. Now where were we?"

He reached for me as the phone rang again.

"Sorry." I stood to answer it.

"I'm out of here." He walked toward the front door.

"Brian, wait!" I called over my shoulder as I headed in the opposite direction. "Hello. Who is this?" I demanded.

"Lexie, it's me, Al."

"Be right back."

I plunked down the phone and chased after Brian, who was half out the door. "Don't be mad. I'm sorry things are so hectic around here."

"Go back to your phone call," he said, kissing the top of my head.

"When will I see you?" I asked.

"Next Sunday." He grinned. "If not before."

Relieved that he wasn't angry, I returned to the kitchen and to Al. "My apologies. I was just seeing someone out."

"Are you all right, Lexie? You sounded so brusque when you

answered the phone."

"Sorry. I've been on edge lately, with everything that's happening around here."

"That's understandable. Have they caught that handyman's killer yet?" Al asked.

"No."

"See much of Brian Donovan?" he asked, then quickly added, "You did say he's in charge of the investigation."

"He's no longer on the case," I said, then wished I hadn't.

"Oh? Did he screw things up?"

"Of course not! Another detective took over because Brian's busy with another homicide," I said. "The police have been interviewing everyone, including the members of the book club."

"I hope you're not on their list of suspects," Al said, sounding worried.

"I'm not." *But my sister is*, I thought, and wondered why I didn't want to share my concerns about Gayle with him.

Al gave a little laugh. "Lexie, tell me you're not playing detective again."

"Don't be silly. How are things in Great Britain?"

"I'm pleased to say they're going swimmingly well."

"How wonderful!" I enthused, glad to be happy about something.

"The company's more than pleased with my plans, and they've referred me to their sister company. It looks like I'll be in London a few weeks longer than I'd planned."

"That's all right," I said agreeably. "Take as long as you need."

"Lexie! Don't you miss me even a little?"

I felt a twinge of guilt. "Of course I do! I'm not very good on long distance phone calls."

"We'll talk about things once I'm home again."

"Of course we will," I agreed. I suddenly realized the time difference. "Al, isn't it very late where you are?"

"It's past two in the morning. All this excitement has kept me awake, but I should get to sleep. We've a long drive to the other company tomorrow. I'll call you very soon. Love you."

"Take care of yourself," was the best I could manage.

I hung up, irritable and out of sorts. I now knew I didn't love

Allistair West and never would. I was crazy head-over-heels about Brian Donovan, and pretty sure he was crazy about me. I had no idea where our relationship was going, though I was aware that getting involved with a cop had all sorts of built-in problems.

I should have told Al the truth. He sensed it, I knew, but I'd wait until he was home again to end our relationship. It was the decent thing to do.

And the most cowardly. Besides, a little voice jibed at me, you don't want him to tell you to leave this house before The Case of the Dead Handyman is solved.

CHAPTER ELEVEN

I dragged a very full garbage pail to the curb. As I headed back to the house, I waved to Corinne, who was outside performing the same chore. She stopped and gestured to the pail behind her.

"Can you believe Felicity and I make enough garbage to fill two large pails in as many days? And half the time I eat dinner out."

I laughed. "I've wondered the same thing. In my case, it must be all those microwave dinners."

"Are you going to Sadie and Tim's party?"

"Yes. What about you and Felicity?"

"I suppose so. I think it will do her some good to get out and be with people. She was terribly upset when they found that dead man so close to our house."

"I can imagine. Felicity's very sensitive."

Corinne edged closer to me. "Have you heard anything about the police finding the person who did it?"

"No. Nothing."

"Strange that he was killed in your backyard."

"I thought so. See you next Sunday."

I'd started for the house, when Corinne called to me. "How's your sister?"

I stopped in my tracks and turned. "Gayle's fine. I spoke to her this afternoon."

Corinne closed the gap between us. "She seems very sweet. Kind of a lost soul."

I shrugged. "Gayle and I are very different. She's been going through a rough patch, and I'm afraid I haven't been much help."

"You're her older sister. She expects you to make things right." Corinne snorted. "Take it from one who knows."

"We haven't been close since we were kids."

"Younger sisters are a pain in the butt. Still, it's our job to look after them."

It sounded as though she were chastising me for not knowing the rules. Well, I didn't—not her rules, anyway. Clearly, Corinne's point of reference was very different from mine. Felicity was borderline unstable while Gayle had a habit of making the wrong choices.

Back inside, I mused how each of us viewed life through a uniquely distorted lens. I opted for a life of freedom and usually chose lovers who proved to be unavailable one way or another. Al wanted a stable, ongoing relationship. Did I find that boring or confining? Was that why I'd convinced myself I couldn't love him? Brian was warm, and I had no reason to believe he had commitment issues. But his job ran his life, and there would be times he wouldn't be able to be there for me. Was that my reason for choosing him over Al? Not this time, I decided, and hoped I was right.

As for the others, Sadie coveted material possessions, Tim loved to gamble. Even Joy, who had chosen to be a full-time mom instead of an active FBI agent, was so paranoid she'd imagined her husband was having an affair.

Who was normal? What was normal?

*****

I set out early Saturday morning to shop for our Halloween costumes. I mentally ran through my list as I pulled out of the garage: an eye patch, a blousy white shirt, a sword, and a pirate's hat for Brian. A peasant-type blouse, an eye patch, and a sword for me. I had the perfect skirt and boots in my closet.

I couldn't find what I wanted in the nearby mall, so I drove to a costume store a few towns away. The extent of their stock boggled my mind. So many choices! Too many choices! I grabbed an armful of blouses and was on my way to the try-on room when someone called my name.

I spun around, startled to find Marge and Evan Billings beaming at me.

"Hi, Marge. Hi, Evan. Getting costumes for Sadie and Tim's party?"

"Uh-huh," Marge said. "We can't decide who to go as—Tarzan and Jane or Wonder Woman and Superman."

I covered my mouth to hide my grin. Considering their girth and white hair, they'd look better dressed as Mr. and Mrs. Santa Claus.

"Can't help you there," I said, to be tactful.

"Of course, you can't!" Evan glared at his wife. "We'll look like damn fools as super heroes or jungle people."

Marge patted his arm. "All right, dear. Don't fret. We'll go as our usual."

Evan looked relieved. "I'm glad you're being reasonable. Let's see if they have a new head for me. The old one's gotten mangy-looking."

"All right, Evan. And I can use a new pair of braids."

Curious, I asked, "What are you two going as?"

"The wolf and Little Red Riding Hood," Evan said.

The three of us shared a good long laugh. *Such nice people, and they've been through so much. Surely, neither Marge nor Evan could have stabbed Len Lyons to death.*

But just because I liked them didn't mean they were innocent. The Billingses were about to walk off, when I asked, "Would you like to go out for coffee when we're through here?"

Evan looked at his watch. "It's a quarter past eleven. I wouldn't mind a bite of lunch."

Marge cast a fond wifely glance at her husband. "Evan still keeps farmer's hours. He's usually up at five each morning."

"Even though I've no cows to see to," he added.

Awake at five in the morning! And they lived a few blocks from my house.

"How about the diner down the street?" I asked. "I'll try on these blouses, pick out a few other items, and be good to go."

"We'll meet you at the cash register," Evan agreed.

Half an hour later we settled into a booth roomy enough for six. We studied the menu and ordered. I asked for a Greek omelet and coffee. Marge and Evan ordered cheeseburgers, well-done with the works, and large sodas.

"I should have told her to leave off the fries," Marge said when the waitress was well out of hearing.

"Next time," Evan answered, putting his hand over hers. "We'll skip dessert tonight."

I sighed. That had to be the most romantic line I'd heard in ages.

Marge gave me a bittersweet smile. "We both ought to lose a ton of weight, but we're making little headway."

Thinking of their three dead children, I said, "It's difficult to diet when you're under stress. Then I added, "I imagine Len Lyons' murder has made us all nervous."

"Good riddance, I say." Evan scowled. "Robbing us and the others must have been penny ante to him. We heard he was involved in criminal activity up to his eyeballs."

I leaned closer. "Like what?"

"You name it," Marge said. "Len had connections to every type of gangster—from loan shark to hit man, and took a percentage from everyone he referred."

Evan nodded. "He was connected, all right."

I pretended to have a flash of insight. "When he was fixing my dishwasher, I happened to mention I was running short of cash. Len said he knew a man who could help me out, but I never pursued it."

"Neither did we," Marge said quickly. "Maybe that's why he robbed us."

"Naw." Evan shook his head. "He burgled Tim's house, and they've done their share of business together."

"Evan!" Marge scolded.

He looked abashed, but said, "Relax, Marge. Everyone knows Tim loves to gamble. Len set him up with a bookie."

"And Sadie lives above her means," I added.

They gave me knowing smiles.

I hesitated, then asked, "Len never referred you to anyone?"

"Ah, here's our food!" Marge exclaimed as our waitress brought over three oval plates.

My omelet was delicious—fluffy and light. As I ate, I wracked my brain for a way to get them to tell me the truth about the giant thug Evan was talking to outside the bowling alley.

I sipped my coffee, then ventured a gambit. "Still, I can see where knowing someone like Len might be useful. Especially after you've tried every legal avenue and can't get what you need."

Marge and Evan exchanged glances.

"If people needed his services," I continued, "I can't imagine why someone would want to kill him?"

Evan laughed. It wasn't a pleasant sound. "I can. Len Lyons was a greedy son-of-a-bitch. He'd agree to a price, you'd pay it, then later he'd ask for more."

"How do you know?" I asked.

"We heard he pulled that stunt over and over," Evan said angrily, not meeting my gaze. "I bet that's what got him killed. It might have been any one of twenty, thirty people—so I've heard."

We walked back to our cars parked behind the costume shop and said our good-byes. I drove home slowly rerunning my conversation with the Billingses in my head. Evan's fury at Len Lyons was too raw not to be personal. Putting together what I knew, I'd venture Len had introduced the Billingses to the man at the bowling alley. When Len asked for more money and the Billingses couldn't or wouldn't pay up, Len retaliated by burgling their home.

And Evan killed him?

Or Evan was right. The murderer had been another of Len's victims. Someone who wasn't a member of the book club.

CHAPTER TWELVE

"I'm not going to any stupid Halloween party!" Felicity said with more heat than I'd ever heard her express. "I don't care *what* Corinne says."

We were sitting in the Roberts' den. I was beginning to regret my decision to stop by on the off-chance that Felicity hadn't gone to work this afternoon.

"Is it because you're mourning Len's death?" I asked gently.

She nodded, her eyes filled with unshed tears. "You're the only person who knows about Leo besides Carol, my boss."

I cleared my throat. "I know Len was very good to you, but I've heard some things about him that, well, are rather disturbing."

"Like what!" Felicity's sadness quickly changed to suspicion.

"You heard yourself—the Billingses and Tim are pretty sure he burgled their houses after doing work for them. And he was involved in other criminal activities."

Felicity pressed her lips together and nodded. "I may as well tell you. It's true. But Leo was going to turn his life around! He swore he would." Her smile was bittersweet when she said, "And then we were going away and getting married. And I wouldn't have to live with Corinne any more and do what she says."

I was taken aback by her vehemence. "Does Corinne always tell you what to do?"

"Every day she makes a list of things I should do and say and another list of what I shouldn't do and say. I'm sick and tired of it!"

This time the tears spilled over, accompanied by shuddering wails. I stood beside Felicity and rubbed her back until she grew calm.

"Here," I said, handing her a tissue.

She blew her nose, and tried for a smile. "Sorry. Corinne says I have to learn to control my feelings."

"It must be difficult to control them when your boyfriend just died."

"Fiancé," Felicity corrected me.

"Fiancé," I repeated. "And you're probably wondering who killed him."

She flinched. I felt like a monster for upsetting her, but Felicity probably knew more about Len than anyone else. From what I'd learned about him, she was the only person he cared for. He might have let down his guard and revealed something that could lead to his murderer. A small detail she wasn't even aware that she knew.

"I know who killed him," she mumbled.

I gave a start, then told myself I'd imagined what I'd heard. "What did you say?"

"I know who killed Leo."

I gaped at her.

"It was Johnny."

"The man who killed your ferret?"

She nodded. "Yes."

I felt a rush of excitement. "Did you see him the morning Len was killed?"

She shook her head. "I just know."

She was delusional, talking about someone from her past. There was no way she could be right. Still, I had to find out more.

"When did you last see Johnny?"

Felicity shrugged. "A few years ago. Three years. Or maybe five."

"Oh." Disappointment washed over me. I was an idiot, trying to get information from a person with such a tenuous hold on reality. "Perhaps someone other than Johnny killed Len,

83

someone here in town."

Felicity nodded. "Could be. Leo told me lots of people didn't appreciate the services he provided."

I bet! "Some of those people may be coming to Sadie's Halloween party," I said, my optimism reviving with every word I uttered. It suddenly seemed vitally important that Felicity attend the party. "They'll be drinking and not watching what they say. Maybe one of them will make a comment connected to Len's death, a comment the police can use to catch his murderer."

Felicity stared at me as though she were reading my soul. Finally, she said, "You think the murderer will be at the party?"

"There's a good chance," I said.

After a long minute, she nodded. "I think I'll go as Cinderella."

"Excellent choice," I told her. "I'll help you with your costume, if you like."

*****

Nothing much happened the week before the party. I had the strongest urge to bump into Tim accidentally on purpose and question him about Len, but figured I'd be more successful Halloween night.

I spent Thursday afternoon helping Felicity sew her costume. She was remarkably creative, and had bought a blonde wig and glass high heels. I prodded her about Len, but she wasn't very forthcoming, either about how the two of them had met or naming anyone whom Len considered trouble. I mentioned that Brian would be coming to the party.

Her eyes twinkled. "You mean, as your plus one?"

"Uh huh," I said, surprised that she knew the expression.

She gave me an elfin grin. "How cool is that! Will he be wearing a costume?"

"Of course," I said.

Felicity turned serious. "I'm glad Detective Donovan will be there. This way we'll have three pairs of eyes looking for the murderer."

"Yes, we will," I agreed, not bothering to add that Brian was no longer in charge of the investigation. I hoped I wasn't making a mistake by encouraging her to play detective. "Is Corinne bringing a date to the party?" I asked, more to change the subject than because I was interested.

"Are you kidding?" Felicity said scornfully. "Corinne hasn't had a boyfriend since—"

"Since when?" I prodded.

"Since Johnny."

"Johnny!" I exclaimed. "The guy who killed your pet ferret?"

"Yes," she answered in her little-girl voice. "They used to go together. A long time ago."

Felicity's lip trembled. *Oh, no!*

"What's Corinne going as to the party?" I asked, hoping to stem the waterworks.

She wrinkled up her face. "A witch."

I burst out laughing.

"She *is* a witch," Felicity said. "Half the time she knows what I'm thinking before I say it out loud. And she's always telling me what to do. I know I get too emotional sometimes, but I can handle more than she gives me credit."

It was the most adult thing I've ever heard her say. "Did you try telling her that?"

"A few times."

"What happened?"

"Corinne says she does what she does for my own good. She's my older sister, and I'm supposed to listen to her. That upsets me so I start to cry. Then Corinne says, 'See. You're too emotional to make your own decisions.'" Felicity shrugged. "Maybe she's right, since it always ends up like that."

"Maybe you're both right."

"What do you mean?" Felicity asked.

"Maybe you can take charge of your own affairs gradually. Little by little."

Felicity threw her arms around me. "You're so smart, Lexie! I'm so glad you're my friend."

*****

Sunday evening, Brian came over at six o'clock. We polished

85

off the avocado and tuna salads I'd prepared, along with a bottle of chardonnay. Then it was time to put on our pirate costumes. We stripped down to our underwear and, for some reason or other, started kissing.

We ended up in bed. It was our first time together and it went pretty well, I thought—thoroughly enjoyable, sexy, and friendly. I found myself still smiling as I cuddled up against Brian, his arm firmly around me under the quilt. I turned to look at him, and he kissed me lightly on the lips.

"I've been wanting to do this ever since we met," he said.

"And now you have."

He moved above me and grinned. "Again?"

"Mmm," I answered. "Why not?"

CHAPTER THIRTEEN

Judging by the thumping rock music escaping from Sadie's house, the party was in full swing when Brian and I arrived. Sadie met us at the door in a purple harem costume that showed off her slender figure. She downed the contents of her wine glass and giggled.

"Well, hello, Lexie. Tim and I were beginning to think you were a no show."

I returned her air kiss. "Are you kidding? Brian and I wouldn't miss your party for the world."

I handed her the bottle of wine we'd brought, and almost laughed aloud at her alarmed expression when she recognized the man beneath the eye patch and buccaneer's hat.

"Detective Donovan," she murmured. "How nice to see you."

Tim, looking dashing in the colorful costume of a circus ringmaster, approached us with outstretched arms.

He winked as he bussed my cheek. "You look gorgeous in your sexy pirate costume. A welcome relief from your usual professorial attire."

He shook Brian's hand. "Welcome, Detective Donovan. I had no idea the police would be here tonight!"

I couldn't tell if Tim was put out or being his usual wry self. I fluttered my mascaraed lashes in the best Betty Boop manner. "I hope that doesn't present a problem." I slipped my arm into Brian's. "Sadie said to bring a date."

"Lexie and I are a couple," Brian said, setting my heart aflutter, "as you and Sadie appear to be."

"So we are!" Sadie declared, grabbing my hand and leading me down the hall. "Lexie, let's get a drink for you and the lieutenant."

"Sure" I said as we headed for the kitchen.

"A scotch on the rocks would be great," Brian called to me.

I glanced at the milling crowd of thirty or forty people dressed in elaborate costumes and finally caught sight of Felicity. The witch standing beside her had to be Corinne. I'd have plenty of time to be sociable later. Now Sadie had her own agenda.

She halted at the kitchen entrance and demanded, "Since when are you and the lieutenant an item?"

I shrugged, trying for casual. "We've known each other for a while now."

Sadie laughed. "You are one *femme fatale*, Dr. Driscoll. I thought Allistair West, world-renown architect, was your main squeeze."

The heat rose to my face. "Al and I are…friends," I said, silently vowing to tell him the situation the next time we spoke.

"Whatever pleases you," Sadie declared with a wave of her hand. "It's Halloween and we're here to have fun! No sad stories. No talk of murder."

"Of course not," I agreed.

We moved on to the kitchen table, which had been turned into a bar. A burly bearded man in a red devil suit was acting as bartender.

"Hey there, Ron," Sadie greeted him. "This is my friend, Lexie. Lexie, Ron Alvarez. Give her what she wants."

"A chardonnay, and a scotch on the rocks, please."

"Coming right up," Ron said and grinned.

I thanked him for the drinks and turned, intent on returning to Brian, but Sadie wasn't through with me yet. She led me over to the refrigerator and asked if the cops were any closer to finding Len Lyons' killer.

I laughed. "I thought we weren't going to talk about murder."

"I meant no new murders. Len's is unfinished business."

"Brian's no longer in charge of the case."

"Ah," was Sadie's inscrutable reply.

"The police have no suspect that I know of, but I find it interesting that everyone in our book club knew Len, including you."

Harem Girl shrugged. "I met him a couple of times. I certainly didn't kill him."

"Everyone says that," I muttered.

A vampire couple came over to talk to Sadie. I grabbed my chance to escape.

"Have fun!" Sadie called as I walked off with my drinks.

"I will," I answered, telling myself not to be disappointed. What did I expect? Sadie to own up that after Len set her up with a loan shark, he demanded money from both of them, and either Sadie or the loan shark knifed him to death?

I found Brian chatting with Joy and Mike, who were dressed alike as two Charlie Chaplin tramps. I handed Brian his drink, and he wrapped his arm around my waist.

"Oh?" Joy asked. "What's this?"

"Nothing," I said the same moment Brian said, "What do you think it is?"

Joy grinned broadly. She waited for the two men to resume their animated conversation, then pumped her fist in the air.

"How can you tell?" I whispered.

"It's written all over you," she whispered back. "Good luck. Brian's adorable, even if all men are bastards."

"You don't mean that," I said.

Joy shrugged.

"Learn anything new?" I asked.

She shook her head. "Nothing conclusive." She glared at Mike. "Except he's still acting like someone in the throes of a new love affair. Kind of like you."

I let out a huff of exasperation. "I meant, have you learned anything new regarding Len's murder?"

"Not a thing." She lowered her voice. "They have no new leads so they're doing their best to track down your sister. What a bunch of idiots! That knife had to have been planted."

I grimaced. "The Utah police want her, too, and I'm worried that they'll find her first. I haven't heard from Gayle in days. I keep hoping she'll come back here and deal with our police department, but I've no idea what she'll do."

"She'll be safer here, even if they book her until we find the murderer."

"I've been talking to Felicity. She's the one person Len Lyons would have confided in. I'm hoping eventually she'll tell me something important. Something real."

Joy sent me a look of disbelief. "What do you mean—real? Is Felicity delusional?"

I gave a little laugh. "I wonder. She told me that Johnny killed Len."

"Who's Johnny? Oh, the guy who killed her ferret."

"Right. And when I pressed her, she admitted she hasn't seen him in years."

Joy sighed. "We can't depend on anything Felicity tells you. She hates this Johnny for what he did to her pet. Now she thinks he's the source of every bad thing that's happened to her."

"Maybe you're right. But she said something even stranger. When I asked if Corinne would be bringing a date, she said her sister hasn't dated anyone since her last boyfriend, who happens to be this Johnny."

"Hmmm," Joy mused. "She's obsessed with this Johnny."

"He's someone from their past."

"But not Len Lyons' past," Joy pointed out.

"Too bad we don't know his last name. Then maybe you could track him down."

Joy grinned. "Right. Life should be that simple."

I meandered back into the kitchen and handed Ron, the Red Devil, my wine glass for a refill. Tim and Evan, his wolf head tucked under one arm, stood in the small alcove beyond the kitchen. I considered joining them until I realized that despite their low voices, they were arguing. I thanked Ron for my drink and moved closer to the men, ostensibly to allow the couple behind me reach Ron.

"We paid good money, to you and to him," Evan said. He caught sight of me and turned his back.

Tim glanced at me, then answered Evan in a tone too low for me to make out his words. But I'd heard enough to know it was Tim and not Len Lyons who had introduced the Billingses to the man they hoped would bring them their granddaughter.

I wandered back into the living room, and made my way to Marge and the Roberts sisters sitting in the far corner of the room. We exchanged greetings and compliments about one another's costumes.

Felicity beamed at me. "Lexie helped me with mine," she told Marge.

"And don't you look beautiful?" Marge commented. "Maybe you'll win best costume."

Felicity blushed. "I-I don't know."

Corinne leered at us, showing off her blackened teeth.

I burst out laughing. "You look beautiful, too, Corinne."

The four of us chatted about innocuous topics. I sent Felicity meaningful glances, but she didn't notice. Clearly, she was enjoying herself too much to remember our conversation about her checking out the guests in hopes of learning something about her dead fiancé's murder. I couldn't blame her. For the first time since I'd met her, she seemed to be enjoying herself. I was about to leave the women and move on, when we heard the opening of Beethoven's Fifth.

"That's me," Corinne apologized. She reached inside her copious black robe and pulled out her cell phone. She turned away, covering her other ear to block out the party noise.

"What?" she exclaimed. She listened, then asked, "How did they get in?"

"Oh, no! How much did they take?"

She covered her face with her hand. "You called Mr. Grissom? And the police? Call our insurance company, too." She rattled off a name and phone number.

After another pause she said, "Yes, I'm leaving now," and clicked off her phone.

Corinne turned around to find her sister, Marge, and me staring at her. "The bank's been robbed. I have to go." She glanced down at her black costume. "I'll stop by the house first and change. Felicity, ready to leave?"

Without waiting for Felicity to answer, I said, "I'll take Felicity home. Brian and I will," I amended.

Corinne cocked her eye at me. "Brian?"

"My date," I said.

That satisfied Corinne. She made a beeline for the front door, her black robes flapping in her wake.

"Where's the witch rushing off to?" Tim asked.

"Corinne's bank was robbed," Felicity told him. "Isn't that awful?"

"On Halloween night?" Tim asked. "Were the thieves dressed in costume?"

Marge, Evan, and I glared at him.

"Please forgive my flippancy," Tim said. "It's the gin talking. But I must say, I'm glad I don't keep my safety deposit box in that branch."

"It's not Corinne's fault!" Felicity insisted.

"Of course not," I said, patting her arm.

"She's going to be so upset." Felicity's lips quivered. I prayed she wasn't about to start bawling.

I stared meaningfully at Tim. He quickly shifted gears.

"We're about to vote for best costumes. Gather around me, children, while we make our choices for prettiest, funniest, and most ghoulish." He winked. "A bottle of wine for the winners!"

Sadie handed out pencils and slips of papers marked with the three categories. I wrote in Felicity for the prettiest, Joy and Mike for the funniest, and Glenn Harris, a teacher in Sadie's school in a hideous green costume, for the most ghoulish.

To my astonishment, I'd picked three winners.

Felicity was the first to receive her prize. "Thank you! Thank you so much!" she gushed, holding the bottle of cabernet to her chest. "This is the first prize I've ever won in my life!"

I squeezed Brian's hand. "I'm so happy for her," I whispered.

"Is she for real?" he whispered back.

"Cynic!" I hissed.

After that we played silly kids' games, most of which involved apples, pie, or water, and had us all giggling. Sadie asked Joy, Marge and me to help set up the desserts in the dining room for coffee and cake.

"This is fun," Joy said as we sliced cakes on the dining room table. "I almost forgot what it's like to mingle with adults."

I laughed. "You come to our book club meetings."

Joy wrinkled up her face. "True. But you never serve wine."

"My bad," I admitted.

She edged closer to me. "Brian seems to be having a good

time chatting with the various suspects."

"Our fellow guests, you mean. Most of the people here work with Sadie or are Tim's friends. I'm willing to bet they have nothing to do with Len Lyons' murder."

"Whatever," Joy conceded. "Brian and Mike get along great." She scanned the room. "Speaking of which, where is my two-timing husband?"

"I've no idea."

"There he is—in the hall, laughing and whooping it up on his cell phone. Wanna bet he's talking to his bimbo?"

I'd had enough of this nonsense! If Mike didn't have the brains to reassure Joy that he wasn't having an affair, I'd do it for him!

But I wasn't fast enough! I stared in horror as Joy lifted the pitcher of cider from the table and made a beeline for her husband. She knocked off his hat and spilled the contents on his head.

Mike let out a shriek. Brian, who'd been talking to Tim on the other side of the living room, dashed over to see what had happened. Was that his gun he'd drawn and was quickly putting out of sight?

I ran over to Mike, now slumped in a chair, his hair slicked down in such a way, I hardly recognized him. Joy stood over him berating the poor guy for chasing after his slut of a girlfriend when he had her and their three children to think about.

Sadie brought Mike a large towel. The rest of us stood and watched. Mike rubbed his head vigorously. He patted down his shirt, then grabbed both of Joy's hands to stop her from beating furiously on his chest.

"Listen, you idiot, I'm not having an affair."

Joy reared back. I thought she was going to punch him in the face.

"Be a man! Tell the truth! I'm throwing you out of the house, whatever you say."

"Oh, yeah?" Mike stuck his face into hers. "I was talking to your sister."

Joy's expressions changed from outrage to puzzlement and back to fury. "Oh, sure! You're talking to my sister right now! At eleven at night."

Mike shrugged. "That's when she called me. Want to say hello? That is, if she didn't hang up when you went crazy."

Joy looked at his cell phone, now on the floor, as if it were a tarantula. Slowly, she picked it up. "Hello?" She listened to the person on the other end.

"Hi, Heather. No, nothing's wrong. But tell me, why did you call Mike?"

After a minute, she nodded, "All right, I'll ask him. Good-bye."

Joy disconnected the call and stared at her husband. "Want to tell me what this is all about?"

We stood in silence, watching and waiting. There was no way Mike could squirm out of this without ruining his surprise.

A broad grin broke out on his face as he reached for Joy and settled her on his lap. "It's a surprise for you, and I don't want to spoil it. But I'll have to if you insist."

She suddenly understood. Joy turned to me, and I gave her the okay signal.

"Oh, Mike," she sighed. "I'm such an idiot. You are the best husband in the world."

They locked lips and kissed the way movie stars used to at the end of romantic movies. The rest of us applauded what had to be the best show in town.

CHAPTER FOURTEEN

The bank robbery made Newsday's front page the following morning, along with a photo of the thieves taken by the surveillance camera. Not that it revealed their identities. As it turned out, they *had* worn Halloween masks. Page three showed a photograph of Corinne and the branch president, along with his quote: "We trust the police will find the thieves and our money."

"He's very trusting for a bank president," Joy commented, pointing to the newspaper article. She reached into her daughter's stash of Halloween candy lying open on my living room coffee table and popped her fifth Reese's Pieces into her mouth. "And how did a robbery that occurred after ten p.m. make today's headline?" I shrugged. "I've no idea."

"It's practically publicity."

"What do you mean?" I asked. "You can't possibly think the bank president had anything to do with the robbery."

"Who knows?" she said, reaching for another candy in the huge plastic bag.

I slapped her hand away. "You've eaten enough of Ruthie's Halloween candy. And you shouldn't have brought it to my house."

Joy grinned. "I told you—Ruthie said to share her loot with Aunt Lexie."

"Why?" I demanded. "Do I look undernourished?"

"My kids feel sorry for you because you have no little ones at home."

"Sweet," I said, reaching for a Mars bar. "Your children are very thoughtful."

"Not Zack. He won't part with one piece of candy, not even for his dad. Poor Mike! The kid almost bit off his head when he asked for a Milky Way."

"I'm glad to see you're supporting your spouse once again."

Joy grinned the grin of a well-satisfied woman. "Of course, now that I know he deserves my love and support."

"He's an idiot," I mumbled.

"What did you say?" Joy asked sharply.

"Nothing."

She nudged me. "Care to share what he has planned?"

"I do not. Don't ask me again."

She nudged me again. "Will you be bringing Brian to whatever it is?"

"Maybe. Maybe not."

Joy grabbed my arm. "Why wouldn't you?"

"Ouch!"

"Sorry, but I had no idea there was trouble in paradise. I got the impression you were crazy about Brian."

"Oh, I am, but I've been thinking that being crazy about Brian Donovan isn't a very good idea."

"Why not?"

"The usual—with homicide cops, the job comes first. They keep irregular hours. None of which is very helpful to a budding relationship."

Joy eyed me keenly. "I wouldn't think you'd mind since you keep odd hours. And you're not especially traditional. You wouldn't care much if your Saturday night plans were canceled because Brian had to go to the scene of a murder."

"True."

"Then what is it? Al?"

"For one thing. I hate talking to him across the Atlantic Ocean, letting him believe I'm considering moving in with him." I grimaced. "Oh, I'll be moving, all right. When he comes home and I tell him I'm involved with Brian, he'll tell me to leave this house."

Joy laughed. "I doubt it. So what's the real reason you're

fighting your feelings for Brian?"

I sighed. "For me, romantic involvements have always been rather complicated. I go for guys who are interesting, but not especially responsible. I hope I'm not choosing someone like that again. I mean, Al is responsible!" I didn't mean to shout the last word.

"And therefore you should fall in love with Al?"

"He's reliable, dependable, and wants a long-term relationship."

"I don't claim to know Brian well, but I consider him reliable and responsible. So does Mike."

I grimaced. "Maybe I'm just nervous."

"Deal with it, and don't screw things up," Joy said, getting to her feet. "Time to head home. The school bus will be dropping the kids off soon. Then I have to pick up Brandon at his play group." She giggled. "I lied and said I had a doctor's appointment so I could come here instead of coffee-klatching with the young mothers. They bore me."

"Bad mommy," I said, hugging her. I handed over Ruthie's depleted stash of candy. "Don't forget this. And thank Ruthie for me."

Joy left me mulling over what she'd said about Brian. I knew he was good guy, but it was nice hearing it confirmed by Mike, who had been in the police department. Not that Brian's character had me worried. It was my caring for him that set me on edge. I'd made so many mistakes in the past, I no longer trusted my judgment when it came to relationships.

That settled for the moment, I thought about Joy's comment regarding the bank robbery. Did she think the bank president was involved? Or Corinne? I chuckled. What a preposterous idea!

Puss ambled by, meowing to inform me it was feeding time. Actually, it was two hours too early for his dinner, but I put some food in his plate and left him purring as he ate.

I graded a few papers, then took out my work in progress. I felt bad that I hadn't done any writing in weeks. I reread the last two chapters, changed a few sentences, then decided it was time to start dinner.

I made a Swiss cheese omelet, which I ate watching the news in the den. The police had no leads on the bank robbers. There was no word about Len Lyons' murder. I supposed this was considered old news, and wouldn't be mentioned until new information leading to his murderer was uncovered.

Brian called. We chatted about our day, and he invited me out for dinner Thursday night. "I've lots of paper work to catch up. My desk should be cleared by then." He hung up shortly after, leaving me with a smile on my face.

I stretched out on the couch and watched a few mindless shows on TV. When Puss jumped onto my chest and began kneading me like dough, I glanced at the clock. It was close to eleven. Bedtime.

Three staccato sounds rang out. Gunshots? I ran to the window, but saw nothing but the lights of the house across the street. A car zoomed away. A minute later, someone was pounding on the front door.

"Who is it?" I asked, praying Pete Rogers hadn't returned.

"It's me, Lexie! Please open the door!"

Felicity stumbled into the hall, her face white with terror.

"What happened?"

"Johnny Scarvino drove by and shot up the house! One of the bullets went through Corinne's bedroom window!"

"Oh, no! Did he hurt her? Is she all right?"

Felicity began to hyperventilate, drawing deep, rasping breaths that shook her body. I sat her down on the living room couch and raced into the kitchen for brandy.

All the while my brain was spinning.

Should I call 911 or go next door to see if Corinne was hurt? For all I knew, she could be lying in a pool of blood as her life faded away.

I wanted to do both, but dared not leave Felicity, who was close to hysterical.

She pushed the brandy aside, almost spilling it over herself, then gulped it down and set off a coughing fit.

Finally, she was calm enough to speak. "Corinne's not home."

I wanted to shake her for frightening me so. Instead, I said, "That's a relief! Where is she?"

"She had a dinner meeting with some bank bigwigs in Manhattan. She called around nine-thirty to say she'd be taking the next train home, and not to wait up for her."

"She should have been home by now."

Felicity shrugged. "She must have stopped at the supermarket. We needed a few things."

"So late?"

"Corinne's a night owl. She often goes for a drive at night. She says it clears her head after being cooped up in the bank all day."

"How do you know it was Johnny who shot at your house?" I asked.

"Who else would want to hurt Corinne?"

I was fed up with her weird sense of logic. I headed for the kitchen. "I'm calling Detective Donovan."

Felicity yanked my arm, bringing me to an abrupt stop. Her strength surprised me. "Why call *him*, Lexie? This has nothing to do with Len's murder."

It was late. Though I knew she was upset, she was sorely trying my patience.

"I know, but Brian will make sure the police come immediately." I glared at her. "You do want them to know what happened, don't you? So they can protect you and Corinne from Johnny or whoever it was that shot at you."

I hadn't meant to come across as a bully, and was appalled at how my sharp tone deflated her. She gripped my arm, her eyes wide with terror.

"Please don't call him, Lexie. Corinne will be so angry."

"Why will Corinne be angry?"

Felicity shook her head from side to side as tears streamed down her cheeks. "I never should have come here. Pretend I never came here. Please, Lexie. For my sake."

I tried to lead her into the kitchen, but she squirmed out of my reach and ran out the front door. I considered following her home, then decided that would only upset her more. Puzzled, I called Brian and told him everything that had happened.

"I'm glad you called me, whether Felicity wanted you to or not. I'll send a car over there to check things out and file a report."

Minutes later I heard them arrive, three black and whites, their sirens blasting the silence of the neighborhood. *Not necessary!* I thought as I peered out my front door to watch. Car doors slammed and six officers approached the Roberts sisters' house. Guilt shot through me as they descended on Felicity, about to cause her untold anguish. A cop rang the bell. The door opened, and Felicity exchanged words with two of the officers. They entered the house. Relieved that the other four cops remained outside, no doubt to wait for the crime scene technicians, I stepped inside and tried not to think of what was happening next door.

I felt uneasy as I got ready for bed. Felicity needed emotional support, yet shied away from it when the police were involved. Her Johnny sounded like a gangster to me, yet he'd worked for the girls' father. And Corinne used to date him. For some reason Brat Farrar flashed into my head. He'd appeared on the scene under false pretenses. Were the Roberts sisters not who they said they were? Were they in hiding because they'd witnessed a crime?

Another thought occurred to me: had Johnny found Corinne through her photo in the newspaper?

A thumping at the front door interrupted my musings. "Coming!" I called as I ran to see who was there. Not Pete Rogers, thank God, but a furious Corinne. Reluctant to let her in, I cracked the door a few inches.

But Corinne had no desire to come inside. "I'll thank you to keep out of my family's business!" she screamed.

"Felicity came here. She was terrified because someone took shots at your house."

"She told you not to call the cops, but you called them, anyway. Keep away from my sister and me, Lexie, or I'll take out an order of protection against you!"

Feeling demoralized and ill-treated, I crept into bed vowing to have nothing more to do with the Roberts sisters. I hated to abandon Felicity, but our relationship was limited by all sorts of restrictions, the major one being Corrine.

I was half asleep when I realized Felicity had given me a clue when she'd mentioned Johnny's last name. Scarvino. Tomorrow I'd Google him as soon as I returned home from my classes.

CHAPTER FIFTEEN

The sound of pounding woke me from a deep sleep. *What now?* I jumped out of bed, scaring Puss, who had snuggled up beside me during the night. I glanced at the clock. Three-thirty. Frightened, I headed for the front door.

"Lexie! Thank God you heard me! I was afraid you wouldn't."

Gayle grabbed me in a tight embrace that started me coughing.

She let go. "Sorry. I have to park the SUV in your garage so no one knows I'm here."

I held off on my "call the police" lecture. Gayle looked stressed out and thoroughly beat.

"I'll move my car to one side of the garage. That should give you just about enough room. Or better yet, I'll park on the street," I said.

"No! Don't do anything out of the ordinary! Pull your car to one side of the garage. I'll park next to you."

My sister followed me into the garage, where we maneuvered both vehicles side by side with barely two inches between them. Gayle lifted her duffle bag from the back of her SUV and carried it into the house.

"Do you have anything to eat?" she asked.

"Sure. I'll make you a sandwich."

She dropped off the bag in her room, used the bathroom, then joined me in the kitchen. I had a dozen questions I was dying to ask, but I settled on one.

"Where did you stay this past week?"

Gayle finished chewing the huge bite she'd taken of her tuna salad sandwich and washed it down with soda.

"With friends of my friends whose nanny left suddenly. They needed someone to watch their kids until the new nanny could start, so it worked out. I was glad not to have to drive anywhere, since you said the cops put out a BOLO for me."

I nodded. "The new detective on the case called a few times to find out if I'd heard from you. I told him about your last call. They tried to trace it, but came up with zilch."

She gave me a bittersweet smile. "So now that you're dating a cop, you're on their side. Are you going to turn me in, Lexie?"

"Don't be stupid." I took a deep breath. "What are you planning to do?"

Gayle shook her head. "I've no idea. It's all I think about, night and day, and I still can't come up with an answer. I can't go back to Utah. Not with Shawn Estes on the loose."

"Did you ever consider contacting a higher official in Utah? Someone like the Attorney General?"

"I've heard he's a decent guy. Maybe if your boyfriend contacted him and convinced him to investigate Shawn Estes, I'd take my chances. But now there are these new charges." She looked so sad. My heart ached for her.

"Lexie, I swear I didn't kill Len Lyons. I don't know how I got entangled in two messes, but I'm innocent." She reached for my hand. "Do you believe me?"

"I do." I squeezed her hand and, though I swore to myself I wouldn't, launched in on my "call the police" spiel. "But you're going to have to speak to Detective Paulson."

"Why, if I didn't kill that man who ended up dead in your backyard? I never saw the knife I was supposed to have hidden."

"Because they're questioning everyone who might have had anything to do with the murder. And the possible murder weapon was found in the room you slept in."

Gayle frowned. "Screwy logic, if you ask me."

I could see her point, but the police had their policies and procedures.

"You have to cooperate and answer their questions, Gayle. I'm sure the crime lab will report the knife doesn't have your fingerprints. Then you'll be free of all this."

"No, I won't! It will only prove someone wiped the fingerprints off the knife. They can throw me in jail if they like."

"I don't think so," I said, but I was beginning to wonder if Gayle was right.

"Lexie, I can't do this now. Give me a day to think about everything. Either I'll talk to this Detective Paulson or I'll disappear from your life."

I nodded to put an end to the discussion and not because I agreed. I sat quietly watching Gayle wolf down the rest of her sandwich, then we both went to bed.

She was still sleeping when my alarm woke me, tired and disgruntled. I left her a note and set out for school, a new idea forming in my head. Why not have Brian contact the District Attorney or Attorney General in Utah and tell him everything Gayle told me? Explain that the man who'd murdered her boyfriend had sent someone to threaten Gayle and she was too terrified to return home. It was too early to call now. I decided to talk to Brian on my drive home.

"I most certainly will not!" my loving boyfriend shouted before I'd finished all I'd planned to say. "For one thing, what happened in Utah stays in Utah. I've no jurisdiction outside of New York. Outside of Nassau County, for that matter!"

"But—"

"In the second place, I've no idea if any of what Gayle said is true. She wasn't exactly honest with you, was she?"

"Not at first, but—"

"In the third place, she's wanted by my department for questioning regarding an ongoing homicide. She'd better get her butt over to Paulson's office before sundown today."

"Sundown!" I shouted back. "This isn't a western! Gayle's terrified and she's innocent." I lowered my voice. "And she's my sister, Brian."

"Dammit, I know she's your sister!" He went silent. I knew not to say another word.

Seconds passed. "Tell you what," he continued calmly, conciliatory, "if Gayle talks to Paulson today, I'll make some calls to Utah to check out the situation."

I released the breath I hadn't realized I'd been holding. "Thanks, Brian. And tell them about that Pete Rogers."

"Oh, I intend to," he said, his tone letting me know he'd already given the subject some thought. "Gotta go." I heard something just before he hung up.

Was that a kissing sound? I wondered as a grin spread across my face.

I drove into the garage, relieved that Gayle's SUV was where she'd parked it. I'd left her sleeping soundly and didn't expect her to take off, but my sister was capable of rash behavior–not including murder, I reminded myself.

I found her playing with Puss on the living room floor. She was dangling my bathroom belt above him, and the silly cat was leaping up after it. It was the most activity he'd had since the day we moved in, when he'd raced around the house leading me a merry chase.

I told Gayle that Brian would help her deal with the Utah police if she agreed to talk to Detective Paulson.

"Okay. I'll do it," she said, to my surprise and great relief.

I handed her his card. "You'll call him?"

"Right now."

She went into her room and closed the door.

I headed for my computer and checked my email. Then I Googled "Johnny Scarvino."

"Oh!" I exclaimed, surprised at the many pages the name brought up.

He was a thug, all right, and had been arrested for racketeering and other mob-related activities in New Jersey. There were many newspaper articles about other Scarvinos. I would have ignored them, but many of them concerned a murder trial I'd read about a few years back. John Scarvino—was that Johnny's father?—had been charged and found guilty for killing another mobster and his wife.

"Lexie?"

I turned to Gayle. "You spoke to Detective Paulson?"

She nodded. "I'm going down to the precinct now."

I suddenly felt chilled. Gayle was doing this because I told her to. But what if someone had screwed up the evidence and she got indicted for the crime? Labs made all kinds of mistakes. There were dirty cops who planted evidence. What if this Detective Paulson wanted to nail the murderer ASAP and wouldn't hesitate to pin it on his only viable suspect?

"Want me to come with you?" I asked.

She paused, then shook her head. "Thanks, Lexie. You've done enough. I'll call if I need you."

Or need a lawyer, I thought as we hugged. I watched her drive away, feeling as I'd felt the morning I'd watched my son Jesse walk to school by himself for the very first time.

CHAPTER SIXTEEN

I called Joy, eager to tell her Gayle had returned and that I'd found out quite a lot about Felicity's Johnny. I got as far as "hello" when she cut me off.

"Talk to you later. I'm on the phone with the school nurse. Zack got hurt during recess."

"I'm here if you need me."

She called back a minute later. "Can you come over now? I have to take Zack to the emergency room. Things will go smoother if I don't bring Brandon."

"Of course," I said, though I hated not being here when Gayle returned.

"I'd bring him over to you, but he just fell asleep."

"No problem. I'm on my way."

I left Gayle a note, grabbed my satchel of quizzes that needed grading and threw on a jacket.

"See you later," I told Puss, who ignored me.

Joy was waiting for me outside her open garage. "Thanks, Lexie. Zack fell and hit his head playing soccer during recess. He might have a concussion, so I'm taking him to the ER. I left you a note on the kitchen table—what to feed Brandon when he wakes up." She grinned. "I know it's a lot to ask, but would you please change him if necessary? You do remember how to do that, don't you?"

"I'll do my best, though I may have blocked it from my

memory. What about
Ruthie?" I asked as Joy climbed into her SUV.

"She's going to her friend Robin's house. Robin's mom is driving them to dance class. Marcia said she'll bring them home, too, and if I'm running late, I'll ask her to keep Ruthie and feed her dinner. Ruthie won't like the dinner part. Mike's supposed to take the kids to Family Swim Night."

"Busy, busy," I commented.

"You don't know the half of it," Joy said before slamming the car door.

I checked on Brandon, who was fast asleep in his crib, then wandered through the house, trying to find a comfortable nook where I could settle down and mark papers. Every room, including the kitchen, was cluttered with toys and kiddie paraphernalia. I suddenly remembered the leather lounge chair Mike had bought for his office, and headed for the back of the house.

His desk was strewn with papers, but the rest of the room was tidy, except for a few dog-eared sports magazines at the foot of the new chair. I set them aside and, red pen and quiz papers in hand, climbed aboard and pushed the lever way back. Comfy.

I finished off the two sets of papers, and got up to stretch. Time to check on the sleeping baby. As I passed Mike's messy desk, I couldn't resist giving it the once over.

There was a box with bills to be paid, magazine subscriptions to be refilled, an application for a home equity loan, and a pile of coupons for local restaurants. In the corner against the wall was an open weekly calendar. Snoop that I was, I peered at this week's schedule. Tonight's Family Swim was down, along with the address of this week's Friday night poker game.

I flipped through the three previous weeks. "Make calls" was jotted down several times, no doubt a reminder to call guests for Joy's surprise party. I noticed a dentist appointment, the times he had to pick up Zack or Ruthie from some activity, and one "call LL."

My heart began to pound. "LL" could only mean Len Lyons! I checked the date and my pulse raced even faster. It was last Wednesday. The day before Len Lyons was murdered.

I paced in circles. Should I mention this to Joy? To Brian? To

Detective Paulson? I felt like the worst kind of traitor. Here I was babysitting his son as I wondered if sweet, loving Mike Lincoln was a murderer!

And why shouldn't I? Right now the police were interrogating my sister because someone I knew had hidden the murder weapon in the room Gayle had used, no doubt to incriminate her.

A loud wail broke into my thoughts. I hurried to Brandon's room to change his Pamper, then fed him some apple sauce and bananas.

Joy arrived home two hours later with a cranky Zack, who couldn't understand why he had to miss basketball practice. She settled him on the couch in the den and turned on the TV, then called me into the kitchen. I gave her a detailed report of Brandon's intake of food and elimination, and received a huge hug of appreciation.

"Want a cup of coffee?" she asked. "It's the least I can do for you."

"No thanks. Gayle's been down at the precinct for hours talking to Paulson. I want to be home when she gets back."

Joy's eyes widened. "I hope everything works out well for her. I've the name of a good criminal lawyer, if you need one."

"Thanks. We might."

Or you might, I thought as I shrugged into my jacket and gathered up my papers.

"Mom?" Zack shouted from the den.

"What?" Joy ran to see what was wrong. I trailed after her.

"Can I still go to Family Swim Night with Dad and Ruthie?"

"You most certainly cannot!" Joy felt his forehead for fever. "You'll stay home and spend a quiet evening with Brandon and me."

"But that's hours from now. I'll be fine then."

"You'll rest tonight and we'll see if you go to school tomorrow."

Joy walked me to the front door. "Have you heard? Corinne and Felicity are putting their house on the market, just as soon as they fix the damage that idiot caused the other night."

I stared at her. "Where did you hear that?"

"The school nurse told me. Her sister-in-law works in the

realty office in town."

"I can't blame them for wanting to move," I said.

Joy's eyes took on a calculating look. "Me, neither. But why did someone shoot up their house, and so soon after the bank robbery?"

I gave a gasp of surprise. "You think the two are related?"

"Only in the sense that they're both really way-out events."

Now was the time to tell Joy about Johnny Scarvino and what I'd learned about his father, but I had other, more pressing matters on my mind.

What did honest, decent Mike—former cop and Joy's husband—want with the likes of Len Lyons, conniver, thief, and thug?

Super investigator that she was, Joy must have seen Mike's notation to call Len Lyons while snooping around in search of evidence of his infidelity. We'd held lengthy discussions regarding who knew the murder victim, yet she'd never mentioned seeing the victim's initials in her husband's diary. Was she protecting him or what?

Should I mention it to Brian? To Detective Paulson?

Should I confront Joy?

"Lexie?"

I gave a start. "What?"

"Weren't you going to tell me something you discovered online?"

"Oh, that!" I waved my hand. "I decided it's not relevant to the case."

Joy's face scrunched up in puzzlement. "But you sounded excited when you called this afternoon. Sometimes it's the little things that break a case."

The little things. Were finding the dead man's initials in her husband's diary a little thing?

"We'll talk tomorrow," I say, edging closer to the door. "Now I want to get home to Gayle."

"Of course," Joy said, sounding disappointed. "The cops could sure use some new leads."

We hugged and I walked home. Gayle pulled into the driveway as I was unlocking the front door. She looked drained. I opened the garage so she could park there, then steered her toward the kitchen and filled the kettle for tea.

"How did it go?"

She offered me a wan smile. "I'm here, aren't I?"

"So Paulson doesn't consider you a suspect."

Gayle shrugged. "One of many. The results of the knife came back. Evidence of blood. No fingerprints."

"No surprise there," I said, but inwardly I breathed a sigh of relief. I told her about finding Len Lyons' initials in Mike's weekly diary.

Gayle simply shrugged. "It doesn't mean a thing. For all you know, Mike might have wanted him to fix a faucet or some such thing. Lyons was a handyman, right?"

I laughed, suddenly relieved. "I never thought of that."

"Everyone in your book group is connected one way or another to Len Lyons," Gayle said.

I grimaced. "Just like in an Agatha Christie novel."

"But not in one by Josephine Tey?" Gayle asked, surprising me by remembering her name.

I shook my head. "Though Tey wrote a few traditional mystery novels, the two our group read and discussed are most original. One involves the solving of a five- hundred-year-old mystery; the other, *Brat Farrar*, concerns a stolen identity and an eight-year-old murder."

"Murders that took place in the past," Gayle mused. "Len Lyons was a career criminal and involved in plenty of illegal activities. What if he was murdered because of something that happened some time ago?"

I shrugged. "We'll never know."

The kettle whistled. I poured hot water into our mugs. As I set out an array of teabags and cookies, another thought occurred to me.

"Josephine Tey believed facial expressions reveal a person's character," I said. "In *The Daughter of Time*, Alan Grant takes on the task of proving Richard the Third's innocence based solely on a photograph of a portrait painting. He works on the premise that Richard looked extremely unhappy and responsible, that he suffered illness as a child and wasn't the sort of man who would kill his nephews for the crown."

"Okay," Gayle said, not knowing what I was leading up to.

"I think I'll give it a go."

"Lexie, what on earth are you talking about?"

"Even better, I'll have the person in the flesh to work with, not some photograph of a painting." I grinned. "I'm going swimming this evening, Gayle. Stay here and hold down the fort."

CHAPTER SEVENTEEN

I entered the pool area wondering how a person could feel hot, damp and chilled, all at the same time. I wrinkled my nose at the strong chlorine fumes, one of the many reasons I avoided coming to the high school pool, which remained open Tuesday evenings for Ryesdale residents throughout the school year. Though I was a good enough swimmer, the idea of going out into the cold after being in an environment suitable for delicate flowers, restricted my swimming to dips in friends' pools during the summer months. But I couldn't pass up the chance to speak to Mike tonight.

There were about thirty people in the pool, mostly parents and their elementary school-aged children. One man in his sixties was trying to swim laps, and seemed annoyed whenever a splashing child got in his way.

I walked over to the shallow end and stepped down. Though the water wasn't cold, I shivered at the idea of wetting my entire body as well as my hair, then having to dry off before dressing again and stepping out into the nippy November evening.

"Lexie! I didn't know you came to Family Swim Night?"

I forced myself down the next two steps, and walked over to where Mike was holding on to Ruthie while she kicked her feet vigorously.

"I thought it would be fun," I said, trying to smile though Ruthie was getting me all wet.

"Hi, Lexie," Ruthie said.

"Hi there, kiddo."

"I heard you babysat for Brandon today," Mike said.

"Thanks."

"How's Zack?"

"He's good." Mike grinned. "Carried on something fierce about missing swimming tonight. I started to say that maybe he could come after all, but Joy squashed that idea pronto."

"A mother knows best. Zack had a concussion. He needs to remain quiet for as long as the doctor says he should."

"I guess."

"Daddy, can I go over and play with Jodie?" Ruthie asked.

"Sure, sweetie. Remember our pool rules."

"Yes, Daddy," she tossed over her shoulder as she dog-paddled away.

I moved a bit in order to face Mike directly. I wanted to study his every expression as we spoke, though I felt silly. Mike looked the way he always did—friendly, cheerful, as though he had nothing to hide. I opened my mouth to ask if he needed any help with Joy's party, when he beat me to the punch.

"Joy tells me Paulson grilled Gayle this afternoon."

"Yes. They found Len Lyons' blood on the knife, but no fingerprints."

"Meaning they can't hold her."

I grimaced. "As Gayle put it, she's now one suspect of many." I looked him in the eye. "Do you realize every person who's in the book club, including Joy and me, knew Len Lyons?"

Mike shrugged. "Why not? He did handyman-type jobs around town."

"Right. Did you know him?"

"Sure. I guess so. Why do you ask?"

My turn to shrug. "No reason. I just wondered. Joy said he never did any work for you guys."

Mike drew in a deep breath and let it out slowly. "Some of my former brothers in blue thought he was responsible for local B & E's. Couldn't prove it, though."

"Tim Draigon and Evan Billings are pretty sure he burgled their homes." I lowered my voice. "Turns out Len had all sorts of criminal connections."

Mike's laugh was as phony as a two cent coin. "Brian shouldn't be telling tales out of school."

"It wasn't Brian," I said. "I heard Len hooked people up with loan sharks and other illegal providers, then held up the deal if they didn't fork over more cash."

He gave me an indulgent smile. "Crooks are killed every day for being too greedy."

"Did Len arrange a loan for you?" I asked.

"Of course not." The smile disappeared. Shutters clamped over Mike's eyes like mirrored sunglasses. "And would I tell you if I did?"

"You just told me," I said softly. "Do the cops know? Does Joy know?"

He grabbed my arm. "Hey! You got the wrong idea!"

I jerked my arm free, suddenly aware of his large size. "I think the cops have no idea you went to Len for a loan or some such thing."

"I didn't!" he shouted.

People stopped conversations to stare at us. Mike reached out to place his hands on my shoulders then thought better of it.

"I've no idea why you'd think I had anything to do with Len Lyons," he said.

"So many people we know used his services," I said, hoping Mike wouldn't realize I'd snooped in his diary. "It almost seems logical that you would have, too."

He let out a defeated sigh. "I considered asking him to arrange a loan with this guy he knows. We sure could use it."

My mouth fell open in surprise. "I had no idea. Sorry."

Mike's lips pushed in and out. "With Joy not working and three kids to feed, the cash doesn't flow like it did before Brandon appeared on the scene. I'm up for a raise, but it won't come through for several months. I heard Len knew a guy who made short-term loans, but you had to go through Len." He shook his head as though he couldn't believe his own actions. "Stupid, I know, but I was feeling desperate. Then I found out Len played dirty, so I never called him. I should have known he was unreliable scum."

His bittersweet smile told me he was speaking the truth.

"Please don't tell Joy," Mike said softly. "She'll feel guilty enough to rush back to work when she wants to stay home with the kids. And she'll insist that I cancel her birthday surprise."

"I won't say a word," I promised. I turned to go, but he put out a hand to stop me.

"I know you're worried sick about your sister being charged, but I wouldn't worry too much." Mike's grin was back in place. "Word on the street is the cops are looking for a mob connection for Lyons' murder."

"A mob connection," I echoed. "Thanks, Mike." I returned his grin. "I never figured you for a murderer, anyway."

Back home, I found Gayle in her room, packing her duffel bag.

"What are you doing?" I asked.

"Brian's coming by in half an hour to drive me to a safe house."

My heart started pounding. "Why! What happened?"

Gayle sank onto the bed. "He caught up with Pete Rogers and they butt heads." She let out a heartfelt sigh. "Pete won't leave Long Island and Brian can't make him. But the Nassau Police can put me in a safe house as a person of interest."

I sat down beside her and held her close. "If it makes you feel any better, the cops here don't think you killed the handyman."

Gayle shrugged. I didn't realize she was crying until her tears dribbled down my neck. I rubbed her back.

"Don't worry. We'll get this all sorted out."

"Two murder cases," she mumbled. "How did I ever get involved in two murder cases?"

Brian arrived. He kissed me then headed for Gayle's room and closed the door behind him. He came out ten minutes later, carrying her duffel bag. Gayle's face was wet with tears. She threw her arms around me.

"You'll be all right," I crooned. "Everything will work out in the end."

I looked over her shoulder at Brian. "Will she be able to call me?"

He shook his head. "Sorry, Lexie. Any electronic communication puts the safe house in danger. But I expect Gayle won't be staying there long. If you don't mind, we'll leave her

SUV in your garage."

"Sure." I bit back the questions I longed to ask for fear they'd only upset Gayle, and watched my sister and my lover leave the house.

"I'll get her settled and come back," Brian whispered. Still, I felt bereft and totally useless as I closed the door behind them.

Brian called me an hour and a half later to let me know he was on his way over. When he arrived, I flew into his arms. Tears spilled down my cheeks.

"Oh, no," he said gently as he traced a tear with his finger. "I can't have both Gruen sisters sobbing on my shoulder in one night."

"How is she?"

"Fine. She's in good hands. The woman who runs the safe house has plenty of experience looking after wounded birds."

I took Brian's hand and led him to the living room couch where I nestled against his chest. If only we could stay this way for hours. I'd been looking forward to filling him in on everything that had happened these last few days—Felicity and Corinne's weird behavior, Johnny Scarvino, Mike's almost calling Len Lyons the day before he was killed—but now none of that seemed urgent. I needed this tranquil respite, and was miffed when he opened his mouth for a jaw-cracking yawn.

I sat up and huffed. "Sorry if I'm boring you."

Brian let out a deep belly laugh. "Lexie, asleep you couldn't bore me. I'm dead on my feet. I've been up since four-thirty this morning."

I grinned at him. "You could stay here for the night."

"I could. And get up early to go home, shower, and change my clothes."

"Or you could get up even earlier," I suggested. "We'll make love, then you can shower with me."

"Sounds like a great idea," he said, turning to kiss me.

Suddenly, both of us were wide awake and raring to go. Brian moved his hands under my sweater. "Or we can make love now *and* in the morning."

Which was what we were in the middle of doing when his phone rang. He reached for it. "Donovan."

I watched his face grow grim as he listened to the caller. "Be right there," he said. He stood and adjusted his clothing.

"Gotta go," he said, bussing my cheek. "There's been a homicide."

"Oh." He was getting into his jacket when I thought to ask. "Anyone I know?"

"Timothy Draigon. Someone shot him as he was leaving Sadie Lu's house."

CHAPTER EIGHTEEN

I turned out the light and tried to sleep, but my brain spun like a hamster on a wheel as it churned out reasons why someone might want Tim Draigon dead. His was the second local homicide in as many weeks. Even more relevant, Tim had been a member of our mystery book club.

Had the same person who killed Len Lyons also murdered Tim? Tim had business dealings with Len. He'd borrowed money from Len's money lender. But assuming Len had burgled Tim's house meant they weren't close friends.

I flipped on my side and rearranged the quilt. Maybe there was no direct connection between the two murders, but some kind of horrible coincidence. After all, Len had been knifed and Tim had been shot.

According to Felicity, the girls next door had been shot at by Johnny Scarvino. He was a gangbanger. Maybe Tim had done business with Scarvino.

Maybe Scarvino also killed Len Lyons. After all, they were both in the same line of work. Which made me wonder if Tim had another connection to Corinne and Felicity other than the book club.

Finally, pure exhaustion took over and I fell into a fitful sleep only to be awakened by a horrific crashing sound. I leaped out of bed and raced into the living room. My mouth fell open at the sight of the large bay window in ruins, shards of glass scattered all over the floor.

The security alarm sounded, filling the house with an ear-splitting siren that went on and on. Puss let out a screech, the likes of which I'd never heard before. I lifted him into my arms and turned off the alarm. Then I ran into the kitchen to call Brian.

He sounded groggy with sleep. He must have just gotten to bed, given the new homicide, and here I was waking him up at three-thirty in the morning. I ignored the pang of guilt and told him what had happened.

"Be right over," he said. "Don't touch a thing."

"I wasn't planning to," I said, but he'd already hung up.

The phone rang. It was the alarm company telling me they were sending an officer over to check the house. I was about to tell them a police detective was on his way, but decided not to. Gusts of cold air blew into the house, sending shivers down my back. For all I knew, the person who had thrown the stone was still outside, planning to climb in through the broken window.

Officer Johnston, a handsome black man who seemed remarkably alert considering the hour, arrived first. I told him the little I knew regarding the incident. He was asking me if I had any idea who might have done this when Brian arrived. He introduced himself and Officer Johnston repeated his question. I looked at Brian, not certain if I should answer.

"There have been two homicides in the neighborhood," Brian said. "This may or may not be related."

"And I'm obliged to fill out a report for my precinct and the alarm company,"

The men eyed one another like two rams about to butt horns. I had to cover my mouth to stop the giggles from frothing over and making matters worse. Brian called the officer into the kitchen, where they conversed in tones too low for me to hear. I assumed they'd reached a compromise, because after asking me a few basic questions and jotting down the answers, Officer Johnston left. He grunted something to Brian and gave me a lilting smile.

"Good-bye, Ms. Driscoll. Hope you have a good rest of the night."

So much for solidarity among all men in blue.

I found Brian at the kitchen table, slumped over and rubbing his eyes. "Coffee, please," he said.

"Are you sure? It's after four. You could go to sleep here."

"Coffee, please. I don't plan to go back to sleep any time soon."

I filled the coffee maker as Brian staggered toward the front door.

"Where are you going?" I cried.

"To take a look outside. Then I'll check the living room. Don't go in there. We'll clean up the mess when I've finished."

"Nothing outside," he reported some minutes later, then disappeared from view.

I held off pouring out his coffee until he returned to the kitchen with a small statue of a dog in his gloved hands.

"This is what someone tossed through your window."

"I think it comes from the rock garden of my neighbor across the street."

"We'll return it after it's checked for prints. A note was tied around his neck." He unfolded the paper and read aloud: "Stop interfering or die."

"Oh."

Brian looked fierce when he asked. "Care to tell me what that means?"

"I'm not sure. Maybe it's that awful Pete Rogers." I poured myself a cup of coffee, put some cookies on a plate, and sat down.

"Maybe," Brian agreed. "He was pissed when I told him we were looking after your sister." He gulped down half of his coffee and turned to me, now as alert as Officer Johnston. "Or maybe it has to do with your playing Miss Marple."

I cleared my throat. "Possibly."

"Care to tell me about it?"

Reluctantly, I started telling him all that I'd looked forward to sharing with him earlier in the day. "First off, you'll remember that Felicity came running over here the night their house got shot up."

"Of course. You called me and I put out the call. Three cars went over there."

"What I never got to tell you is Felicity was insistent that she knew who'd done the shooting."

"Really? She never told that to the officers."

"I'm not surprised. As upset as she was when she first came over here, she was half out of her mind because I'd called you. Later, big sister Corinne came over to give me a piece of her mind. I should have respected Felicity's wishes and kept my mouth shut instead of calling the cops."

Brian stroked his chin. "This gets weirder and weirder." He shot me a glance. "And who is this person Felicity believes is responsible for shooting up their house?"

"His name's Johnny Scarvino."

He frowned. "Now why does that name sound familiar?"

I felt a tingling of excitement as I told him what Felicity had told me about Johnny Scarvino, plus what I'd found out about his father being in prison for killing a Mafia leader and his wife.

"You've been a busy little researcher," he said dryly. "Does anyone know what you've been up to?"

"I was about to tell Joy when she asked me to baby sit for Brandon. Zack got hurt at school, and she had to bring him to the ER." My face grew warm as I told him what I'd come across in Mike's diary.

"But Mike had nothing to do with Len Lyons' murder," I exclaimed. "He told me so in the high school pool tonight."

Brian burst out laughing. "Add two more to the list of people who want you to mind your own business."

I stared at him, horrified. "Mike and Joy would never throw a rock through my window."

"Well, someone did." He stood up. "Time to clean up the glass and tape the window shut, and get whatever sleep we can catch. I'll question everyone you ticked off in the morning."

It was close to five o'clock when we finished cleaning up the glass shards and crept into bed. I left a message with the English Department secretary that an emergency prevented me from coming in for my classes, but that I'd be able to attend the department meeting later that afternoon. My plan was to call a glazier and have him install a new window before I left the house. I slept until ten-thirty, not surprised to find myself alone. I smiled when I read Brian's note:

"I fed the feline and called this glazier I know. He'll be over soon as he can. B"

I grinned. Fed the cat and called the repairman. What more could a girl ask for?

The doorbell rang, and I went to let in the glazier and his two assistants. We spoke about cost and insurance. I called the insurance company, then I showered and got dressed.

The workmen finished around one, leaving me enough time to go food shopping before my department meeting. I walked across the street and rang Mrs. Seidman's bell. The old woman came to the door and squinted up at me.

"Is that you, Lexie?"

"Yes, Mrs. Seidman. Did you hear the noise last night?"

She shook her head vigorously. "Nope. Heard nothing. Why, what happened?"

"Someone took your dog statue and tossed it through my front window."

Mrs. Seidman pursed her lips. "it must be those hooligans who live down the block. During the summer, they moved it to Joy and Mike's front yard." She cocked her head. "So where is Winston? Didn't you bring him home?"

"The police have him. They're checking for fingerprints."

"Good! Maybe this time they'll catch those bad kids and throw them in juvie hall."

"I hope so. Good-bye, Mrs. Seidman."

I turned around and crossed the street.

"Lexie."

Corinne waved at me from her driveway, taking me by surprise. The Roberts sisters had moved into an undisclosed hotel a few days after the shooting. Corinne had probably stopped by the house just now to pack up some of their possessions.

I made a beeline for my front door. I wanted nothing to do with Corinne. She'd accused me of interfering in her family's privacy when I was only trying to help Felicity. For all I knew, she'd tossed Winston through my window.

"Lexie!" she called again as she dashed across my lawn. I'd unlocked the door and was stepping inside when she grabbed hold of my arm.

"Lexie, I'm sorry about the other day. I know you only

wanted to help us. I had no business attacking you as I did."

I met her gaze straight on. "Why did you?"

Corinne hunched into herself. For the first time, I saw the family resemblance she shared with Felicity—the same well-shaped nose and perfectly sculpted chin. When she looked up, there were tears in her eyes.

"My sister and I have been through so much because of—that person. We know from experience that calling the police to chase after him only makes matters worse. It incites him to commit more spiteful acts."

"Shooting up your home is more than a spiteful act. He could have killed one of you."

Corinne nodded. "He must have seen my picture in the paper."

"Johnny Scarvino?"

Corinne gave a start. "Felicity told you his name."

I nodded. "She told me you used to go out with him."

She gave a sad little laugh. "What a mistake that was."

"Is that why he did it? Is he stalking you?"

Corinne nodded. "I can't even tell you where we're staying. I've put the house up for sale. A realtor's holding an open house this weekend."

"Corinne, you can't let him drive you away! Let the police handle it."

She shook her head. "He's too wily for the cops. There's no stopping Johnny Scarvino when he sets his mind to something."

"But you need police protection!"

She let out a humorless bark of laughter. "Went that route. Let me give you my cell number."

I pulled out my cell phone and entered her number.

"Don't give it to anyone, all right?"

"Of course not."

Corinne pointed at my bay window. "What the hell happened?"

"Someone tossed Mrs. Seidman's dog statue through my window in the middle of the night. She thinks it was the kids down the block."

Corinne shook her head. "First the murder, then attacks on both our houses. Maybe it's a good thing I'm leaving this neighborhood," she tossed over her shoulder as she headed for home.

Maybe moving wasn't a bad idea, at all.

CHAPTER NINETEEN

It was a relief to find myself sitting in a roomful of my colleagues amid humdrum discussions of finance, syllabus changes, and new directives from the administration. The rise and fall of familiar voices lulled me into a state close to oblivion. No smashed windows, threatening repo-type men or murderers on the loose. But a drifting mind pays the consequences. Lorrie Pruitt, my sly department chairman, took advantage of my inattention and I found myself heading a committee for students with special needs. I gulped to attention, nodded my reluctant agreement, and said I'd get moving on it ASAP.

Joy called me the minute I hit the Northern State. "Can you talk?" she asked.

"Uh-huh. What's up?"

I braced myself for a tirade for having cornered her hubby at the pool, only it never came. Mike must have felt guilty for even considering getting a loan through Len Lyons and didn't tell Joy I'd checked him out as a suspect.

"What's up?" she tossed back at me. "I saw the glazier at your house. This is the first free moment I've had to call."

"Oh, that." I drew in a deep breath. "Someone heaved Mrs. Seidman's pooch statue through my window in the early hours."

"Do the police know who did it?"

"I haven't spoken to them in the past few hours. It could be any number of people—that Pete Rogers who's after Gayle, the murderer running loose around town." *Your husband, pissed because I considered him a murder suspect.*

"I heard about Tim. Isn't it awful?"

"Terrible," I agreed. "Do you think the two murders are connected?"

"Could be. Come over soon and tell me what you were so excited about yesterday."

I sighed. "Now I wonder if it's relevant. It's like the Wild West around here. I can't believe everything's related."

"Maybe, maybe not. Zack's feeling better," Joy said. "Of course I kept him home from school."

"I'm glad he's okay."

"How's Gayle doing?"

"All right, I hope. Brian escorted her to a safe house last night."

"Where she'll be safe," Joy pointed out. "Now we have to work on keeping you safe. Step number one: stop asking questions."

Joy's words shot out like a warning. A chill ran down my spine. "Why do you say that?"

"Why do you think, dummy? The note."

I braked hard at the red light and, despite the belt across my chest, jerked forward in my seat. "Who told you there was a note?" I demanded.

"Who do you think? Your boyfriend. Brian asked Mike and me to keep an eye on you."

Which he wouldn't have done if he considered Mike a suspect. But how humiliating—friends being asked to watch out for me like I needed a baby sitter! I was caught between being annoyed by Brian's presumption and happy that he cared. Happy won out. I felt a huge smile break out on my face.

"I won't go snooping," I promised.

"We'll talk and figure out what we can do," Joy said. "Tonight, if you're free."

"Sounds good," I said. "Right now I want to run something by you."

"Sure. What is it?"

"Our book club's scheduled to meet to discuss one more Josephine Tey mystery."

"Right. *Miss Pym Disposes* next Wednesday."

"Do you think I should hold the meeting?"

"I don't see why not."

I let loose a sigh of exasperation. "Joy, Tim's dead. The Roberts sisters are talking about moving. Our group is dwindling."

"A meeting's a great idea. It will take people's minds off reality. Shoot off emails as reminders. Include that I'll be bringing a red velvet cake and lemon squares. That will hook them for sure."

The wisdom of her words made me smile. "Joy, you're a treasure."

I drove home slowly, trying to sort through everything that had happened since we'd met to talk about *The Daughter of Time*. Two murders—three if I included Gayle's boyfriend—and two houses vandalized. It was like living in a battle zone. However, Joy was right. A book club meeting would take our minds off these awful events. I'd start emailing everyone as soon as I got home.

But first I needed to stop for groceries. I turned onto Main Street and parked in the lot behind our most popular supermarket.

Chips and dip, I told myself, mentally preparing for our next meeting and my future dinners. Cheese. Bagels and bialys. Cat food. Chicken breasts. Why hadn't I written out a list?

Because I'd been occupied with more serious matters was why. Which left me with the time-eating task of rolling my cart up and down each aisle, starting at fresh produce. I tossed a package of salad, a head of broccoli, and an acorn squash into my cart, then zipped around to the next aisle. A large woman stood with her face pressed into the cereal boxes as she sobbed her heart out. With a pang, I recognized her.

"Marge?" I hesitated before patting her broad back. It felt surprisingly muscular.

She gave a start. "What?"

I apologized. "I didn't mean to intrude."

Marge wiped her nose on the sleeve of her jacket. "They took him away."

The bawling started again.

"You mean…Evan?"

"Ye-e-e-s-s."

"The police took him?"

She nodded vigorously.

It clicked. "They took Evan in to question him about Tim's murder?"

"I told that Detective Donovan, the one you brought to the Halloween Party, that the only gun we ever owned was a rifle. And Evan gave that to our neighbor when we moved to Long Island. But it made no difference. He nodded and thanked me, then dragged poor Evan down to the station. I didn't know who to call to act as our lawyer since Tim was our lawyer, kind of."

She sniffed. I rummaged in my pocketbook for a tissue. She took it and blew her nose loud enough for people two aisles over to hear.

"How could they think Evan killed Tim?" I said. "That's crazy."

"Your boyfriend saw them arguing at the Halloween party. But that was *weeks* ago." She glowered at me. "Why did you have to bring him to the party?"

I shrugged, not having an answer she'd appreciate. Instead, I asked, "What were they arguing about?"

Marge scrunched up her face and hunkered down, then gestured that I join her. I felt foolish, huddled as if we were two football players setting up a play, but I had to know.

"We weren't getting any results from that fellow Tim had set us up with to bring our granddaughter to the States. The guy wanted more money. He said he had to pay off more people than he realized. Also, he would have to go back to Peru, which he claimed was highly dangerous." Marge gave a grunt of frustration.

"We told Tim, and he agreed to speak to the guy. He came back to say if we wanted our granddaughter we had to pay another ten thousand dollars, which we were to give to Tim." She shook her head. "I never saw Evan so furious. We'd paid that fellow forty thousand dollars already. Evan got to thinking Tim was in on the scam to squeeze us for more money."

"Wow!" I exclaimed.

"Wow is right," Marge agreed. "At the party, Evan told Tim

128

he wouldn't pay another cent. He accused Tim of cashing in on our misery."

"And then someone shot Tim to death," I mused.

"Turns out Tim was as crooked at Len Lyons."

"Do you really think so?" I asked.

Marge bit her lip. "I don't know what to believe anymore, except I know my husband didn't kill Tim. I think Tim and Len both stiffed someone and that person got very angry and killed them both. That's what I think."

"Could be you're right," I said.

At home I put away the groceries, then composed an email regarding our next mystery book club meeting, making it as appealing as I knew how. I mentioned Joy's home-made goodies, and said we needed to be together in companionship at this time of stress and sadness to escape the harsh realities fate had bestowed upon us.

But who would come? Tim was dead. Corinne and Felicity planned to move ASAP. Evan was Suspect Número Uno. Sadie was in mourning.

Unless she'd killed Tim. Now what made me think that? Sadie and Tim appeared to be a happy couple at the Halloween party. But they both had had financial dealings with Len Lyons. What Marge told me made me wonder if Tim was taking over where Len Lyons had left off—scamming people who needed his services. Sadie was compassionate the way a good guidance counselor should be. But she also was accustomed to living above her means.

I sent my email into cyber space and picked up the ringing telephone.

"Hi, Lexie, it's Sadie."

For a moment I was afraid she'd read my mind and had called to insist she was innocent.

"I was talking to Tim's sister about the funeral. Moira asked me to call some of his friends regarding the arrangements."

She gave me the particulars of the wake and the funeral, and I said I'd be there.

"I'm surprised the ME's office is releasing the body so quickly," I said.

"Things are slow at the morgue," was her wry answer. "And

Moira said the police are almost certain he was shot at close range." Sadie sniffed. "I can't believe Tim's dead. Why would someone want to kill my Tim?"

Her Tim? "Could it have been one of his clients?"

"Why would you think that?" she asked, her tone defensive.

I stifled my irritation. "Tim never talked about his family, and as far as I know, you're his closest friend. So I wondered if a client could have been angry with him for some reason."

"I see." Sadie paused, then said, "Tim didn't have any clients."

"Really? I knew he was an attorney. I hadn't realized he'd retired."

"He'd been disbarred a few years ago. Only a few people knew."

"He mentioned going to his office," I said.

"He did work for other lawyers, and consulted on various projects."

Like the Billingses' attempt to find their missing granddaughter. I wondered if they knew Tim wasn't a *bona fide* attorney.

"I'll see you at the wake," I said, about to hang up.

"Oh, I see you've sent me an email," Sadie said.

"Yes. About next Wednesday's meeting. The day after Tim's funeral."

"I'll be there!" Sadie said, her tone brightening. "It will be a relief to talk about something other than what's happening in real life."

Joy was right, I thought a few hours later after I'd received a positive response from all our mystery club members. Marge had added a heartfelt line that the police just released Evan and led him to believe that he wasn't a serious suspect.

The following evening I drove Joy to Tim's wake. Thirty or forty people milled around the room, though Sadie was the only person I knew. She introduced us to Tim's sister, brothers, and their families and we extended our condolences. I refused to go near the body, and stood several feet from the open casket, making small talk with Joy and a few neighbors.

"Hello there, Lexie," a burly man greeted me, surprising me with a kiss on the cheek.

I gaped at him. He seemed familiar but I couldn't place him.

"Ron Alvarez. I teach English at the high school."

I shook my head.

He grinned. "You might recognize me in my other guise—as Lucifer. The red devil, to be precise."

Then I remembered. Ron had been the bartender at Tim and Sadie's Halloween party.

"Of course. You look different, dressed like this."

Ron turned to survey the room. "It's too bad about Tim being gunned down that way."

"Yes," I agreed. "Did you know him well?"

"Well, enough. He did some work for me, before he stopped lawyering." He leaned closer to say conspiratorially, "A fun guy, but I prefer a lawyer who follows the straight and narrow."

So, Tim's reputation was known to all. "I wonder if one of his projects backfired and got him into trouble," I prompted, hoping Ron would say more.

He laughed. "It wouldn't surprise me. By the way, Sadie mentioned you guys are having a mystery book club meeting next Wednesday night."

"Did she?"

"And you're going to discuss *Miss Pym Disposes*. That's one of my all-time Tey favorites."

"Mine, too," I agreed. "After *Brat Farrar*."

"*A Daughter in Time* is my number one."

I looked at him, surprised. "You are up on your Josephine Tey."

"I used to be. May I come to your meeting and bring a friend? We'll be happy to pay, of course."

"Sure." I gave him the information regarding our next meeting, including my fee.

Ron flashed me a wide grin. "Viola and I look forward to next Wednesday night." He patted my shoulder and disappeared into the crowd.

Joy turned from her conversation with a neighbor to ask, "Was that the devil?"

"Sure was." He's coming to our next book club meeting and bringing someone name Viola."

Joy pursed her lips. "Viola's coming? That should be

131

interesting."

"Why?"

"Because Viola's Tim's ex-wife. Their divorce was anything but friendly."

"Is she here?" I asked, looking around.

"I doubt she'll show up here, though I wouldn't be surprised if she attends the funeral. To make sure Tim's really put in the ground."

I shook my head. "That bad, was it?"

"So I heard." Joy lowered her voice. "They had her down at the precinct for hours, but there was no evidence so they couldn't keep her."

"I never knew she existed till now," I said, stung. "Brian never mentioned her to me."

Joy burst out laughing. "Don't expect him to tell you one fraction of everything he finds out—especially since you knew Tim."

The next few days passed quietly. The police had no new leads regarding Tim's murder, at least none that Brian shared with me. As Joy predicted, Viola showed up at his funeral on Tuesday wearing a long, black dress that flattered her slim figure. Her jet black hair hung halfway down her back, giving her a vampire look.

"It's a wig," Joy whispered to me. "Viola's hair is blonde and curly."

"How do you know her?" I whispered back.

"She belongs to my gym. Teaches French in the high school."

"Ah," I said as Ron slipped into the row to stand beside her. "I see they're a couple."

"Have been for years—since Viola left Tim."

I tried to digest this new information and fit it in with everything else I knew. "But she didn't come to Sadie and Tim's Halloween party."

"If I remember correctly, Ron told me Viola had gone to visit her sister that weekend."

"So, she would have come to the party if she'd been in town?"

"I doubt it. It wasn't a friendly divorce. Ron came to the party because he and Sadie are good pals."

"And Viola and Sadie?" I asked.

"They hate each other's guts."

"Oh, no!" I moaned as the organ sounded, informing us the service had begun. *What had I done, giving Ron the okay to bring Viola to our meeting tomorrow night? Would a cat fight break out—or something worse?*

That night I ran through *Miss Pym Disposes* and drew up a list of topics I wanted to discuss. It was a delightful novel, though I found the first half slow-going. I wondered if a mystery publisher would have bought it in the twenty-first century, given today's readers' need for instant suspense and a dead body by the end of Chapter Three.

Wednesday afternoon, I picked up a gallon of chocolate chip ice cream and paper plates at the supermarket, and a fresh lemon merengue pie at my favorite bakery. I was filling candy dishes and setting out mugs when the phone rang.

"Hi, Lexie. Al here."

"Hello!" I chirped as brightly as I could manage.

"How have you been? It's been almost a week since we spoke last."

"Has it been that long?" I asked.

"I've been busy, tying up matters. I've just made reservations to fly home the first week in December."

"Oh." I felt a fluttering in my stomach. That was a few weeks from now. "I thought you were staying on longer."

"I'm coming in for a fortnight, then I fly back to London. I'll be here for Christmas. You can fly over and visit me."

"Sounds like a plan."

"Lexie, is everything all right?"

"Yes. I've a mystery club meeting here tonight. There's been another murder here in town."

"Oh, no! I've been too occupied to watch the news. I hope the victim wasn't anyone you knew."

"Tim Draigon. He was in the book club."

"I remember him. A shady lawyer. Got disbarred a few years ago."

"Right."

"Remember, these murders have nothing to do with you!"

"I know they don't."

"I have to go. Stay safe and don't go off sleuthing."

"Of course not."

I hung up, puzzled by Al's attitude. When we first met, he was more than eager to help me find Sylvia's killer. Maybe men turned protective when they started caring about someone in a romantic way. The thought gave me an attack of the guilts. I didn't want Al to think of me in a romantic way any longer. Perhaps it was a good thing he was coming home. The sooner I let him know the score, the better.

CHAPTER TWENTY

"How many of you liked *Miss Pym Disposes*?" I asked by way of opening up our evening discussion.

Four of the eight members sitting around my living room—Felicity, Marge, Viola, and Ron—raised their hands.

"Sorry, I didn't get a chance to read the book," Sadie mumbled. We sent her glances of sympathy, but she sat slumped in her chair and never noticed.

"I put it down after twenty pages," Evan said. "Too long-winded by far."

Joy mouthed that she hadn't had time to finish the book. Corinne merely shrugged her shoulders.

I laughed. "You're not alone. Many of today's readers find the book slow going. Lots of setting the scene, letting us see the senior girls' routines, and the mystery doesn't appear until the final third of the novel. But keep in mind *Miss Pym Disposes* was published in 1947. People were more disposed—if I may share that word with our author—to read slower-paced books. The story builds up gradually and grows tenser with each page."

"I loved the book," Felicity enthused. "As I read, I felt I was a student at Leys College and knew all those girls." She gulped and turned a bright red. "Sorry, Lexie. I didn't mean to interrupt."

I grinned at her, delighted by her contribution. "No need to apologize. I love the book, too. Tey's style of writing is both brilliant and original. By the time we've finished reading the novel, we realize why she went to such trouble to familiarize us with the students and faculty at the school.

"To recap for those who didn't read or finish reading the book: *Miss Pym Disposes* takes place in Leys Physical Training College, which is very much like the college that Josephine Tey attended. Lucy Pym, a mousy spinster, has written a book on psychology refuting the well-known schools of Freud and other greats. To her surprise, the book turned into a best seller. Lucy's been invited by the college's schoolmistress, Henrietta Hodge, a former schoolmate, to gave a lecture on psychology. Lucy becomes the pet of the senior class, and ends up staying for two weeks instead of heading home as planned. Never popular when she was a schoolgirl, Lucy is pleased by this attention. She's impressed by the spirit and ability of the fourteen senior girls who rise at five-thirty to begin an exhausting day that includes gymnastics, dance, sports, physical therapy, and more.

"Anyone want to comment on the various students?"

We talked about the wealthy and beautiful Beau Nash, the talents of her friend Mary Innes, the unlikable Barbara Rouse, and the vivacious Teresa Desterro, The Nut Tart from Brazil.

"The college finds employment for the seniors. Word gets out that a top school has requested a Leys graduate to fill a position. Students and teachers alike assume the brilliant Innes will get the job. But Henrietta has decided this plum position will go to Rouse, a smarmy girl, whom Lucy believes has cheated her way to A Levels.

"Rouse is injured when the beam she practices on every morning gives way, and eventually dies. Lucy finds a small shoe ornament near the gym, which she's certain belongs to the murderer."

I looked around the room, pleased that I had everyone's attention. "Comments, anyone?"

We talked about the various suspects, the girl Miss Pym thinks murdered Rouse and how she's proven wrong.

Ron chuckled. "The murderer's never punished for the crime."

We discussed the murderer's character, then I brought the discussion back to Miss Pym. "What does the title, *Miss Pym*

Disposes, mean?"

To my surprise, Joy fielded the question. "I didn't get a chance to read most of the book, but it comes from the saying 'Man proposes, but God disposes.'"

"Exactly!" I beamed at her.

"How does that relate to the novel?" Joy asked.

"Miss Pym withholds information from the authorities," Marge said. "She thinks she's protecting the murderer, only she's gotten it all wrong."

Viola waved a hand. "She realizes her psychology theories are full of holes. No doubt, this is Josephine Tey's way of telling us what she thinks of this less-than-exact science that was so popular in the forties."

"Well said," I commented, thinking that Viola was a wonderful addition to the group. I read aloud from the end of the novel where Miss Pym vows to give up lecturing on psychology, and instead is considering writing a book about reading faces.

Felicity raised a tentative hand. "I suppose it shows that Miss Pym never should have played God. When she did, she made a mistake."

"That's one way of looking at it," Ron said. "Miss Pym believes the girl who inadvertently killed Rouse didn't mean for her to die. She says nothing to the authorities because she doesn't want to ruin her life or upset her parents."

"Not a very good reason to withhold information about a crime," Evan offered. "If someone kills someone, purposely or accidentally, they should be punished!"

Marge shot her husband a look of disbelief. "I'm surprised at you, Evan Billings! There's such a thing as accidental death. Should someone who accidentally kills someone be put in jail?"

Evan shrugged. "Sure. Why not? Dead is dead."

I laughed. "That's not how our legal system works."

"More drunk drivers and speeders who cause vehicular deaths are going to prison," Viola said. "I agree with Evan—dead is dead."

"Those aren't accidents!" Marge retorted. "They're acts of reckless disregard for life."

"They are accidents, in a way," Corinne said.

Time to pull them back on track. "Why do you think

Henrietta Hodge chose Barbara Rouse for the position, though her faculty thought Innes deserved it?"

"Maybe she had a sexual thing for Rouse," Viola suggested.

"I don't think that was it," I said. "I got the impression Henrietta considered Rouse a hard worker who deserved the post."

"Maybe she felt sorry for Rouse," Ron said. "Rouse had no family. No friends."

"Regardless, Henrietta was pig-headed," Marge said. "Her staff opposed giving Rouse the appointment, and Henrietta pulled rank. She disregarded what Lucy Pym said about Rouse's cheating on her exams."

"Henrietta was blind to what everyone else saw in Rouse," I said. "She made her decision and set a plan into motion."

"But we can't blame her for Rouse's murder!" Felicity said.

Sadie suddenly came alive. "Oh, yes we can!" she shouted, glaring at Viola. "People can be responsible for killing someone, even if they don't pull the trigger!"

Viola went pale. "What are you trying to say?"

"You know *exactly* what I'm saying."

Viola clutched at her throat. "I had nothing to do with Tim's murder."

"You threatened to have his car impounded if he didn't repay his loan on time."

"Sadie, Viola, please! Now isn't the time for this," I protested, but neither of them so much as looked my way.

"Your lover boy owed me money," Viola spat out. "Lots of it. He would have had it, too, if he'd worked instead of gambling it away."

Sadie's hands formed fists. I hoped they weren't about to start flying. "Tim was out of his mind with worry! He was desperate to raise the money for you."

"And why not? He owed me that money." Viola tossed her dark mane over her shoulder, seemingly unconcerned that Sadie might act on her fury. "He went to those gangsters he liked to think of as his friends." She laughed. "But he must have pissed them off because not one of them loaned him one cent! It's not my fault if one of them killed him."

Sadie let out a moan. I put my arm around her, but she

shrugged it off and turned her anger on me. "Lexie, if you don't throw that woman out, I'm leaving!"

Viola walked over to face Sadie. Hand on hip, she declared, "I paid to come here, same as you."

"In which case, I won't stay here another minute."

Sadie pushed past Viola and made a beeline for the spare bedroom, where I'd tossed everyone's jackets. I chased after her.

"Please, Sadie. Don't leave like this."

She stopped shoving her arms into her parka to throw me a murderous scowl. "How could you ask that woman to join our group, with Tim barely laid in his grave?"

"I had no idea..." I started to explain as Sadie made a beeline for the front door.

Viola and Ron left on her heels, and the others wandered into the kitchen for coffee and dessert, which they carried back into the living room.

"That was an unexpected flash of excitement," Corrine said. "The ex-wife and the girlfriend battle it out."

"I had no idea Viola was ever married to Tim," I said. "Ron asked if he could come to the meeting and said he was bringing a friend."

Joy grimaced. "Ron's a trouble maker. He knows Sadie and Viola can't stand each other."

"But Tim and Sadie only started dating a short while ago," Marge said.

"They couldn't stand each other before Tim and Viola got divorced," Joy explained. She lowered her voice. "Sadie was going out with Ron until Viola went after him. While she was married to Tim."

Evan laughed. "Ryesdale's beginning to sound like Peyton Place."

"Why?" Corrine asked. "Ryesdale's like any other place-- people fall in love; they divorce."

"And some are murdered," Joy murmured.

Everyone turned to stare at her. Though I knew Joy's comment was meant to provoke a discussion about the murders, I felt obliged to smooth things over.

"There's been talk that both Len Lyons and Tim had mob connections," I said. "Maybe someone in organized crime killed them."

"How do you figure that?" Connie scoffed. "A loan shark wouldn't kill Tim for trying to borrow money. And Len was the local burglar. You're barking up the wrong tree."

Felicity let out a heart-wrenching groan. "That Viola woman said Tim went to gangsters to borrow money. I bet Johnny killed him!"

"Felicity, sweetie." Corinne reached out to take her sister's hands in hers. "Why would you think such a thing?"

"Because Johnny kills people," Felicity whispered. "He killed Len." Her eyes widened. "And he wants to see you dead."

"We're safe now, remember?" Corinne said softly. "We have guards escorting us to work and back to the hotel."

Felicity jerked her hands free to cover her face. "We'll never be safe. Never!"

*****

"Felicity Roberts thinks Johnny Scarvino killed her boyfriend and Tim Draigon," I told Brian the following evening. We were sitting in a booth in my local diner, munching on cheeseburgers.

"Really?" Brian grinned. "And you believe her?"

I shrugged. "I wouldn't know, but Corinne's tough and she's terrified of the guy. She and Felicity are living in a hotel. The house is up for sale."

Brian frowned. "That's too bad. We can take steps against intimidation, but only if they file a complaint."

"Which they won't. Corinne said it only made things worse. Have you found out anything new about Johnny Scarvino."

"He's a gangster. Lives in New Jersey."

"Thanks." I let out a huff of exasperation. "Tell me something I don't know."

"I can't, Lexie."

I pursed my lips. "That isn't very sporting of you. I report conversations. In return you withhold information."

He nodded. "It's not fair, I admit, but I don't want to have to step back from another case."

"I get it. I've no intention of jeopardizing your career." *In which case, Joy and I will check Johnny out.*

Brian pulled back in mock surprise. "That's mighty kind of you, Lexie. Too kind, in fact. Which makes me think you're up to something."

I grinned. "The 'don't ask, don't tell' policy was created for couples like us."

He sent me a thoughtful glance. "I can't stop that devious mind of yours from spinning and plotting, but I'm telling you— don't antagonize the murderer by snooping around and asking questions. You've gotten one warning already."

"Do you think the same person killed Tim and Len Lyons?"

Brian's nostrils flared, and I knew I'd gone too far. "Maybe yes, maybe no. This conversation is over."

"All right," I said, stung by his reaction.

"Sorry," he muttered, and covered my hand with his.

We finished our food in silence. Brian downed the last of his coffee and asked for the check. The waitress dropped it on the table, and he pulled out his wallet. I slid along my seat, ready to stand, when Brian looked up.

"Wait a minute, Lexie. I have to tell you something."

He's going to break up with me! My heart plummeted to my stomach. I swallowed. "What is it?" I croaked.

Brian leaned across the table to speak softly. "Gayle's going home to Utah in two days, and I'm going with her."

"Oh!" Relief and dismay vied for top position in my heart. Dismay won out. "Will it be safe for her to go back there? Is that Shawn Estes still intent on having her brought back so he can...." I couldn't bring myself to utter the word I was thinking.

"I've been in contact with the Utah police chief and the County Attorney. They've suspended Estes while they investigate Chester Fenton's murder."

"Suspended him? You mean to tell me he's not in jail?"

"They never found the knife used to kill Fenton, so it's his word against Gayle's. But the department's also looking into other criminal activities Gayle said Estes was involved in. And they're still searching for the murder weapon."

I shivered. "Estes must be more determined than ever to see the last of Gayle. She's the only person willing to tell the truth about him."

"He's a dangerous S.O.B. Which is why I'm escorting her to

Utah," Brian said. "There's something else. The cops hope Estes' former girlfriend will provide corroborating evidence of all he's been up to. An ambulance rushed her to a hospital a few weeks ago with severe internal injuries. He'd been using her as a punching bag."

"What about Pete Rogers!" I demanded. "For all we know, Estes gave him orders to shoot Gayle on sight."

Brian rolled his eyes. "According to the Utah police, Rogers is exactly what he claims to be. I wouldn't be surprised if he went home. We haven't seen hide nor hair of him or his truck for three days now."

I nodded. "I thought I spotted his truck a few times last week, but not recently."

Now he was grinning. "How about I bring Gayle over to your house tomorrow around dinner time? You can share a meal, stay up talking all night. I'll swing by for her six-fifteen the next morning. We've a ten o'clock flight. She'll fly back to Long Island in a week or two to pick up her SUV."

I hugged Brian and planted a big smooch on his lips. "Detective Donovan, you are the best thing that's happened to me in a long, long time."

CHAPTER TWENTY-ONE

As much as I looked forward to spending time with my sister before she left for Utah, I couldn't stop thinking about Johnny Scarvino. He was the linchpin that linked the two murders.

As soon as Brian dropped me off at home, I pulled out a pad and paper and jotted down everything I knew about the mysterious Johnny:

He was a mobster, which meant he was a killer.

He lived in New Jersey, but had no compunction about coming to Long Island,

He used to date Corinne, which made him no older than thirty-five.

His father went to prison for killing another gangster and his wife.

He killed Felicity's pet ferret.

He probably shot up Corinne and Felicity's house.

Corinne and Felicity were terrified of him.

Did he kill Len Lyons? Did he kill Tim? Both Len and Tim had mob connections, which didn't make them mobsters. Besides, not all mobsters knew one another. I thought of the Logic class I'd taken in my freshman year of college, and realized the problem didn't add up logically. But, like Felicity, I believed the two murders were related.

I called Joy. She answered, sounding grumpy and exhausted.

"We have to do further research on Johnny Scarvino," I told

her.

"Tomorrow. I'm off to bed as soon as I make the kids' lunches."

"It's nine-thirty," I pointed out.

"Thanks for the time check. I've been up since six a.m., if you don't count the two times Brandon woke me up during the night."

"Sorry," I apologized. "I'll come over tomorrow, after my classes."

"I'll be human again then."

As promised, Joy was her usual sweet self the following afternoon when she led me to her tiny computer room.

"I looked up Johnny Scarvino. Didn't find much more than what we'd read about him last time. He was arrested for various mob-related crimes. His father, John, must have killed dozens of people, but went to prison for killing an older couple."

"Who?" I removed the papers on the bridge chair and sat down beside her.

"A Big Enchilada in the mob world," Joy answered as she clicked through several newspaper articles.

"Pick the longest article," I said. "It will have the most information."

"Will do." She was already printing out the article.

I studied the photos before I started reading. John Scarvino was a handsome if grim-looking man about fifty, with a full head of graying hair. The other photo was of the murdered couple, Salvatore Vito (Salvey) and Rose Fusco, seated at a table in a suit and fancy dress at some elegant affair. The photo was too grainy for me to make out their facial features, but the way they held themselves spoke pages. Salvatore Vito loomed big and brawny in the foreground; Rose hunched back in her seat as though shrinking from the camera's lens. *A bully and his victim,* I thought.

I read the text slowly. Salvey Fusco was a boss, and Johnny's father was his underboss. The Fuscos were found shot in the head, execution-style, in the elegant bedroom of their New Jersey mansion. Fusco's fingerprints were found on the gun.

"I didn't do it, I swear! Why would I want to hurt Salvey and Rosie?" Scarvino told the cops when they arrived because an anonymous caller had reported the murders. "Sure I picked up the gun. So what? You think I'm stupid? You think I'd leave my fingerprints if I killed them?"

Scarvino swore the Fuscos were family. He'd never in a million years harm them. But the police and DA's office saw it differently. They figured Scarvino was fed up taking Fusco's orders and wanted to be in charge. They were sure he'd have wiped his fingerprints off the gun, given the chance.

I finished the article and looked at Joy. "It does seem pretty lame that a guy like John Scarvino would leave fingerprints."

Joy laughed. "The cops saw their chance and arrested him. The DA threw the book at him. With that kind of evidence, he didn't have a chance in hell of going free. Catching him on this made up for all the cases they couldn't pin on him."

"Then who made the call? Who knew John Scarvino was at the Fuscos' house?"

Joy shrugged. "Who knows? Someone loyal to Fusco? One of his capos?"

"But why kill Rose Fusco?" I asked. "In the photo she looks terrified of her husband."

"Who knows. Maybe because she was there."

"Did they have children?"

"There's no mention of any kids," Joy said.

Frustrated, I slammed my hand down on the desk. "We still know practically nothing. We've no idea why Johnny Scarvino's angry at Corinne."

"For breaking up with him?"

"That happened years ago."

Joy shrugged. "Some men hold a grudge."

"They do, but shooting up Corinne and Felicity's house seemed to come out of the blue."

"Right after Corinne's bank was robbed," Joy mused.

"And her picture was in the paper."

Again I thought of Brat Farrar and how he longed to be part of the Ashby family. The family! What if the Roberts sisters were part of the family?

"I have it!"

"What?"

I grinned broadly at Joy. "Do you remember when Felicity

told us at one of the meetings that Johnny Scarvino killed her ferret?"

"Of course."

"Corinne tried to calm her down. She said Johnny had done it at their father's orders."

Joy bit her lip as she thought. "So she did."

I nodded. "What if Salvey Fusco is Corinne and Felicity's father?"

Joy's eyes flit back and forth as she considered this possibility. "You mean their names aren't Corinne and Felicity Roberts?"

"Probably not."

"Felicity does go on and on about Johnny Scarvino," Joy mused. "She's terrified of him."

"And Corinne admitted she used to date him."

Joy shook her head in disbelief. "It can't be. This is too weird."

"Why?" I demanded. "Because it's happening on Magnolia Lane where you live, and not in one of your FBI cases?"

"We've no proof," she said weakly.

"Of course we don't. But it adds up! It makes sense, doesn't it?"

Joy nodded. "I'll call one of my buddies, find out what I can about Salvey Fusco's family."

"And I'm going home to start Gayle's farewell dinner. Brian's dropping her off in a couple of hours."

Since Gayle was a vegan who occasionally ate fish, I'd picked up some Chilean sea bass, salad, and several winter vegetables, which I planned to roast in olive oil and garlic cloves. My sister had no rules against imbibing wine, so I bought two lovely bottles of chardonnay, along with a gallon of extra rich chocolate ice cream.

Brian and Gayle showed up at my doorstep at six-fifteen. I invited Brian to join us, but he said he had to catch up on paper work before flying to Utah, and he'd take a rain check for when he returned to Long Island. While Gayle carried her duffle into the guest bedroom, Brian pulled me into the den for a long, passionate kiss.

"So you won't forget me," he whispered and nipped my

146

earlobe, sending me swooning. He released me so suddenly, I nearly toppled over as he strode into the hall.

"What are you doing?" I called after him.

"Checking all your windows and doors. Make sure you double-lock the front door when I leave."

Five minutes later, he was gone. Still dazed, I wandered into the kitchen, trying to remember what attention my carefully-planned meal required. None whatsoever. I smiled at Gayle, already seated at the table.

"Hungry?" I asked.

"Starving." She grinned. "And thirsty."

I turned the oven temperature down and removed a bottle of chardonnay from the refrigerator door. I uncorked it and filled our glasses.

Gayle swallowed a healthy mouthful of wine and sighed. "I'm going to miss you, Lexie."

I patted her arm. "We'll see each other. I'll come out to Utah. I promise."

"You'd better." She gulped down the rest of her wine. "I'm terrified of going back. Shawn has plenty of influence in town. Regardless of what they find against him, he won't take this lying down."

I suppressed a shudder. "Brian's talked to the County Attorney several times. He believes you, but can't take further action until he interviews you face-to-face."

Gayle burst into tears. "Wally Foster's new at the job. Shawn's been in the police department for almost twenty years. He has friends. All I need is for one of them to tamper with the evidence and I'll be charged with Chet's murder."

I put my arms around her. "That's why Brian's going with you. To make sure you get treated fairly." I thought a moment. "If you'd like, I'll come, too."

Gayle shook her head so fiercely, I expected to see her turquoise earrings fly across the room. "You stay right here, Lexie, where you belong. I feel better knowing you're safe at home."

"If that's what you want," I murmured, thinking that with two unsolved homicides, life wasn't exactly safe in Ryesdale, either.

Gayle loved the sea bass and accompaniments, and ate

heartily. We finished off the bottle of chardonnay, and I was about to open a second when Gayle stopped me.

"I'd rather have coffee and dessert."

"Your wish is my command," I said, rising to fill the coffee maker. I was delighted that either the wine, the food, or a combination of the two had mellowed her mood. She cleared the table while I ladled out huge portions of ice cream, which I drenched with chocolate syrup and nuts.

"Let's have dessert in the den," I said, grabbing a handful of napkins and leading the way.

We settled on both ends of the couch and polished off our ice cream as we reminisced about our childhood.

"Did you know how jealous I was of you when we were kids?" Gayle blurted out.

I stared at her to see if she was kidding. "Really? Why on earth?"

"Why on earth?" she exploded. "Because you were older. And close to Mom. And to Sylvia. I remember the three of you going off on shopping sprees or to Manhattan, while I had to stay home with the baby sitter because I was too young."

"But you're six years younger than me," I said, remembering one incident when I was fifteen. Gayle had screamed and hollered when Mom said she couldn't see a Broadway show with us because she was only nine.

"And sometimes acted even younger?" she asked with a bittersweet smile.

"Sometimes," I admitted.

"That came from being so damn frustrated. Whenever I wanted to go out with you and Mom, she always said I was too young. And so I ended up making the loudest fuss I could. Then when I was old enough, you went off to college."

"I'm sorry," I said softly. "I had no idea."

"And it didn't help that you were brilliant in school. The teachers were so damn disappointed when I didn't turn out to be another Alexis," she said bitterly.

"But you had other strengths," I said lamely.

"Yeah. Folk dancing and pottery making, while you got a PhD in English."

"Years after I had Jesse," I pointed out. "I was a single

mother juggling a job and taking classes. It was a long haul and not easy."

Gayle made a face. "I even screwed up in that department—never marrying, never raising a child."

I shot her a look of disbelief. "And I was great at it? Come on, Gayle! Look at my record. Godfrey wasn't husband material; at least not at twenty-three. He left me right after Jesse was born. And now both he and Jesse live in California, as chummy as any father and son." I sighed. "As for Gerald—he was a total nut case. Why I ever married him is beyond my comprehension."

"You claimed he was brilliant, sexy, and charming, remember?"

I nodded. "So he seemed. Three months into our marriage, I realized how selfish and immature he really was. And spiteful. Look how he ended up accidentally causing his own death."

"By burning down your house."

"To a crisp."

We looked at each other. Our lips turned up into smiles, and a minute later we were laughing hysterically.

"He-ee killed himself," Gayle said. "That's not funny."

"It certainly isn't," I agreed between bouts of laughter. "It's tragic."

"You don't keep husbands for very long," Gayle pointed out unnecessarily.

"Did I ever claim to be good marriage material?" I demanded, tears streaming from my eyes. "As you can see, I'm far from perfect," I said when our laughter subsided.

"But the best sister in the world," Gayle said, hugging me tight.

The sound of a truck idling outside the house caught my attention. I switched off the light, then ran to the window to tweak back the drape.

"What is it?" Gayle demanded.

"Trouble," I said, watching two men cross the lawn. I raced to the hall table where I'd left my cell phone and dialed Joy's number. Ruthie answered.

"Ruthie honey, it's Lexie. Let me speak to your mom or dad."

"Mom's at the gym. Daddy's in Zack's room fixing something."

"Get him, okay?"

"He told me not to bother them unless it was an emergency."

The doorbell rang. "Gayle, open the damn door!" shouted an angry male voice.

"Keep away from the door!" I told Gayle.

"What's happening?" Ruthie asked.

"Get you dad. Hurry, please."

The pounding on the door reverberated through the house. Would the door hold? Could whoever it was break his way in?

"Don't!" I shouted at my sister, but it was too late. Gayle was peering through the peep hole.

She let out a shriek. "It's Shawn. He's going to kill me!"

Mike was on the line. "What's wrong, Lexie?"

"Shawn Estes's come for Gayle," I said. "I don't know how he found out she was here—"

"Take her down to the basement and lock yourselves in the cedar closet. Now!"

"But—"

"Do as I say! I'm coming over."

"There are two men…" I started, but Mike had hung up. I pressed Brian's number. It went to voice mail. I ended the call.

The thumping and shouting grew louder. As scared as I was, I had to see Shawn Estes for myself. No big surprise. He was a scowling, burly man with a Fu Manchu mustache and bushy eyebrows under his cowboy hat. The pistol strapped to his hip sent a ripple of fear down my spine.

"Open the door, Gayle!"

"He's going to break it down!" Gayle moaned as she crumpled to the ground.

"Get away from my house!" I shouted. "You have no jurisdiction here."

"Gayle's wanted for questioning in a homicide case back in Utah. She had no business running away."

"I've called the police!" I shouted. "They're on their way."

Shawn's hearty laughter gave me the chills. "We'll be halfway home by the time they arrive. Now open the damn door or I'll break it down!"

I covered my ears, then realized I had better things to do with my hands. I wrapped my arms around my keening sister. "He won't get us," I whispered. "We'll hide in the basement."

"He'll find us."

"Then we'll go out the back door and make a dash for Joy's house."

I prodded Gayle to her feet and half-shoved her through the kitchen. I was about to unlock the door when she grabbed my arm. "Pete's out there!"

"And using the butt end of his gun to smash in the glass panel!"

I pulled my favorite knife from the knife rack. It had a long slender blade with a sharp point. When the gun's grip broke through the glass, I stuck the knife point into the back of Pete's hand. His yowl made me grin.

"Damn!" We both jumped as Shawn's brutal attack on the front door resounded in the kitchen.

Gayle whimpered. "He'll break the door down!"

"Mike will be here any second." *Where was he?* my mind screamed.

Shawn's next assault came louder than ever. Wood splintered. It was only a matter of time before the door gave way and he grabbed my sister.

And killed her?

I racked my brain to come up with a plan to save Gayle. *Think! Mike's on his way. Any delay is worth a try.*

I grabbed Gayle's arm. "I'll jab Pete again if he tries to break in. Go down to the cedar closet in the basement. The key's in the drawer next to the closet. Take it and lock yourself inside.

She shrugged free of my grasp. "Why bother? Shawn's armed. He won't hesitate to shoot us both. I may as well go with him."

"No!" I took hold of Gayle's chin and forced her meet my gaze. "I won't let him take you. Help's on the way."

After a long minute, she nodded.

"Wait here!" I said when I realized the noise had stopped. "I'll go check, see what he's up to."

"Don't go, Lexie." Gayle squeezed my fingers.

Gently, I plied them free. I headed for the front door, wondering if Shawn was coming around the house to break down the kitchen door instead.

Trembling, I peered through the peephole. The sight before my eyes gave me a case of the giggles. I laughed and laughed until my sides ached, but I couldn't stop.

"What is it?" Gayle demanded.

I had to swallow a few times before I could speak. "Mike's holding a gun on Shawn. His hands are raised like you see in the movies."

I slid open the door in time to see Joy prodding Pete before her, his hands raised in defeat. The giggles returned. The gun the bounty hunter thought she held on him was nothing more than the top part of a hockey stick.

A police siren cut through the air. Gayle and I stood there, our arms wrapped around each other, as police officers piled out of three cars and surrounded the two men from Utah.

"You're safe," I whispered to my sister.

"For now."

CHAPTER TWENTY-TWO

"After that stunt Estes and Rogers pulled at your house, the County Attorney's buying Gayle's story from start to finish," Brian reported Monday evening. "And Estes' girlfriend's came through. She's talking and there's no stopping her."

"I'm glad. The more witnesses against him, the stronger the case. How's Gayle holding up?"

"You'd be real proud of her, Lexie. They let me sit in on some of the briefings. She spoke clearly and coherently. No hysterics."

I leaned against the back of the sofa and sighed with relief. "I'm glad you were there for her. When are you coming home?"

"Pretty soon, babe. I have to give my testimony as well."

I laughed. "What testimony? You came in at the tail end of things the other night."

"I'm grateful Mike and Joy secured the situation till we got there."

"Me, too. I'm still reeling from Joy's part in it!" I shook my head in disbelief. "Mike called to tell her what was happening. She drove here, grabbed Zack's hockey stick from the back seat of the car, and used it to take down Pete Rogers."

Brian chuckled. "No wonder the bureau keeps trying to coax her back to work."

"But she won't go. At least not till Brandon's in school full time."

We let a moment of silence go by. How I wished he were here beside me.

"I never got a chance to tell you—Joy and I figured out Johnny Scarvino's connection to Corinne and Felicity Roberts."

"What are you talking about?" Brian asked curtly.

I took a deep breath. "Johnny Scarvino's father killed a gangster, Salvey Fusco and his wife."

"And?"

My voice wavered because suddenly I wasn't certain of what I was about to say. "We think Felicity and Corinne are their daughters."

Brian laughed. "The Roberts sisters! How did you reach that conclusion?"

"Corinne used to go out with Johnny Scarvino. Felicity told us that he killed her ferret on their father's orders. And Felicity's positive he shot up their house."

Silence from Utah.

"Brian?"

He let out an exasperated sigh. "Lexie, none of what you just said makes any sense. You're basing most of it on what Felicity told you, right?"

"Mostly," I admitted.

"And Corinne could have gone out with Scarvino, whether or not she's from a crime family."

"I suppose."

"Though he may have shot up their house. Ballistics show the bullets found in the house match one of Scarvino's guns."

"So I am right!" I said gleefully.

"Only that Scarvino and the Roberts sisters knew one another, not that the girls are Fusco's daughters." His voice was suddenly hoarse, a sign he was feeling distressed. "Scarvino's one bad dude, Lexie. The good news is the cops in New Jersey are holding him on various charges. But he'll probably be out on bail in a few days."

"And roaming the streets again," I said mournfully.

"Looks that way." He sighed loudly. "Do me a favor—keep out of this. Don't so much as Google him, much less borrow a cup of sugar from your neighbors."

"I couldn't if I wanted to. Corinne and Felicity are staying at a hotel, I've no idea where."

"Glad to hear it. Gotta go." He hung up.

I stared at the phone, not at all happy the way our conversation had ended. Then I realized what had put Brian in such a foul mood. I'd hit upon the truth about Corinne and Felicity, and he wished I hadn't.

"Yay!" I shouted, thrusting my arm in the air. I was a pretty damn good detective. Slowly but surely, the pieces were falling into place.

I had no intention of doing anything stupid like driving over to Corinne's bank and opening up a new account so I could question her about her past. Besides, if I were being honest, I only wanted to know if the girls were Fusco's daughters for the same reason people read gossip columns. It made no difference to me if they'd grown up in a crime family. They were only a link to Johnny Scarvino, whom I suspected of murdering Len and Tim. Knives and guns were mobsters' weapons of choice.

I wondered if it was a coincidence that the police had Johnny Scarvino under lock and key. No doubt, they were questioning him about the two murders. I shivered to think he'd broken into my house to hide the knife behind the bookcase in the guest room. When had he managed to do that?

I spent the rest of the week doing ordinary activities that had nothing to do with homicide. I taught my classes, looked after Puss, and spent Saturday morning shopping with Mike for favors for Joy's birthday party. We wandered through several shops in a nearby town until we settled on mini Godiva chocolate boxes.

"Everyone loves chocolate," I pointed out.

"I'll buy a few extra for the kids," he said.

"How many people are coming?" I asked

"Thirty-five. Forty. I don't have to call in the final count for two weeks."

I left him signing his charge card, and drove back to Ryesdale to do my weekly shopping at the supermarket. I was about to enter the store when someone called to me.

"Hi, Lexie!"

I wasn't sure if I wanted to flee from Felicity or give her a hug. Corinne was with her. I waited for them to approach, telling myself I wouldn't ask any probing questions.

"Hi," I greeted them. "What are you doing here?"

"Like you, food shopping. We need to eat, don't we?" Corinne said, yanking a cart free from the metal lineup.

"Oh." For a moment I was flustered. "I thought you were staying at a hotel."

"We were," Corinne said, "and today we're moving back home."

"Because Johnny Scarvino's in jail?"

Both sisters gaped at me.

"I-I heard the police are holding him on various charges," I stammered.

They exchanged glances and came to a conclusion, a conclusion that lowered the level of tension considerably.

Felicity grinned. "Johnny's locked up in jail, so Barbara said we could get rid of our guards and move back home."

"Is Barbara your WITSEC handler, or whatever they call them?" I hadn't meant to say that, but the words flew from my mouth on their own volition. Brian wouldn't be pleased.

Nor was Corinne. She grabbed my arm none too gently and ordered me to keep my voice down.

"Sorry," I said softly. "I just figured out who you guys really are. How awful for you. I mean, your parents getting killed that way."

Corinne's mouth formed a severe line. "John Scarvino murdered them."

Felicity placed her hands over her ears. "Don't talk about it, Corinne. Please don't talk about it."

Corinne pulled out a handkerchief and wiped the tears spilling down her sister's cheeks. "Not another word, sweetie. Let's pick up a few things for dinner, then go home and forget about everything unpleasant."

Her expression changed to a glare when she turned to me. "Good-bye, Lexie. I trust you'll keep your mouth shut about our identities until we've moved from Ryesdale."

"You're still planning to sell the house?"

"Of course. Jail won't stop Johnny from tormenting us. He'll come after us the minute he's free."

Why is he tormenting you? I wanted to ask, but they were already passing through the automatic doors of the supermarket.

I don't even know their real names, I mused as I grabbed a wagon and followed them into the store. They were two strange birds, but who could blame them, given their background? I felt sorry for Felicity, but every time I tried to help her I had to deal with Corinne's smoldering fury. Corinne controlled her sister like a domineering parent. But Felicity was fragile and probably needed her sister's guidance. I'd no doubt the two were devoted to one another. The only times I'd seen Corinne soften was when she was comforting Felicity.

I had no regrets that they were moving. I hoped the people they sold their house to were nice and normal.

As I tossed a box of oatmeal into my wagon, it dawned to me I needn't wonder about my future neighbors because I had no idea how much longer I'd be living on Magnolia Lane. Al was due home from England right after Thanksgiving, at which time I planned to tell him I was involved with Brian.

Where would I go? What would I do? Buy a house? Rent somewhere? I'd be homeless again, which disturbed me no end.

A tremor ran down my spine as I considered another possibility: what if Brian asked me to move in with him?

A thrilling but terrifying thought. I was crazy about Brian, but the idea of getting serious with anyone sent my hyperventilating. Here I was, approaching the half century mark, and I didn't have one male-female relationship I could point to that had lasted longer than a year. As for Brian and me—we got along fine, but we weren't spending time together on a regular basis. Once we did that, he'd get to know just how quirky I was. Even worse, I'd discover his flaws and take off like a bat out of hell.

I told myself not to get carried away. Brian and I were just getting to know each other. I'm sure the idea of our moving in together had never crossed his mind. And if it did, he was sure to quash the impulse once he found out I'd questioned Felicity and Corinne about their past after he'd told me not to.

It was obvious Brian knew about the girls' background and their history with Johnny Scarvino. So why did he pretend what I'd discovered about them was preposterous? And when he could no longer deny the possible relevance to the case, he sounded downright annoyed.

I felt my smile growing wider as I moved on to pastas and

sauces. Brian had acted that way because he cared about me and wanted to keep me safe. I appreciated the sentiment.

From him, but not from Al.

I called Joy when I got home and told her about my conversation with the Roberts sisters.

"Their real names are Catherine and Francisca Fusco," she told me.

"Good job! How did you find out? Their names weren't mentioned in any of the articles."

"Of course not. WITSEC managed to keep them out of the paper."

"WITSEC," I echoed. "Were the sisters put into protective custody because they gave evidence when their parents were murdered?"

"Corinne—Catherine did. She saw Scarvino Senior leaving her parents' home. She found them brutally murdered in their bedroom and called the police."

"A strange thing for a Mafia princess to do," I commented.

Joy laughed. "You're so jaded, Lexie."

"I'm trying to figure out why Johnny Scarvino's been tormenting them, to borrow Corinne's expression."

"Maybe because his father went to prison based on Corinne's testimony," Joy said.

"And he hates her for it? But what would he expect her to do?" I asked.

"Logic doesn't come into the picture," Joy said.

"What else did you find out about the two sisters?"

"Not much," Joy admitted. "Their parents kept them out of the spotlight. In fact, they went to boarding school and were away from home most of the time."

"I bet that was their mother's doing," I said. "She probably did her best to keep them far from crime and murder."

"Francisca—Felicity—had a nervous breakdown and left boarding school when she was fifteen," Joy said. "She had tutors home schooling her until she was eighteen."

"Have they been living in the house next to me since their parents were killed?"

"No. They've lived in two other locations. Each time Johnny Scarvino found where they were and harassed them. He often tailed Corrine when she was driving, made menacing calls. Stuff like that."

"It doesn't sound like he was out to kill them," I said.

"Not until he shot up their house last month."

"I wonder what made him angry enough to do that," I mused.

Joy laughed. "Who knows what lurks in a gorilla's mind."

CHAPTER TWENTY-THREE

Two days later I found myself in Toys R Us, of all places, with Joy at my side. We'd come in search of baby gifts and party supplies. The night before, Marge had phoned the book club members with the most wonderful news. Between tears, sobs, and exclamations she told us *doña* Marisol, the woman who'd been taking care of their three-year-old granddaughter, had arranged for a neighbor to call them. In broken English, the neighbor asked the Billingses to email photos of themselves, their daughter, and to spell out in detail how they planned to raise Eloisa. This would help Marisol decide if it was safe to hand over Eloisa *a sus abuelos en los Estados Unidos*.

Puzzled but elated by this sudden request, they quickly obliged. *Doña* Marisol's email response came within hours. In Spanish, she wrote that she looked forward to meeting Eloisa's mother's parents as soon as possible, and she had the proper papers that enabled her to release the child to her closest blood relatives. A government official assured her that if all papers were in order, the Billingses would be permitted to bring Eloisa home with them.

Marge and Evan ordered baby furniture for their spare room, and Joy and I arranged to host a baby shower at my house tomorrow evening, the night before the Billingses flew to Lima.

"What do you think of this?" I held up a child's-size plastic shopping cart.

"It's okay, isn't it, Brandy Boy?" Joy said. She stuck her grinning face into her son's carriage and earned herself a toothless grin. I welcomed Brandon's company today, since almost twenty years had passed since I'd last shopped in Toys R Us. Having him along helped me feel less like a fish out of water.

"What's wrong with the cart?" I demanded. "I'm also planning to buy a set of toy groceries. They've a nice selection to choose from."

"Actually, the shopping cart's a great gift," Joy said. "It allows for creative role playing while using familiar objects. Though we don't know if the objects in the cart will be familiar to Eloisa, or if she'll know what to do with the cart. We've no idea what her life experiences have been up until now."

"And she'll be speaking Spanish, not English," I muttered as I put the shopping cart back on the shelf.

"Watch and see how quickly she picks up English," Joy said airily. "It's the other changes in her life that will take time."

"What are you getting Eloisa?" I asked to ward off more child psychology observations.

Joy sent me a self-satisfied smile. "An age-appropriate computer. All kids love computers."

"Smart-ass soccer mom."

"Sorry," Joy said, not looking sorry at all.

We turned down another aisle, and suddenly I was surrounded by dolls—large dolls, small dolls; brown dolls, white dolls; some dressed in finery, others in a nightie. I loved dolls and hadn't bought a single one for Jesse while he was growing up because he didn't even like to play with action figures.

I reached for a life-sized baby doll smiling at me behind cellophane in a half box. "Maybe Eloisa would like this."

Joy scrutinized the doll as if it were a piece of evidence. "I bet every doll she's had till now was made of cloth or wood. And not one of them had blue eyes *or* blonde hair like this one."

I pressed my lips together. "Is that a problem?"

"Maybe not, but to be on the safe side, get the shopping cart. She's bound to love the shopping cart."

Reluctantly, I set the doll back on the shelf. "I'll go back for the cart after you choose a computer."

Brandon started to fuss, but quieted down when we resumed walking. I grabbed an empty wagon, and we began filling it with our presents and decorations for the shower. Fifteen minutes later, we had everything we'd come for.

"I still can't get over how quickly their granddaughter's situation changed, and on such short notice," I said.

"Me, neither," Joy agreed. "It isn't the sort of issue that's easily resolved. It's as though someone stepped in and took over from the money-hungry people Tim had found for them."

"Who could that somebody be?"

Joy shrugged. "Beats me. Marge promised to explain everything tomorrow night."

"Getting their granddaughter means everything to Marge and Evan. I hope they're not flying all the way to Peru only to be disappointed."

"Which is why Evan asked *doña* Marisol for assurance that no one will prevent them from bringing Eloisa home with them. She had him contact an official in the village where she lives."

When we reached the check-out line counter, Brandon began to cry. Joy shook a rattle. He grabbed it and put the teething end in his mouth.

"Good boy!" She helped me unload our purchases onto the conveyer belt. "Brandon wants his lunch, a change, and a nap."

"Lucky little boy, having a mom who understands him."

"It's easy, after Zack and Ruthie."

"Every day with Jesse meant learning something new," I said as we walked toward Joy's SUV.

"It gets easier with each kid. You start to know what to expect." Joy backed expertly out of the parking spot and we headed for home.

"Do you miss working?" I asked when we'd stopped for a red light.

The question surprised her. "Occasionally, but after being in the field all those years, I'm happy to be home when the kids get off the bus. I'm glad I can tell the class mother or teacher, 'sure, I'll bake a dozen cupcakes' or 'I'm free to chaperone a class trip.'"

"And you're available to help me solve local homicides," I joked.

Joy nodded. "Especially since our friends in blue haven't made much progress. No clear-cut evidence, DNA, or eye witnesses to point a finger at anyone."

"Josephine Tey believed facial characteristics reveal character," I said. "If a murderer's face gives him away, then who killed Len and Tim? No one we know looks especially malevolent or ominous."

Joy pursed her lips as she thought. "Sadie's been rather grim since Tim died, but that's to be expected."

"And Corinne's perfectly frightful, spewing one of her Medea-like rages when she feels Felicity needs protecting." I grimaced. "And I'm usually her victim. You'd think by now she'd have caught on that I want to help her sister, not upset her."

"You'll be rid of Corinne soon enough," Joy said. "WITSEC will be whisking them off to a new home with new IDs."

I felt a twinge of guilt. "Because I told them I knew they were Fusco's daughters?"

"Primarily because Corinne testified at John Scarvino's trial. The government's obligated to give them new identities and keep them safe from the likes of Johnny Scarvino."

I sighed. "Relocation. New jobs. New friends. It must be difficult."

"Luckily, the two sisters are devoted to one another," Joy said. "They have to be, to get through this."

I shook my head. "Poor Felicity. She's not the brightest bulb, and she probably needs Corinne to look out for her, but she needs some leeway if she's going to develop self-reliance. Corinne's so overbearing."

Joy winked at me. "I'm sure you don't treat Gayle that way."

"Lately, Gayle thinks I'm the best thing since chopped liver. She called last night to thank me for seeing her through this mess. Estes is in jail on several charges. This time his own department won't let him post bail."

Joy sent me a knowing look. "Probably because of what your boyfriend told them. When is Brian coming home?"

"The day after tomorrow. Gayle's flying to Long Island next week to pick up her SUV. I'm hoping she'll stay to spend Thanksgiving with me. We should spend holidays together when we can."

Joy reached over to pat my hand. "You've done good, Lexie, reconnecting with your sister."

"I'm glad we've forged a new kind of relationship. Besides Jesse, Gayle's the only family I have." A pang of sadness dinged my heart. "Now that he lives in California, he sees more of his father than he did in all his growing-up years."

"Jesse needs to spend time with Godfrey," Joy said. "He knows he has you."

"I suppose," I conceded.

As she turned down Magnolia Lane, we discussed how much cake and cookies I was to buy when I went shopping again later that afternoon.

"Don't go crazy, Lexie. No one expects much on such short notice. How many are we?"

"There's you, me, Marge, Felicity, Corinne, Sadie, and Viola. Seven in all."

Joy pursed her lips as she pulled into my driveway. "I hope Sadie doesn't throw a fit because we've included Viola."

"Viola's part of our book club now and welcome to come to the shower," I said firmly. "Besides, I think Sadie's overdoing the widowed girlfriend bit."

"Really?" Joy mused, her expression thoughtful. "Do you think Sadie killed Tim and is putting on an act so we won't suspect her?"

"Anything's possible." I pointed at her. "You, better than anyone, should know that."

Joy sighed. "Still, I hate to have to go around suspecting people we like."

I laughed. "We'd rather all murderers looked like Shawn Estes. He fits Tey's formula."

"Perfectly!"

I blew Joy a kiss, then carried the cart and party supplies inside.

*****

Preparing for a shower was much easier than preparing for a meeting of the book club. All I had to do was put out the goodies and keep the decaf coffee and tea going. I was glad to take part in this joyous occasion. Little Eloisa was finally meeting her American grandparents, and they would make sure she led a happy, cared-for childhood.

I scrambled a few eggs for dinner, then cleared the table to set out the pretty paper plates and napkins we'd bought earlier. A faint sound coming from the back yard sent a shiver down my back. I turned off the light switch and peered outside. Nothing.

No one's out to hurt you. Estes is locked up in a Utah jail. I caught sight of the swaying tree branches and smiled. It must have been the wind I heard. *Besides, you're safe inside, and friends are on their way.*

I returned to my baby shower preparations. Thinking someone might like wine, I took an unopened bottle of chardonnay from the fridge and set it beside the cookies, cakes and mugs. I placed the toy shopping cart I'd bought for Eloisa on the small table I'd set up for gifts. Because of its odd shape, I hadn't wrapped it, though I taped a large welcome card to one of the sides.

As I worked, I couldn't stop wondering if there really had been a legal problem preventing Eloisa from leaving Peru. Whether the problem had to do with immigration or was a ploy by the group trying to get more of the Billingses' money, someone had stepped in to cut through the red tape. Someone powerful with plenty of clout.

The doorbell rang. I glanced at my watch. Ten to eight. A bit early, but no big deal. I went to welcome my first guest.

"Sorry. I didn't realize the time," Sadie said, her breath coming in gasps.

"No problem. Everything's ready. Come on in."

"I had so much to do, I was afraid I'd be late," she said, shrugging out of her coat. She was still dressed for school—mid-calf leather boots, a long tan sweater she wore belted over a skirt. Sadie looked down at the beautifully-wrapped gift in her hands. "Where can...? I see."

She placed her gift on the table and picked up the shopping cart, which suddenly looked naked in its unwrapped state. "How precious! I had one of these when I was little."

"What did you buy her?"

"An age-appropriate educational toy." Sadie gave me a wan smile. "A friend who's a child psychologist suggested it."

"I'm sure Eloisa will love all her gifts," I said. "Want a cup of coffee?"

"I'd love one! I never got a chance to eat dinner."

Sadie followed me into the kitchen and poured herself a mug of regular coffee. I filled one with decaf.

"Would you like me to make you a sandwich? I've tuna fish, turkey, and Swiss cheese."

"Coffee's fine." She let out a sigh. "I'm not able to eat much these days."

"How have you been?" I asked, wondering if she was truly upset or trying to make me *think* she was.

Sadie blinked back tears and offered me a brave smile. "Losing Tim knocked me for a loop. Though we only started dating weeks ago, we've been friends for ages. I had no idea how essential he was to my life."

"Shall we sit down?"

She followed me into the living room.

"I know everything thinks Tim was a shyster lawyer who pulled all kinds of deals and made money in sleazy ways, but he was a wonderful person."

I nodded, feeling a sense of *déjà vu*. I'd heard similar words recently. When? Where? Of course! When Felicity was mourning Len Lyons.

"Do you have any idea who might have killed him?" I asked.

"The detectives keep asking me that. I'll tell you what I tell them each time: I don't know. Tim never told me anything about his business."

How very convenient. "They probably keep asking because you both borrowed money from someone in the mob."

Sadie's eyes flashed with anger. She was about to lash out and ask how I knew her business. Instead, her aggressiveness dissipated, and she merely shook her head.

"I went on a stupid spending spree, buying items I couldn't afford." She gave a humorless laugh. "My reaction to a relationship gone sour. And suddenly I was in debt. Owed more money than I ever had in my life! Tim understood and offered to help me out. He arranged for me to borrow money without my having to meet with the person doing the loaning. He promised that as long as I made my payments, I'd be fine."

She glanced at me. "He took care of everything for me. And now he's gone."

"The honorable money lender," I murmured.

"Don't mock what you know nothing about! And the worst part is, it's far from over."

"What do you mean?"

"Today I got a phone call telling me to pay up everything I owe. With interest."

She sent me a glance of pure terror. "But how can I pay back money I don't have? I can't even sell my house in two weeks."

"Whoever he is, he means business. I hope you've called the police."

Sadie's nostrils flared as she shook her head vehemently to ward off my suggestion. "I know who killed Tim! The pieces all came together as I drove here. How dumb of me not to have seen it before."

I swallowed, dreading what I was about to hear. "Who killed him?"

"Viola."

I shivered as if ice cubes were dripping down my back. "What makes you say that?"

"She's the only person who wanted Tim dead. So she could stop paying him alimony."

Sadie's words made no sense. "At our last meeting, Viola said Tim owed *her* money."

"He did. He'd been gambling a bit and had a streak of bad luck, so he asked Viola for an advance to pay some bills. She gave it to him. Then suddenly she wanted her money. He had to borrow from a money lender to pay some of it back."

Sadie let out what sounded like a hiss. "It's not like she needed it. Viola doesn't give a damn about the money! She only wanted to see Tim miserable." She glared at me. "Her father's a billionaire, and she has a side business that brings in thousands every week."

I bit my lip. *Why had I invited Viola to join our group?* "But that doesn't mean she'd *kill* Tim."

"Viola hated him. She told Tim she'd kill him if he ruined the life of another woman." Sadie gave me a wan smile. "And then we started going out."

"Think, Sadie." I placed my hand on her shoulder. "You're only saying this—"

The doorbell rang, cutting off the rest of my sentence.

CHAPTER TWENTY-FOUR

The others started to arrive, chattering away as they shed jackets and covered the small table with gifts for Eloisa. Viola appeared, lugging the largest gift of all. I turned to Sadie, afraid that she'd suddenly shout accusations and ruin the festive mood, but she merely stared at her nemesis, jaw clamped tight in fury.

"I've brought Eloise a doll carriage," Viola said, putting it on the table with the other presents. "Every little girl needs a carriage for her babies."

I got caught up in my hostess duties and lost track of Sadie.

Marge, overcome with emotion, went around hugging everyone. "Thank you all! I can't begin to express how much your kindness means to Evan and me."

We bombarded her with questions, most of them regarding the sudden ease with which they were now able to bring Eloisa to the U. S.

In response, Marge pulled a magnum of champagne from her tote bag. Grinning broadly, she said, "All in good time. Lexie, could you get us a couple of glasses? I want everyone to drink a toast to our angel."

Joy accompanied me into the kitchen. "What's the big mystery?" she grumbled as we filled two trays with wine glasses. "Who's this wonderful savior?

"Aren't you the impatient one?" I teased. "You'll find out in a minute."

Marge surprised me by opening the bottle with finesse. She poured a generous amount of champagne into each glass and handed them around. We stood in a tight group, watching Marge and waiting for what came next.

"I want to drink a toast to our darling little Eloisa, and to the wonderful person responsible for bringing her home to Evan and me."

I raised my glass, prepared to imbibe the moment I heard the mysterious person's name, when the doorbell rang.

"Sorry. Won't be a minute," I apologized, dashing to the front door. I looked through the peephole and saw a delivery man holding a gift-wrapped package.

"Delivery for Mrs. Evan Billings."

I opened the door and stared longer than I should have at the gorgeous Adonis standing before me. He was around thirty and had the broad shouldered-trim body of a swimmer, black curly hair and wonderful features.

"How-how did anyone know to send a gift to this address?" I sputtered.

"Beats me," he said. "Do you want to sign for it or not?"

"I'll take it. Thanks." I scrawled my name on his gizmo and shut the door.

Joy walked toward me, a scowl on her face. "Is that Mike, asking for help with a problem he can't handle?"

"It's a gift for Eloisa," I said, carrying the box into the dining room.

"Who from?"

"It must be from Marge's granddaughter. She's the only person we invited who couldn't make it tonight."

"Lexie! Joy! We're waiting."

"Sorry," I mumbled as we rejoined the others.

"Now," Marge said, "as I was about to tell you, our joy and happiness is due to one special person—our dear friend, Corinne Roberts."

Six necks swiveled to stare at Corinne. The object of our attention met our stares with a hint of a smile. We raised our glasses and toasted her in silence. When I found my voice, I said, "Corinne, please tell us how you performed this miracle."

She shrugged. "Marge gives me much too much credit. I

merely got things rolling. The other day was quiet at the bank, so I had time to examine a few of our big personal accounts—something we're asked to do periodically for our customers' benefit as well as ours. I came across the account belonging to a rather nice gentleman high up in the state department. I remembered what Marge and Evan were going through, so I called him to ask if he could help resolve the matter."

"She's full of it," Joy whispered.

She had to be. The story sounded too good to be real, but I *had* to hear more. "You called and he offered to work out all the kinks?" I asked Corinne, not bothering to hide how incredulous I found her story.

She grinned back, as if she knew what I was thinking and didn't give a damn. "More or less. The problem appealed to him, probably because it involved a young child. He promised to see what he could do, and called back two days later, matter resolved."

"Amazing," I muttered.

"Totally amazing!" Marge agreed. "The woman looking after Eloisa needed reassurance that we'd be good guardians. After all, she's a distant cousin of the little girl's father. Money wasn't the prime concern."

Prime concern? "Are you and Evan paying her?"

"Of course. For taking care of Eloisa all this time. Doña Marisol is a widow. She earns barely enough money to feed her three children and herself, let alone feed and clothe Eloisa."

I bit back what I really thought, for fear of ruining Marge's special evening. "The important thing is bringing your granddaughter home."

At that point, everyone had something to say. Something was wrong with this picture. No doubt, this *doña* Marisol was receiving big bucks, as were other people. But none of it mattered if Eloisa was brought safely to the U. S. Feeling restless, I picked up the dishes of cookies and cakes and went around offering them to my guests.

"Coffee and tea are in the kitchen," I said. Minutes later, when everyone was back in the living room munching away, I suggested that we open Eloisa's presents. We oohed and ahed as one after another gift was unwrapped and held up for Marge's approval. And approve she did. At last, the only remaining gift was the one that had just been delivered.

I reached for it. "I think this is from your granddaughter, Marge."

"Really?" Marge's face scrunched in puzzlement. "Callie told me she was sending us a check."

"Then I've no idea who it's from. Maybe the card's inside."

Marge ripped away the paper. "It's a beautiful cloth-bound photo album." She thumbed through the pages. "I can't find a card. Wait, here's something."

I picked up the photograph that had fallen to the carpet. A young woman gazed down at something long and furry in her lap. I gulped when I realized it was a ferret. A dead ferret, judging by the angle of its head.

Then why was the young woman smiling?

"That's Oscar!" Felicity exclaimed. "And that's you, Corinne." Her voice wobbled when she asked, "What did you do to him?"

Corinne put an arm around her sister's shoulders. "I didn't do anything, sweetie. Johnny had just put him to sleep because Daddy..." She removed the photograph from Felicity's trembling fingers. "You shouldn't be looking at this."

She glared at me. "How did this photo get here? Is this your idea of a joke?"

"My idea? You saw for yourself. It fell out of the baby album."

"Who would do such an awful thing?" Marge moaned. She slumped down in her chair. I didn't like the pale color her face had turned.

"Oh!" I exclaimed, suddenly remembering the young man who had delivered the package. Though the tilt of his cap had prevented me from seeing his face, I was willing to bet he was Johnny Scarvino.

I reached for the photo. "May I see that?"

"No! " Corinne held it between the thumb and forefinger of each hand, about to rip it to shreds. Joy broke her grip and grabbed the picture.

"This isn't yours, Corinne. It came in a gift for Eloisa. The police might want it as evidence."

"Evidence! Evidence of what?" Corinne's face burned red with fury. "*I'm* the person in the picture. I'll decide what happens to it. Hand it over!"

Joy shook her head. Corinne looked like a cork ready to pop.

"Come, Felicity. We're going home!"

I followed the sisters into the spare bedroom where the guests' jackets were strewn on the bed.

"But you were smiling, Corinne. Why were you smiling?" Felicity asked.

"Felicity dear, I wasn't smiling. Here's your jacket. Now where's mine?"

CHAPTER TWENTY-FIVE

I picked up Brian at Kennedy Airport the following afternoon. We stopped for an early dinner then drove to my house. Once inside, we ripped off each other's clothes like they do in the movies and headed for the bedroom. Puss meowed when I closed the door in his face, but I was in no mood to worry about his feelings.

After a short bout of cuddling and another round of sex, I showered and dressed while Brian called the precinct and caught up on things. Then we walked hand-in-hand to Joy and Mike's house.

The Lincoln household was quiet at nine o'clock with all the kids in bed. Joy sat us down at the kitchen table, poured us each a mug of coffee, then handed the photo to Brian. He studied it for what seemed like minutes. When I could take the silence no longer, I said,

"Corinne's smiling. No normal person smiles when an animal dies, unless she killed it."

Brian pursed his lips, still staring at the photo. "I can't *swear* that she's smiling. She's not looking at the camera so we can't see her eyes. It could be a grimace of sadness because the ferret's dead."

Joy threw him a scornful look. "Come on, Donovan. You're not on the stand. You know as well as I do Corinne killed that poor creature. *Corinne!* Not Johnny as Felicity believes."

"That's what Johnny wants us, Corinne's neighbors, to know," Mike said. "But why? And in such a convoluted way."

Joy sipped her coffee. "Probably because no one's listened to what he's been saying all these years. Namely, that his father didn't kill the girls' parents."

"How did he find out about the shower?" I asked. "We only planned it a few days ago and Johnny was in jail, according to Corinne and Felicity."

"He must have bugged their phone somehow," Brian said.

"Or bugged one of their cell phones," Mike said. "Either way, he knows people with high tech expertise."

"He's fishing," Brian said. "Without new evidence regarding the murders, he can't expect to get his father out of prison."

I bit into a brownie and chewed thoughtfully. "Johnny's telling us Corinne is evil. Only an evil person would kill someone's pet."

"Only an evil person would kill her own parents," Joy said.

Brian laughed. "That's some wild assumption."

"There's such a thing as logic and common sense!" she snapped. "Murderers who kill without compunction start out by killing animals."

"Ferrets are weasels," Mike pointed out. "Though they're popular pets, many people don't regard them as they do cats and dogs."

"Oscar was Felicity's pet," Joy said.

Mike leaned over to kiss her cheek. "What you need is evidence, my dear, to substantiate your charges."

Joy frowned. "We've no evidence, no clues, no DNA to say that Corinne ever harmed anyone, much less a ferret."

I suddenly remembered. "Speaking of wild assumptions, Sadie has it in her head that Tim's ex-wife, Viola, killed him. For one thing, she was fed up paying him alimony."

Mike grinned at his wife. "That's a good enough reason in my book."

Joy punched his arm.

"Sadie also said Viola threatened to murder him if he ruined another woman financially," I said.

"Well, that didn't happen," Joy said. "Sadie racked up her debt all by herself."

"True, but Tim arranged a loan for Sadie, and didn't tell her with whom. Now that person wants his money back pronto and with interest."

Brian stared at me. "That's serious. Did she go to the police for protection?"

I shook my head. "I told her to report it, but she seemed more concerned with confronting Viola herself."

Brian cursed under his breath.

The phone rang. Joy answered it. From the way her face froze, I could tell the news wasn't good. The three of us stopped talking to listen to the conversation.

"Are you sure? Really? I suppose they can hold him, though—"

She listened some more, then said, "Unfortunately, Homeland Security isn't part of the FBI."

From the little I'd heard, I felt sorry for whomever was on the other end of the phone.

Joy spoke words of comfort to the caller and hung up. She turned to us. "That was Marge. They were checking their luggage for the flight to Lima and Evan was taken away. It seems he's on Homeland Security's 'no fly' list."

The words tumbled around in my brain. "That's absurd. Evan was a dairy farmer, for God's sake. How did he end up on the national terrorist list?"

Joy turned from leafing through her phone book to answer me. "It's a mistake, of course. Probably someone with the same name—ah, here it is!"

"Are you calling Fred?" Mike asked.

She nodded as she punched in numbers. "Of course. He has friends in Homeland Security. I'm hoping one of them can clear Evan in time to get him aboard his plane."

Mike shook his head. "That's not going to happen."

"Are you absolutely positive Evan's who he says he is?" I asked.

Joy scowled at me. "What an awful thing to say!"

"Why? The Mafia princesses live next door to me."

Brian and Mike found that hilarious.

Joy left their friend Fred a message to call her ASAP. After she hung up, she turned to us. "Fred's the only one who might help, and I've no idea when he'll get back to me. Looks like Evan's not leaving the U.S. any time soon."

The phone rang again. Joy explained all this to a very agitated Marge. She ended by saying, "I'm afraid you're going to have to fly to Lima without Evan." She listened, consoled her as best she could, and hung up.

"Poor Marge is devastated, but she's determined to fly to Lima herself," Joy told us.

Brian and I left shortly after that. When we reached my driveway, he pulled me close. "Lexie, babe, I worry about you. You're like a magnet for bad guys, no matter where you live."

Annoyed, I pulled free. "What are you talking about? It's not my fault the Mafia princesses live next door."

I didn't like the smirk on his face. "And the others? A smalltime wise guy ends up dead on your lawn. A book club member's shot to death. Another one's stopped by Homeland Security. Do you call that the usual order of business?"

I drew myself up until I almost faced him eye to eye. "I don't know what's normal. All I know is I didn't bring any of this about."

"You didn't. I only wish you weren't involved."

"Well, I am involved with my book club members!" I strode the remaining yards to my front door and pulled out my key. "Good night, Brian."

When he tried to hug me, I remained rigid as a board.

"Don't be like this," he murmured in my ear.

"Then don't tell me whom to care about, whom to know—"

He kissed me, putting an end to my tirade. Finally, he let me go. Stroking my cheek, he said, "Cops have a hard time when the people they love get caught up in their cases."

Love! I nodded, reeling from his choice of words.

"Stay safe, Lexie," he whispered, not moving until I was safely inside.

*****

Joy called the following afternoon to tell me her friend Fred had managed to contact someone who could do something about Evan's situation.

"Homeland Security's running through every document they have on him, and should be finished later today."

"Poor Evan. Will he be able to fly to Peru, after all?"

"They've told him not till next week the earliest."

"Damn! He has to be there to sign the necessary documents."

Joy laughed. "You didn't let me finish. Fred's friend called in a few favors, and things are moving at lightening speed. Evan should be able to leave tomorrow night."

I grinned. "I'm impressed. I'm glad I know you, in case I get into trouble."

"*Don't* get into trouble!" she said fervently. "My nerves can't take another shock."

Brian called from the precinct, where he was catching up on paperwork.

"Thanks for the tip about Sadie. I stopped by the high school this morning. It took some convincing, but she finally agreed to let the department handle her loan shark."

"I'm glad. I don't want anything to happen to her. Does Sadie still insist that Viola killed Tim?"

He laughed. "You know I can't tell you."

"I love this one-way relationship we have."

"It's only one-way where my work's concerned," he said softly.

I bit back my retort, determined not to make this a festering issue between us. Brian had recused himself from one homicide investigation because of our relationship, and I didn't want him to have to do it again. We discussed our Saturday night dinner plans at a cozy restaurant out East then said good-bye.

I settled down to grade essays, but thoughts about the two unsolved homicide cases, Johnny Scarvino, and the Billingses' trip to Peru kept interrupting my concentration. I riffled through the pile of papers yet to be read and promised myself I'd read eight more before taking matters into my own hands à la Jane Marple and Lucy Pym. It was time to do some sleuthing on my own.

The phone rang. It was Viola.

"Lexie, do you plan to hold more meetings to discuss works by Josephine Tey?"

"With all that's been happening, I haven't given it much

thought."

"You mean like someone shooting my ex-husband, and his hysterical girl friend insisting that I killed him?"

I drew in breath. "Sadie went ahead and accused you? I told her not to."

Viola snorted. "Sadie's not one to listen to reason under the best of circumstances."

"She's distraught over Tim's death—"

"Oh, sure!" Viola shocked me by making a rude sound. "She's convinced herself they were soul mates who tragically found one another before death tore them apart. They shared a passion all right—spending money on things they couldn't afford."

"I think that's a bit harsh," I said.

"Sorry Lexie. I didn't call to bitch about Sadie. Ron and I were hoping you'd consider holding a book club meeting to talk about another Tey novel."

I thought a bit. "I'd be happy to discuss another Tey book, but I'm afraid our book club might be falling by the wayside. Tim's gone, the Billingses won't be back from Peru for another week or so, and the Roberts sisters are moving within the month."

"I've spoken to a few of the teachers in school. At least three people are interested in joining the group. They can make a Wednesday night meeting."

"Sounds good to me," I said. "I'll run it by the others and get back to you regarding the date and the title of the novel we'll be doing."

I rummaged through my Tey novels, wondering which book everyone would enjoy. *The Franchise Affair* appealed to me because it didn't include a murder, though the crime was ugly enough. The story, based on an actual eighteenth century case, concerns a young woman who claims a mother and daughter kidnapped and beat her. The women ask a meek, stick-in-the-mud lawyer named Robert Blair to clear them of the charges. At first reluctant to take on the case, Blair suddenly finds life exhilarating as he unearths the truth and discovers the real story of how the girl managed to get herself beaten and why.

In the end, murder and intrigue won out, and I decided to go with *To Live And Be Wise.* I felt a sense of exhilaration as I reached for the phone to start informing the members of my selection. Hopefully, most of them would be able to attend the meeting, which I decided would take place two weeks from tonight.

CHAPTER TWENTY-SIX

The following evening I was finishing my frozen dinner from Trader Joe's when Joy called, desperate to get out of the house.

"Have you decided to run away and abandon your kids?" I teased.

"Don't mention kids to me! I had nine of them here all afternoon and for dinner! If I don't escape for a few hours, I'll go crazy. Mike saw what a state I'm in and invited his pals over for a poker game."

"I'm in," I told her.

"Pick you up in an hour," she said and rang off.

We decided to go for ice cream. Our neighborhood Friendly's restaurant was crowded with young families and teenagers, no big surprise for a Friday night. We snagged the last empty table and gave our order. I decided on the three scoop sundae. Joy opted for two scoops.

"So, you're planning to discuss another Josephine Tey novel," she said.

I nodded. "*To Love and Be Wise*. It's a delightful, well-written treasure."

"I'll come, but I can't promise to finish it in two weeks. Do you have a copy I can borrow?"

"Our library's requested eight copies from neighboring libraries. You can pick up yours tomorrow."

Joy laughed. "I'm impressed by your pull with the library

brass."

"It's not as impressive as the power you wield, but it comes in handy," I joked.

"Will there be enough people for a meeting, Lex?"

"Viola and Ron are bringing three of their fellow teachers, Sadie said she'll be there, and Marge emailed me from Peru to say she's read the book and plans to come, with or without Evan." I grinned. "And I'm to tell everyone that Eloisa is the most adorable, precocious child in the world."

"I'm happy for them." Joy made a face. "And the Mafia princesses? Will they still be in town?"

I chuckled "You have to stop calling them that. No one answered the phone when I called earlier, and I didn't leave a message."

Our ice cream sundaes arrived, and for a few minutes we were too busy scooping the yummy concoctions into our mouths to talk.

"You know," Joy mused, "This meeting will give us one more stab at figuring out who killed Tim and Len Lyons."

"Great choice of words," I pointed out. "I'm beginning to think the murderer isn't a member of our book club."

"Maybe so, but there's a good chance he's involved with a member of our book club."

I pointed my spoon at her. "You're thinking of Johnny Scarvino, aren't you?"

"He's a gangster, and he does seem to crop up a lot," Joy said.

We finished our sundaes then decided we wanted coffee."

"This is fun," Joy said. "What else can we order?"

I giggled. Joy sounded like a kid let out of class on a school day.

"I'd forgotten how wonderful it is to sit and talk in a public place without someone yanking on my arm for attention."

"Speaking of which, your big birthday celebration's coming up," I said. "Are you buying a new outfit for the occasion?"

Joy shot me a shamefaced grin. "With all the stress leading up to it, I kind of blocked it out. I should get something, I suppose."

"We'll shop one evening next week," I said, and signaled to

our waitress to bring the check.

We drove home, singing along with the radio. It was a quarter to ten when Joy pulled into my driveway.

"Do you have big plans tomorrow night with Brian?" she asked as I opened my car door.

"Just dinner."

"We're playing cards with the Kramers around the corner. Zack and Ruthie love to go there because they have the Wii, which we don't."

The sound of a garage door opening caught our attention. Joy and I stared as a car zipped out of the Roberts' garage and zoomed down Magnolia Lane.

"Corinne must have a late date," I said In jest.

"That was Felicity," Joy said, her voice pure steel. "Get back in the car, Lexie. We're off to investigate." She drove slowly, letting the other car get a block ahead of us.

"But Felicity hardly ever drives anywhere by herself," I muttered. "And never at night."

"Duh. That's why we're following her," Joy said.

"Do you think she has a new boyfriend?" I whispered.

"And doesn't want Corinne to find out?" Joy whispered back.

"Why are we whispering?" I asked in my regular voice.

"Because we don't want Felicity to find out we're following her."

We laughed and rode the rest of the way in silence.

Joy took various turns that struck me as familiar. "Is this the way to—?"

"Sadie's house," Joy finished as Felicity pulled into Sadie's driveway. She pressed the doorbell several times. Sadie opened the door and listened to what appeared to be an emotional tirade. Felicity was sobbing. When Sadie tried to interrupt, Felicity's hands formed fists and struck her thighs repeatedly like an anvil. She never stopped talking, but she spoke too low for us to make out the words. Finally, Sadie stepped back and Felicity entered the house.

"What was all that about?" I said, watching the door slam shut.

Joy shook her head. "Haven't the foggiest. Clearly, Felicity's upset, but I couldn't tell if she's upset with Sadie or in desperate need of a shoulder to cry on."

"I had no idea the two of them were friends."

"Or why Felicity might be angry at Sadie," Joy said.

We stared at the house. Saw nothing. No new lights went on. Neither woman came out.

After ten minutes passed, Joy turned on the motor. "I don't have time for a stake out. I gotta get home."

"I suppose we'll never find out what this was about," I complained as we drove off.

"You never know," Joy said.

It was uncanny how right she was. The ringing phone woke me early Saturday morning. It was Joy, telling me that Sadie had been found unconscious and was in the hospital.

I struggled to sit up and grasp what she was saying, which was a bit too much to take in first thing in the morning.

"How do you know?" I asked. "Who found her? When did this happen?"

"Mike's former partner, Terry, just called. He knows Sadie and I are in the book club together, and that the members are involved in the murders."

I winced as Joy continued. "Ron Alvarez found her around midnight."

"Midnight! What was he doing there at that hour?"

"He claims he's been keeping close tabs on Sadie since Tim died. He called, got no answer, so he went to see if she was all right. He knocked and rang the bell. Nothing. Then he peered through the window and saw her lying on the floor. He broke into the house and called for an ambulance."

"Sounds fishy to me," I said. "Did you tell Terry we followed Felicity?"

"I had to, since we saw her enter the house. When we left, she was still inside."

I swallowed. "That was around ten o'clock. She must have left before Sadie's attacker broke in."

"The doctors think Sadie was unconscious for some time when Ron found her," Joy said gently. "If he hadn't broken into the house when he did, Sadie would have died."

I leaned against the backboard of my bed, suddenly feeling faint. "Are you trying to tell me Felicity struck Sadie?"

"Not definitively, but there's a huge possibility she did.'"

My mind refused to accept the possibility. I had the overwhelming urge to run next door and hold Felicity in my arms. "You can't believe she's capable of harming anyone. She's delicate. And fragile."

"And unstable. Think, Lexie. Unstable people wreak havoc."

I thought, not liking the images that came to mind. Still, I refused to think ill of Felicity. "She's too gentle a soul to hurt Sadie."

"She's from a mob family, Lex. As much as her mother might have protected her, she had to know that people were murdered on her father orders. These are values she learned consciously or unconsciously as she grew up. In the darkest recess of her mind, murder is an all-right solution if the people deserve it."

I opened my mouth to argue, and closed it again. As much as I didn't want to agree, Joy's argument made sense.

"When are they coming for her?"

"Any minute now."

I pulled on jeans and a sweater, determined to be present when the cops arrived to take Felicity in for questioning. I didn't know why I felt so protective toward her, only that I did. Maybe it was to show I believed she wasn't capable of striking Sadie.

Or of murdering Len and Tim.

Now what made me think of that?

I flung open my front door and saw I was too late. Three black and whites were parked helter-skelter in front of the house next door. Corinne, flanked by a man and a woman, stood arguing with two of the cops while another pair of cops escorted Felicity to one of their cars. I couldn't tell if she was in handcuffs.

I reached Felicity just as a cop pushed her head down none too gently so she could climb into the back seat.

"Easy there," I said.

The cop glared at me. "Step back, miss."

I ignored him and peered in at Felicity. She was sobbing noisily. Tears spilled down her cheeks.

"I know you didn't hurt Sadie," I said as soothing as I could manage. "Is that your lawyer with Corinne?"

"Mr. Coffey said he'll be waiting for me at the station."

"Then who's that talking to Corinne?"

"That's Barbara and her partner." Felicity sniffed. "The police won't listen to them."

Barbara? Of course. She was their WITSEC handler, I remembered, as someone yanked me away from the car. I stumbled backward and would have fallen if one of the cops hadn't caught me.

"Keep away from Felicity!" Corinne stood inches from me, her face contorted with rage.

"I only want to—"

"They're dragging her off to jail because of you! I've told you before—stay out of our lives!"

"I didn't tell the police anything!"

Corinne's dark eyes were lasers that seemed to bore right through me. "You! Joy! What's the difference? You both followed Felicity last night and fingered her to the cops."

My mouth fell open. *How did she know?*

Corinne and I watched the car carrying Felicity drive off to the police station. When it disappeared from view, she stepped closer to me until our jackets nearly touched.

"My sister can't take much more of this. If anything happens to her, you and your pal will regret it for the rest of your lives."

Shaken, I ran home and double-locked the door. Corinne's words cut me like a razor. When it came to Felicity, she was a tigress protecting her cub. For all Joy and I knew, Corinne had followed her sister last night and assaulted Sadie after Felicity left. How else could she have known that Joy and I were there, that Joy gave up Felicity to the police?

But why would Corinne hurt Sadie? Was she so overprotective of Felicity that she didn't want anyone else getting close to her? Sadie was a guidance counselor. Perhaps Felicity had turned to her for advice, and Sadie's advice was to break away from her older sister.

Or did it have something to do with Tim's murder?

Whatever the reason, I needed to tell Brian about Corinne's behavior.

Thinking of Brian cheered me up. I ate breakfast and realized I had something else to be cheerful about. Next week my son and his girlfriend were coming for Thanksgiving! Since Gayle was going to be on Long Island for the holiday, I decided to make it a real family occasion. To my great surprise, Jesse said he and Cici would be happy to fly out on Wednesday afternoon and stay until Saturday. How they managed to get tickets at this late date, I didn't dare ask. With Brian, we'd be five.

I ran errands in town, ending up at the supermarket where I filled my wagon with a frozen turkey, cranberries, sweet potatoes, and pineapple. When I got home, I called Rosie.

"How are you, stranger? When do we get to see you?" she asked.

"I'm fine. Things here are hectic."

"Still dating your detective?"

I drew a deep breath. "Yes."

Rosie burst out laughing. "It's that bad, is it? What about Al?"

"I'll explain everything when he's back in the U. S."

"Do they have any leads regarding that man they found murdered in your backyard?"

"No, and another book club member was shot to death."

"Oh, no! I read about it in the newspaper. I didn't realize you knew him, too."

I refrained from telling Rosie about last night's attack on Sadie. Instead, I said, "Jesse's coming for Thanksgiving. He's bringing his girlfriend."

That led to a discussion about my son and Rosie's three daughters. I asked for her Brussels sprouts and easy apple cake recipes, then invited her and Hal over for dinner the night after Thanksgiving. "This way you'll get to meet Gayle and Cici."

"Are you sure you want to make dinner two nights in a row?" she asked.

"I'll have plenty of leftovers."

"Instead, why don't you all come here on Friday night?" Rosie said. "It won't be any trouble. Tara's doing the family honors on Thursday. All I have to do is bring three side dishes."

"Sounds like a plan. I'll bring dessert."

Later that afternoon, I was dressing for my date with Brian, when the phone rang.

"Hello, Lexie."

I swallowed. "Hello, Al."

"I hope I'm not interrupting you. I know it's going on seven o'clock in the States."

"I'm getting ready to go out with a few friends," I lied. "He- they should be picking me up any minute now."

"Then I won't keep you. I wanted to tell you I'm flying home next Friday. I was hoping to make it for Thanksgiving, but there were no flights available Monday through Thursday."

"Too bad," I said as I silently exhaled a sigh of relief.

"Any chance you can pick me up at the airport Friday afternoon?"

My throat constricted. "I'm afraid I can't. Jesse and his girlfriend are here for Thanksgiving weekend. So is my sister. We're all going to Rosie and Hal's for dinner on Friday."

Silence. No doubt Al was waiting for me to invite him to join us. He knew how close Rosie and I were, and that she'd never mind an extra guest. A giggle of nervous laughter nearly escaped as I pictured Al and Brian at her dining room table.

Finally Al spoke. "Don't worry yourself about it. I'll be seeing my daughters on Saturday. We'll have Sunday and Monday. I fly back to London Tuesday morning."

"Actually, Monday will be best," I said, deliberately misunderstanding him. "My company leaves on Sunday. I'm driving Jesse and his girlfriend to the airport."

"Oh," Al said, sounding puzzled and hurt. "In that case, I'll see you on Monday. We've lots of catching up to do."

"Yes, we do," I agreed.

I hung up, feeling awful. I was such a wimp when it came to breaking bad news. Al assumed I was still his girlfriend, which I wasn't. Brian was my guy. Telling Al wasn't going to be easy.

CHAPTER TWENTY-SEVEN

"Corinne didn't knock Sadie unconscious. Viola did."

"What? How could I have gotten it so wrong?" I must have looked foolish with my mouth open, because Brian let out a belly laugh.

It earned him disapproving scowls from the couple sitting next to us along the banquette of the upscale Italian restaurant where we were dining. Brian ignored them. He did, however, lower his voice to a near whisper as he explained.

"You heard me. Viola struck Sadie. She claims she didn't mean to. Her story is she went over to Sadie's to tell her to stop badmouthing her in school. Sadie shoved her, she pushed back, Sadie fell, and Viola ran."

I nodded. "So that's why Ron went over there—to make sure Sadie was all right."

"Viola sent him."

I had trouble letting go of my version of the situation. "Are you sure Corinne didn't attack Sadie?"

Brian reached across the candle-lit table to cover my hand with his. "Positive."

I shuddered. "Corinne's so fierce, she scares me."

"She's usually fired up on her sister's behalf."

I sighed. "I wish they'd move already."

He pursed his lips. "Barbara Stengel, their WITSEC marshal, is working on it, but it's turned into a complicated situation."

"I thought once a cover is blown, WITSEC resettles people in a different location ASAP."

"They do, when their clients cooperate. Corinne wants to leave Ryesdale." He hesitated. "And she wants to quit WITSEC."

I stared at him in surprise. "Really? Why? Isn't she afraid of Johnny Scarvino?"

Brian examined the nails of his right hand. "Johnny Scarvino's out of the picture."

"Dead, you mean?"

"He was shot in a holdup a few days ago. The Jersey police notified WITSEC; their marshal informed Corinne and Felicity."

I shuddered. "Poor Johnny."

Brian laughed. "Why do you say that? You never knew him."

"I saw him, remember? The night he delivered the baby gift. He seemed kind of nice."

"For a thug."

"He didn't strike me as a thug," I mused. "Was he the only person out to get Corinne?"

"Looks that way. Which is why Corinne wants out of WITSEC. Now she refuses to move until a buyer comes along, one who's willing to pay a good price for the house. Barbara Stengel thinks Corinne ought to remain in WITSEC, at least for a while, and she's trying to convince her to reconsider."

The waiter brought our bottle of wine. He decanted and filled our glasses. Brian and I toasted one another silently and sipped.

"Felicity must be relieved Johnny Scarvino's no longer a threat to her sister."

"No doubt," Brian agreed, "but Felicity has her own weird agenda regarding Corinne. When I drove her home from the precinct, she told me she'd gone to Sadie's house to talk to her because Sadie understands how she feels."

"About Corinne?"

Brian nodded. "Felicity wants to stay in Ryesdale. She doesn't want to live with Corinne any longer. She went on and on in this vein." He gave me a sad smile. "When I dropped her at home, she made me promise not to tell Corinne what she's planning, then ran straight into her sister's arms and held on for dear life."

I sighed. "Felicity's conflicted. It's difficult breaking away from a bossy, overprotective sister. Frankly, I wonder if she can manage to live on her own."

Brian smiled. "She's had the good sense to make a start in that direction. She told me her boss, Carol Barnes, is willing to rent her a small apartment over her garage. She'll have privacy yet be living close enough to someone she trusts."

"Is that the word Felicity used—"trusts?"

"It is."

"Which makes me think she doesn't trust Corinne."

"I think you're reading too much into their relationship." Brian raised his glass. "Enough about them. Let's drink up and enjoy ourselves."

*****

The next few days were a whirlwind of activity as I dove into my Thanksgiving preparations. For the first time in months, I set aside thoughts of murder and mayhem to concentrate on domestic matters. A nervous excitement sparked through me as I wandered through Bed, Bath, & Beyond in search of the perfect tablecloth and napkins.

All the while, my mind never stopped churning out questions:

Were things serious between Jesse and Cici?

How would Jesse and Brian get along?

Would my turkey come out of the oven succulent and tender or tough and dried-out?

How would Al respond when I told him we were no longer a couple?

The Billingses brought their granddaughter home on Sunday. Though they were thoroughly exhausted, they insisted on inviting the original book club members to their home on Tuesday evening to meet Eloisa. We agreed on the condition that they allow us to bring in dinner. And so at seven o'clock Joy, Felicity, Corinne, and I knocked on their door, each of us with a casserole or dessert in hand. Sadie wanted to come, but we told her to stay home and rest.

Marge and Evan were exuberant as they presented us to Eloisa, an adorable three-year-old girl with fair skin and dark hair and eyes, wearing pink pajamas. She took one look at us and ran to stand behind Marge's legs, all the while never letting us out of her sight.

I crouched down and smiled. *"Hola, Eloisa. ¿Cómo estás?"*

"Bien," she mumbled, not meeting my gaze.

To my surprise, Corinne knelt beside me and rattled off something in Spanish. It must have been something silly, because Eloisa giggled and answered her. As this continued, the rest of us gathered closer to watch them. Finally, Eloisa dashed away.

"Where is she going?" Joy asked.

"To get some of her new toys for me to see," Corinne explained.

"Isn't Corinne something?" Felicity asked, beaming with pride.

"She's something, all right," I murmured, thinking that Felicity would never muster up enough courage to tell Corinne she wanted to live on her own.

We oohed and ahed over the toys we'd bought for Eloisa. After coffee and cake, we said our good-byes. Evan, his granddaughter in his arms, saw us to the door. Marge embraced Corinne.

"You'll never know how happy you've made us," she said.

Corinne smiled. "I like to see happy families."

*****

I woke up early Thanksgiving Day, happily anticipating the long holiday weekend. Puss meowed as he ushered me into the kitchen. *Full house*, I thought as I passed the closed doors of my two guestrooms. Gayle was asleep in one, Jesse and Cici in the other. For once I felt part of mainstream America, sharing my favorite holiday with my loved ones.

I fed Puss, put up a large pot of coffee, then whipped up my sweet potato casserole. I seasoned the turkey and was sliding it into the oven for a slow roasting, when Jesse padded barefooted into the kitchen. He bent down to kiss my cheek. Then he sniffed the air.

"Smells great, Mom."

"Did you sleep well? I've no idea if the mattress in your room is comfortable or not."

"It's fine, mom. Cici's still zonked out, and she doesn't sleep well in new places."

Interesting.

Jesse peered into the refrigerator. "Do you have any OJ?

"It's on the door."

"Got it."

He was about to drink directly from the plastic container, when my hand shot up to stop him. "Get a glass, please."

Jesse burst out laughing. "Sorry, Mom. I forgot what a stickler you are about following the rules of decorum."

"It's not decorum. Just being sanitary."

He drew back, his expression one of exaggerated surprise. "Afraid you'll catch germs from your only son?"

I grabbed a dish towel to swat him, but Jesse was too fast. He dodged me, then backtracked to hug me from behind. I was glad he couldn't see my grin. He'd stopped being openly affectionate toward me at puberty. I supposed this change was the result of Cici's influence.

Gayle wandered into the kitchen, rubbing her eyes. "Is the coffee made?"

"Sit down. I'll pour you a mug."

I filled three mugs, then brought out the bagels, lox, and cream cheese I'd bought the day before. Jesse finished his coffee and stood.

"See you later. I'm going for a run."

Gayle and I gorged ourselves as we caught up with each other's news. I told her about the second murder and Sadie's injury, and she told me what was happening with Shawn Estes' trial.

"He's in jail right now, but I'm still afraid of him." She shuddered. "I wish I didn't have to testify. Shawn's one scary dude."

"If you don't testify, he might get off. Then you'll really have something to worry about."

Gayle frowned. "That's what I tell myself. And I've had lots of support, even from other cops. There's one who's been extra nice. His name's Ryan Felling."

As I listened to her, I mused how life goes on. People die. People fall in love with new people.

Cici came in silently and joined us at the table. She and Gayle talked about California, then we had a nice chat about how well Jesse was doing with the band. He was writing songs for them and even writing a few for other groups.

I watched Cici as she spoke, a pretty girl with long, brown hair and large brown eyes that reminded me of Sandra Bullock. She seemed solid and normal, and she loved my son. What more could a mother ask?

A wedding. Grandchildren. *All in good time*, I told myself. I chuckled to think I was fast turning into the stereotypical mother, when for so many years I'd done my darnedest to be unique.

Brian called to ask what time he should come by.

"The turkey will be done at four, but come whenever you like."

"I'm bringing a few bottles of wine. How many are we?"

"Just the five of us, but I think we'll eat in the dining room."

"Whatever. It's your show, babe."

As it turned out, we were five for dinner but many more for dessert. After breakfast I called Sadie to find out how she was feeling, and she mentioned she'd been invited to Felicity and Corinne's for dinner at four.

"That's when we're eating," I said. "Why don't the three of you come here for dessert?"

"Sounds good to me," Sadie said. "I'll mention it to Felicity and Corinne."

A few minutes later Corinne called to say she loved the idea. "We'll bring the cakes and pies over to your house."

"Fine, as long as you take whatever's left back home with you."

Since they were coming, I decided to include Joy, Mike, and the kids, who were having an early Thanksgiving meal at Mike's mom's.

"You're sure you want us all?" Joy asked.

"Bring some videos for the kids. They can watch them in the den." I thought a moment. "I'll call Marge and Evan, too."

Marge and Evan were delighted. "Frankly, we're walking around like zombies, afraid to fall asleep in case Eloisa needs us.

But this will give her a chance to be with other kids."

I told everyone to show up between five and five-thirty, which allowed us plenty of time for a leisurely meal. And time to have my family to myself.

My family, I thought, and realized I'd included Brian in the group.

I showered and dressed, then returned to the kitchen to prepare the rest of the meal. I was about to ask Gayle and Cici to help me open the dining room table, when I saw they were already putting in the extra leaves.

"For when everyone comes," Gayle explained. "We can sit at this end for dinner, then set places for the others."

"How did you know I keep the extra leaves in the hall closet" I asked.

"I remembered that's where Mom kept hers."

Gayle and Cici cut up lettuce, tomatoes and other veggies for the salad while I got busy on my butternut soup. Then I made cranberry sauce, adding walnut pieces and sections of mandarin orange while it was still hot. We worked in companionable tandem, chatting and laughing as though we'd done this several times before.

Brian arrived and, after kissing me and hugging Gayle, gave Jesse and Cici each a hearty handshake. He must have bought the wine yesterday, because it was chilled. Jesse was quick to open a bottle and pour out three glasses for Gayle, Cici and me.

"Like a beer?" he asked Brian.

"Sure," Brian said.

Jesse opened their beers, then led the way to the den to watch the football game, as if this were something the two of them had done several times before.

"He's cute," Cici whispered.

"Brian's a godsend," Gayle said.

My heart was beating with pride, but I merely shrugged. "He's all right."

The three of us cracked up laughing. When we'd calmed down, I said, "Al's flying home from England tomorrow."

"Really?" Gayle stuck out her chin in the direction of the den. "Does he know about Brian?"

"No, but I think he suspects. We're getting together on

Monday. I dread it."

"Former boyfriend?" Cici asked.

I nodded. "This is his house I'm renting."

"Oh. Sticky."

I raised my hands. "No more talk about Al. Today we feast and have fun."

"And celebrate being together," Gayle said.

I put an arm around my sister and pulled her close. "And give thanks for having each other," I added.

CHAPTER TWENTY-EIGHT

Gayle and Cici helped bring the many dishes I'd prepared to the table. Cici asked to say grace, so we bowed our heads as she expressed how grateful she was to be sharing this meal with Jesse's family. We passed the dishes around, scooping out much larger portions of food than what we normally ate.

The compliments rained down on me. It was embarrassing how many times I had to say "thank you." But for someone who rarely cooked, I was astonished at how well everything turned out. The turkey was well-roasted yet succulent, the side dishes were perfectly done. We chatted as we ate, took seconds, and then the meal was over. I wanted to reach out and grab hold of something to slow down time, but there was nothing to catch hold of. When would the five of us be together again? Would we ever be together again?

"Take some photos," Gayle suggested.

I retrieved my camera from my bedroom, telling myself not to be maudlin. We took turns snapping one shot after another. Then our meal was officially over. *Life moves on,* I reminded myself as Gayle, Cici, and I cleared the table. *Cherish it in motion.*

They spooned the leftovers into containers while I stacked the dishwasher. Then we joined Jesse and Brian in the den. Why did we bother? I'd no sooner opened my mouth to say something when Jesse shushed me. He jumped to his feet as a great roar emanated from the TV crowd.

I glared at the two males, then turned to my sister and Cici. "I see we're not wanted. Let's sit in the living room."

Brian stretched out his arm. "Stay here, Lexie," he said, his eyes glued to the TV.

"See you later."

The three of us chatted until I realized it was a quarter to five. I put up decaf coffee in my largest coffee maker, and boiled water for tea. Then we arranged slices of cake and cookies on platters and set them on the dining room table.

Half an hour later Ruthie, Zack, and Eloisa were munching on cookies in the den, as a Disney movie was about to begin. The rest of us sat at the dining table, drinking coffee and eyeing the many cakes and pies spread out on the table. Baby Brandon slept in his Pack n Play at his mother's feet.

"Yum. My favorite—chocolate cheesecake," Mike said, his fingers inching toward one of the delicious cakes Corinne had made and brought to share with us.

Joy slapped his hand away. "Don't touch!"

Mike opened his eyes wide, into a reproachful, wounded expression. "I was only admiring."

"You don't know how to admire without touching," Joy said.

We all burst out laughing.

Gayle and I doled out the desserts while Marge and Cici saw to coffee and tea refills. Everyone was in a festive mood, chatting and laughing around the table. Evan beamed as he told us how well Eloisa seemed to be settling in.

"She's picking up English, and her *abuelas* are learning some Spanish."

"Once Eloisa's settled, you should consider sending her to nursery school," Joy said. "I was very happy with the school Zack and Ruthie attended. I'll email you their number."

Marge looked doubtful. "I don't think we should be sending her off to school so soon. Poor Eloisa has been through so much. She's first getting used to us."

"Believe me, the sooner the better," Joy insisted. "Children are resilient. Eloisa will love Teeny Tots."

For a while, we talked about the benefits of nursery school. I caught sight of Sadie, hunched over in her chair.

"Are you all right?"

She gave me a wan smile. "My head hurts, but I'm happy to be with everyone."

Brian looked at her. "You're sure you want to stay? I'll drive you home if you're not feeling well."

Sadie gave a little laugh. "I shouldn't have stuffed myself. The doctor warned me overeating could make the bouts of nausea return."

"Nausea?" I echoed.

A broad grin spread across Joy's face. "Sadie Lu, you're pregnant!"

"I am." Sadie positively glowed as she gazed down at her empty dessert dish. "How did you guess?"

"You gave it away just now," Joy answered. "But having been there recently, I had my suspicions the minute you walked through the door."

I glared at Brian. "You knew Sadie was pregnant!" *And didn't tell me!* hung in the air.

He took it as the accusation it was meant to be, and managed to look both defiant and contrite. "The doctor told me when I went to see Sadie in the hospital. Sorry I couldn't tell you, babe."

"Why not?" A rage built up inside me until I felt like a volcano about to explode. I ignored Joy's warning headshake. "I give you information you'd never learn on your own! The least you could have done was tell me Sadie's news."

"It could have turned out to be part of the investigation."

"Her pregnancy? Give me a break."

We stared at one another until Brian stalked off to the den. I heard the muted sound of the TV.

Felicity crouched down beside Sadie's chair. "Are you happy about the baby, Sadie?"

Sadie looked tearful when she said, "More than anything in the world. Now I have a part of Tim forever." She sniffed. "If only he were here to help me raise the child."

Felicity reached over to stroke Sadie's long, black hair. "Don't worry, Sadie. We'll all help out. I'll babysit for you as often as you like."

Corinne's head shot up. "What are you talking about, Felicity? You'll be long gone from Ryesdale before Sadie gives birth."

Felicity met her sister's gaze across the table, but when she spoke, her voice was barely audible. "I'll still be here, Cathy. I want to stay in Ryesdale."

Cathy? Of course! Catherine is Corinne's real name. Joy and I exchanged glances while the others watched Felicity, puzzled expressions on their faces.

Corinne sent her sister a bemused smile. "But you can't stay in Ryesdale, Felicity. Not after we sell the house."

"Yes, I can. I have friends here, and a place to live."

"Really?" Corinne laughed. "A place to live?" And where's that? You don't have enough money to live in a hotel."

Felicity stared down at the carpet. "Carol said I could stay in her small apartment over the garage."

"And who will take care of you when the black times come? Who will stay up with you all night? Hold you until you stop shaking?"

Felicity trembled. "I'll take medicine."

"How many meds did you try? Ten? Twenty?"

"There are new meds on the market. Maybe one will work. Don't you think?"

Poor Felicity looked like she wanted to sink through the floor. She was about to buckle under and give in to her sister.

"I'll help you, Felicity, in any way I can," I said.

"You can count on me," Joy chimed in.

Evan patted her back. "You're always welcome at our house."

Corinne stared at her sister from across the table. Instead of the fury I expected, her face wore an expression of total devastation. "But you have to come with me. We made a promise to always stay together."

"I'm sorry, Cathy," Felicity said softly. "I don't want to live with you anymore. I have to lead my own life."

Corinne walked around the table. Felicity flinched as she approached.

"You're right," Corinne said. "I haven't been treating you like the grown up woman you've become. You can do anything you like. Go anywhere you want."

Felicity seemed to waver. I sensed she was about to take the path of least resistance. Then she thrust back her shoulders. "It's time I lived by myself. I can't think when I'm living with you."

Corinne gave a false laugh. "What's there to think about?" She put her hand on Felicity's shoulder. Felicity shrugged it off. "Don't, Cathy."

"All right. I'm going home now. Do you want to come with me?"

Felicity shook her head.

"We'll talk when you come home, all right?"

"Yes."

Corinne left and, to my surprise, Felicity perked up. The men joined Brian in the den to watch the end of the football game, and the women helped me clear the table. Then we moved into the living room where we sat around, chatting about everything except my outburst and Corinne's departure.

Too soon, my guests went home. Felicity was the last to go. I hugged her good-bye, then handed her what remained of the cakes she and Corinne had brought over.

"Let me know if you need me," I told her.

"I'll be fine," Felicity said, sounding anxious. "Corinne just needs time to adjust to my news."

"You really mean to stay in Ryesdale? Will you be able to manage?"

"I'll get help as I need it," she said simply.

"That's the right answer," I said, hugging her again.

Brian walked past me and opened the hall closet.

"Hey," I said. "Are you leaving?"

"Looks that way." He slipped on his jacket without turning to me.

I swallowed, feeling ill. He was pissed at me, and now that I'd calmed down, I couldn't blame him.

"Are you coming with us tomorrow to Rosie and Hal's? You're invited, you know."

He turned to me and put his hands on my shoulders. He let loose a deep sigh. "Tell them I appreciate their kind offer, but I can't make it."

I pursed my lips. "You're not coming because I got angry before. I'm sorry. It just slipped out."

He gave a humorless smile. "You can say what you like to

me, but never in front of a group of suspects."

"Suspects?"

His grip grew tighter. "All right. Persons of interest in two homicides. Why on earth did you invite them over when I was here?"

I opened my mouth to explain it just happened, then closed it again. Brian was right. "I'm sorry. I didn't think."

"Lexie, until this case is settled, I think it's best we cool our relationship."

Tears stung behind my eyes. "You're breaking up with me."

"No, I'm pulling back for now. You have your family here. Concentrate on them."

He kissed my cheek and was gone before I could figure out what to say next.

CHAPTER TWENTY-NINE

snifters

Jesse and Cici said good-night and disappeared inside their room. Gayle filled two sifters with brandy and led me into the den. I drank deeply, then sank against the soft back of the sofa.

"He'll get over it," Gayle said from her end of the sofa.

I frowned. "I don't know."

"Sure he will. Brian's crazy about you." She scooted closer to me. "The question is, will you?"

Surprised, I stared at her. "Of course. Why do you ask?"

"You were furious because he didn't tell you something you would have told him. Meanwhile you've passed on every piece of information you uncovered that might be connected to the murders."

I shrugged, conceding her point. "Why shouldn't I be mad? I felt betrayed. Used."

"You invited Brian to dinner then asked your book club members over, knowing some of them were under investigation."

I bit my lip. "They're people I know. I forgot that they're suspects—or persons of interest. Besides, Brian went to the same Halloween party they were at."

Gayle gave me a stern look. "Lexie, this was different. I bet you never told Brian they were coming."

I felt my face grow warm. I should have been more thoughtful. More considerate of my boyfriend. "Hey, you're turning into the big sister here."

Gayle grinned. "It's the least I can do, after all you've done for me."

I reached over to hug her. "Thank *you*, for being my sister."

"And thank you for not being like Corinne. Can you imagine what it must be like for Felicity?"

"I never realized theirs was a symbiotic relationship," I said. "I always thought Corinne was the dominant and Felicity her underling."

"Who knows what they had to endure growing up as Mafia princesses."

"Whatever it was, I doubt they felt like princesses."

*****

It was hours before I slept. I mulled about Brian, hoping our relationship hadn't ended, and eventually managed to convince myself there was nothing I could do. I finally drifted off, telling myself I wouldn't think about him while my family was still with me.

On Friday, the kids wanted to go shopping, so we set out for The Arches, the Tanger outlet mall in Deer Park. It was mobbed, but we all managed to buy a few items. Before we knew it, it was time to drive to Rosie and Hal's.

"Where's Brian?" Rosie demanded after she'd hugged each of us in turn and had me alone in the hall.

"Sorry, he couldn't make it," I said. "He asked me to offer his apologies."

Rosie studied my face. "Why? What happened?"

I shrugged. "We had a bit of an argument." I turned away. "I was pissed because he knew Sadie Lu was pregnant and didn't tell me."

"Ah. And who's Sadie Lu?"

I explained.

Rosie gripped my arm.

"Ouch!"

"You like this Brian Donovan, don't you?"

I nodded.

"Then don't screw it up."

"I didn't set out to screw anything up. I only—"

She squeezed my arm again. "Lexie, you're at the critical stage in this relationship. You're involved, you care about the guy, and you're suddenly terrified because you realize how much you care."

I opened my mouth to argue, then closed it. "I'm not terrified. Just a bit nervous, which I never realized till now."

Rosie gave me her know-it-all grin. I felt like smacking her and grabbing her in a bear hug at the same time. I did neither. Instead, I considered her observation.

"I suppose it never dawned on me because I've been so busy, but the fear was working inside me all the time."

"Which is why you blew up the way you did."

I shrugged. "Could be you're right."

"I *am* right." She hooked her arm into mine, and we walked side-by-side into the living room where everyone else was milling around.

*****

Too soon my houseguests left me and I was on my own. Gayle set out early Sunday morning. We hugged and promised to keep in touch and visit regularly. The kids' flight to L. A. took off in the early evening. I drove back from the airport feeling forlorn and abandoned. Jesse had been especially affectionate when I dropped them off, and tried to get me to promise that I'd come out to California some time during my winter vacation.

"Come on, Mom. You've never seen my digs. And Dad would love to see you."

I made a face. "Sure he would."

"No, really. I've heard him telling Stacey how great things were between the two of you the first few years."

Right. Until you came on the scene. I quivered as a pang of the old hurt passed through me. Then I realized I was pleased. "What an idiotic thing to tell your long-time live-in girlfriend."

Jesse grinned. "You don't know Stacey. She's so cool, a compliment to you wouldn't upset her."

"I suppose that's why she and your father have lasted this long."

Cici surprised me with a big hug. "It was so nice spending a real Thanksgiving with you and your family, Lexie. It's one holiday my family managed to skip all these years."

"My pleasure," I said, meaning it.

"And do fly out to California." She lowered her voice. "It would mean a lot to Jesse."

The house felt like an empty shell when I returned. Even Puss, who usually greeted me when I walked through the door, was fast asleep on a living room cushion. A heavy cloak of self-pity enveloped me. No family, no boyfriend, and tomorrow I had to tell Al that we were through. The way things were going for me, he'd probably tell me to vacate the premises within forty-eight hours.

Stop being a drama queen. Jesse and Gayle went home because all guests go home. As for Brian, you'll straighten things out, or try to.

The phone rang, jarring me from my dismal thoughts. It was Al.

"Hi, Lexie. I thought I'd touch base. Is now a good time?"

"As good as any."

I was relieved if a bit surprised that he hadn't picked up on my somber tone. We exchanged news about our Thanksgiving dinners. I talked about Jesse and Cici, Gayle, and our visit to Rosie and Hal. I omitted mentioning Brian.

"I was hoping we'd be able to get together tomorrow right after your classes, but it looks like I'll be tied up until the evening. How about dinner at L'Etoile?"

My face lit up. "I'd adore dinner at L'Etoile! But isn't it kind of pricy?"

Al laughed. "Nothing but the best for you, my dear. Shall I pick you up at seven?"

We hung up, leaving me looking forward to dining at one of Long Island's finest French restaurants, yet sad because of what lay ahead. Al was a wonderful guy—sweet and kind, bright and cultured. In fact, he was perfect. Unfortunately, I didn't love him.

I switched on the TV, then turned it right off. The phone rang again. It was Brian.

"Has everyone left?" he asked.

"Uh-huh. I'm here on my lonesome." I bit my tongue. *Why did it have to sound like I was begging him to come over?*

"Sounds appealing."

"Really? I thought you were cooling things between us."

That brought on a deep sigh. "So did I."

"And?"

"Maybe I'll come by—if you want me to."

"I'd like that," I said.

Brian came and stayed the night. We said little about what had driven a wedge between us, but our lovemaking was passionate and wild. Makeup sex, people called it. A way for two lovers to say they were sorry they'd quarreled and hoped it never happened again. The following morning, we each drove our own car to the local diner for an early breakfast. From there, we both had to go to work.

In the parking lot, he walked me to my car. "Don't be too hard on West," he said, grinning maniacally. "The poor guy lost out to the Guy in Blue"

"Did he ever," I said, wrapping myself around Brian as if he were a pole dancer's pole. "I only wish people didn't have to get hurt."

"I wish people didn't kill other people," Brian quipped. He dropped a kiss on my nose and left.

I hummed as I drove to the university. Spending time with Brian Donovan left me like a car that had just been tuned to its optimum condition. Though we saw the world differently and Brian rarely read books, let alone the classics, I felt in sync with him and was happiest when we were together. We laughed, we talked, we understood one another.

Was that love?

After my classes, I ran a few errands, so I didn't arrive home until close to two o'clock. The phone was ringing when I walked in the house. Joy wanted to chat. I brought her up to date on my love life.

"I'm glad things are good again with you and Brian," she said. "Are you nervous about breaking it off with Al tonight?"

"A bit," I admitted. "He's a good guy. A wonderful catch, actually, for anyone in her right mind."

"Anyone not in love with someone else."

Love. There was that word again.

I must have been truly sleep deprived because I dozed off while rereading *To Love and Be Wise*, something I never did during daylight hours. I awoke feeling rested. I glanced at my watch. It was a quarter to four.

Puss came ambling by, meowing for an early dinner. I fed him the rest of the can of cat food, then realized I hadn't any more for his breakfast tomorrow. There was plenty of dry cat food in the cupboard. He'd have to make do with that.

Who was I kidding? He'd sniff at his dish, look disdainfully at me, and leave the kitchen, tail in the air. Sighing, I shrugged into my parka and headed for the garage.

All of the parking spots near the pet supplies warehouse were occupied. I drove around to the other side of the lot. The only available space was near a run-down, weather-beaten warehouse. The place looked deserted. I had no idea what, if anything, was stored inside. Fifteen minutes later, I wheeled out my cart filled with three cases of cat food and the few toys I couldn't resist, and loaded them into the trunk of my car. As I slid into the driver's seat, an SUV drove up alongside the front door of the warehouse not twenty feet to my right. Evan Billings stopped out.

I opened my mouth to call out to him, then closed it when I caught sight of his grim expression. Good thing I didn't, because a minute later a huge goliath of a man, as bald as Mr. Clean with a black Vandyke beard, emerged from the warehouse. He spoke to Evan, much too softly for me to hear what he was saying. When Evan started to speak the man turned his back and entered the warehouse.

I'd seen the man before, albeit without facial hair. Of course! It was The Giant, the man Evan had words with in the bowling alley parking lot about bringing Eloisa to the United States.

But all that was resolved! Why was Evan here? I was in such a state of confusion, I almost didn't notice Evan drive his SUV to the back of the warehouse.

I made sure no one was around, and stepped out of my car. I walked quickly to the warehouse, then inched along the side, both terrified and excited at what I might encounter. Brian would kill me if he had any idea of what I was doing, though The Giant would probably kill me first if he caught me spying. There was no doubt in my mind he was a thug and a criminal. I had to find out what hold he had over Evan.

I peered around to the back of the building, and was glad I hadn't gone one inch further. Two men stood beside a van, smoking and laughing. Evan had parked close to the back door of the warehouse. He climbed down from the SUV and retrieved a large duffel bag from the back seat. From the way he held it, I could tell that whatever was inside weighed at least forty pounds.

"Hand it over," The Giant ordered from the open door.

I couldn't hear what Evan said, but clearly he wasn't eager to comply. The Giant zipped open the duffel bag and held up a pair of ornate silver candlesticks three or four feet tall. He examined them with reverence, then placed them back in the bag with care. He turned to Evan, a mock expression of gratitude on his face.

"Thank you, Mr. Billings. We'll let you know when we need your services again."

"I can't do this," Evan mumbled.

"Oh, but you agreed. You knew what you were getting into."

"No, I didn't," Evan insisted.

"People had to be taken care of so you could have your precious granddaughter."

"I had no idea!"

"Don't play the innocent! You had a choice: pay more money or help us acquire items. Now your hands are dirty, same as ours." The Giant pointed a finger at Evan. "Remember, we have you on tape."

Evan opened his mouth to argue, but once again The Giant left him standing as he disappeared inside the warehouse.

What had Evan gotten himself into? I drove home wondering what The Giant meant when he said people had to be taken care of. Paid off? Murdered? Clearly The Giant's gang had boxed Evan in, forcing him to steal for them.

Whoever *they* were.

I drove home, wondering if this gang had been responsible for putting Evan on the "No Fly" list. I shook my head, knowing how improbable that was. Besides, the "no fly" problem had been cleared up.

But why was Evan beholden to The Giant and his gang? It was Corinne who had delivered Eloisa into her grandparents' hands. Or had the people she'd contacted inadvertently employed the gang that had tried to stiff the Billingses, making them angrier than ever?

One question led to another, and I couldn't answer any of them. Frustrated, I put away the cat food and dangled a new toy in front of Puss. He sniffed it and turned away. So much for gratitude.

I called Brian on his cell phone to tell him what I'd observed. He didn't sound happy.

"You actually walked around to the back of the warehouse, Lexie?"

"No. I just peered around the side."

"Did anyone see you?"

"I told you no one saw me."

He gave a snort of exasperation. "That's good, because the thieves who store their loot in that warehouse have security cameras that scan the backyard."

Suddenly I was frightened. "How do you know?"

"Robbery's keeping a close watch on them until they're ready to raid the place."

"How can a gang of thieves use a warehouse in plain sight of everyone?" I said. "It's across the parking lot from where I buy cat food."

"They know who to watch for."

"They probably sent Evan around to the back to catch him on camera and incriminate him further. They said they have proof he stole the candlesticks."

"I'll check it out," Brian promised. "And no, I won't bring your name into it."

"Thanks, Brian."

He laughed. "Go have fun on your date."

"Right," I grumbled.

I enjoyed a long soak in the bath, then put on a cashmere sweater and black trousers for my evening out with Al.

As I blow dried my hair, I practiced how to tell him, as kindly as possible, that our relationship was over.

"Sorry, it just happened," came to mind. Only it hadn't *just* happened. I was attracted to Brian Donovan the moment we met. I liked Al, of course. Liked him a lot. But my feelings for him never had the magical spark I felt when I was with Brian.

Al arrived promptly at seven. We hugged, and I was startled at how glad I was to see him again. He kissed my cheek then held me at arms' length.

"How are you, Lexie? You look terrific."

"You look well yourself."

He was elegantly well dressed as always, his light brown hair a bit longer than the going style. Without his beard he looked younger. A catch, if ever there was one.

Al beamed at me. "Ready to go?"

I nodded, and went to get my coat. Al held it for me as I slipped my arms into the sleeves.

In the car I asked him about his daughters, and he asked me about Jesse's visit. Conversation was comfortable, mundane. Thank goodness he didn't bring up the subject of our moving in together because that would have brought our evening to a crashing halt. For some reason, I felt it was important that we have our last evening together.

Al stopped in front of an elegant manor house. A valet helped me out of the car. Another restaurant employee opened the entrance door of L'Etoile and bid us welcome. "Lovely," I murmured as the *maitre d'* led us to a table in the dimly-lit dining room. Two candles rose above the snowy white tablecloth.

When we were seated, I said, "I've been wanting to eat here for years."

Al reached across the table to squeeze my shoulder. "I'm happy to make your wish come true."

We ordered drinks, then our dinners. I decided on filet mignon, though I rarely ate beef. I wasn't going to let this once-in-a-lifetime opportunity pass me by.

We chatted easily about people we knew in common then about Al's project in London, which he said was going very well. I sensed we were both sidestepping any discussion concerning the two of us. Part of me wanted to tell Al I was madly in love with Brian. Part of me wanted to wait until he introduced the subject or it magically arose on its own.

Instead, I told him the two local murders were still unsolved. Al didn't seemed alarmed that the killer was undoubtedly someone I knew. *Odd*, I thought, until I realized he was probably remembering how I'd reacted the last time he'd advised me not to get involved in any more murder cases. No doubt he wanted our evening to go as smoothly as I did.

Our main course arrived. As usual, we sampled each other's dishes, and were delighted to discover that both had been perfectly prepared. Then I concentrated on savoring everything on my plate. The filet mignon was the best I'd ever tasted. When I finished eating, I glanced across the table and saw that Al had left most of his food untouched. He sat with his hands at his sides, gazing into the distance.

Something's wrong. He must suspect what I'm about to tell him. I promise to tell him over dessert.

Minutes later, our waiter poured our coffee and departed. Al reached for my hand. "Lexie, you are an amazing woman."

"Thank you," I said, feeling foolish.

"You don't deserve what I'm about to say."

I stared at him.

"I feel like such a heel. You and I had an understanding before I left for London. We cared for one another. We had a history of sorts."

I yanked my hand away. "What is it, Al? Spill it out."

"I met someone in London. She's an officer in the company that hired me. We fell in love."

My mouth fell open. "I thought you were in love with me!"

"I thought I was, too," he said. "But Deborah's British. She understands me in a way no American can."

"Oh!" I said, offended on my own behalf and that of my country. I leaned against the well-padded chair, hoping it would absorb some of the shock of his announcement. Though I was madly in love with Brian, Al's news was a stunner on many levels.

He looked appropriately abashed. "I'm terribly sorry, Lexie. The human heart obeys no laws."

I nodded. "I know."

He learned on his elbows and cocked his head at me. "Can you ever forgive me?"

Time for some compassion and maturity, Lexie. Your pride's suffered a blow, but things turned out the way they were supposed to.

I smiled. "Of course I forgive you, Al. Ah, here come our desserts."

CHAPTER THIRTY

"I thought we'd talk a bit about female-to-male gender-crossing before discussing the plot of *To Love and Be Wise*." I was happy my announcement met with nods of approval. This evening the members of the Golden Age of Mystery book club sat around Ron Alvarez's high-beamed Adirondack-style living room on two very long couches. A fire roared in the stone fireplace that covered the entire wall behind me. We were a large group. Five new people, mostly high school teachers, had joined us.

With the exception of Evan, everyone from our last meeting was in attendance. I worried about him. Marge claimed he was baby sitting, then immediately went into raptures recounting some of Eloisa's antics. Was this a ploy to avoid talking about her husband? Was Evan all right? Was he going to be arrested for grand larceny and spend time in prison? I knew Brian had spoken to him, but nothing else. I was totally in the dark regarding matters in my own backyard.

I continued. "Given Josephine Tey's love for the theatre, it's not very surprising to find gender-crossing in one of her novels. After all, Shakespeare uses gender disguise in four of his comedies: 'Two Gentleman from Verona,' 'The Merchant of Venice,' 'As You Like it,' and 'Twelfth Night.'"

Ron let out a deep belly laugh. "Funny that, since in those days all the actors were men. Gender-crossing meant they were men pretending to be women pretending to be male. Confusing when you think about it."

He was our host, so I ignored the interruption and merely fine-tuned his observation. "All actors in Shakespeare's time *were* male, but young boys played the female roles."

Ron winked at me as he put an arm around Viola's shoulders. "I stand corrected."

"Women posed and dressed as men in our Revolutionary and Civil Wars," Joy said. "They had to, if they wanted to fight."

Felicity, seated between Marge and Sadie, shivered. "How silly. Why would anyone *choose* to fight in a war?"

Across the wooden table, Corinne glared at her younger sister. "Because they were patriotic, that's why. And wanted to fight for something they believed in."

Oh-oh. Corinne wasn't onboard with Felicity's new life.

"Don't forget the female pirates," Viola added. "I bet they were a ferocious bunch."

"Cross-gender impersonations go on today," Marge pointed out. "Think of Robin Williams in 'Mrs. Doubtfire'."

"Hey, what about Dustin Hoffman in 'Tootsie?" Joy said. "Mike and I saw it recently on Netflix."

"That was one fantastic movie," Carole, a Spanish teacher agreed. "Hoffman won an Oscar for that role."

"No, he didn't," Marge corrected her. "Sidney Pollack got the award for Best Director."

"Sorry, Marge," Ron said with a grin. "Pollack was a candidate, but the only Oscar for 'Tootsie' went to Jessica Lange for Best Supporting Actress."

I cleared my throat. "To get back on track, we've many examples of cross-gender roles, both in the arts and in real life. And while we've instances of men in drag and dressing as women, let's stick to the topic of women pretending to be men. Why do you think they do it?"

Viola raised her hand. "That's easy. Through the ages, men have always had the freedom to do as they please. Women were supposed to stay home and mind the babies."

"While men risk their lives out in the big, bad world," Ron said, brushing her cheek with the back of his hand. *They must have some sex life*, I thought.

"Hah!" Viola poked him in the ribs with her elbow. "I'm out in the world same as you are."

"Nowadays, women are," I said, "but think of Barbra Streisand in 'Yentl'. She had to pretend to be a boy in order to study."

The comments flew thick with examples. Someone pointed out that Anne Perry had written two mysteries with heroines pretending to be male. Finally, I cleared my throat.

"Getting back to our novel, *To Love and Be Wise*. If you'll remember, the opening scene takes place at a party. It's very much like the opening of a play, isn't it? Inspector Alan Grant is at a literary sherry party where he encounters a strikingly beautiful young man named Leslie Searle who wants to be introduced to the author, Lavinia Fitch. Leslie claims he really wants to meet Lavinia's nephew, Walter Whitmore, because they have a dead friend in common. To Leslie's delight, Lavinia invites him to stay at Trimmings, her estate in the country.

"And so Leslie Searle insinuates himself into the lives of the people at Trimmings. Who are they?"

"Lavinia's sister, Emma, Emma's stepdaughter Liz who is Lavinia's secretary, and Walter," Marge said. "Liz and Walter are engaged."

"So they are," I agreed. "Tell us about Walter."

Corinne fielded that one. "He's kind of a prig with a weekly radio show. He takes Liz for granted."

I nodded. "And who is Marguerite Merriam?"

Ron unfolded his legs. "An actress Walter had been involved with. She killed herself after they broke up. She was also—"

I stopped him. "Let's wait on that. Leslie Searle comes to stay at Trimmings, and causes quite a stir. He and Liz become fast friends, which makes Walter jealous, which is a brand new emotion for him."

I paced in front of the wall on which hung a beautiful Navajo blanket. "Does everyone like Leslie?"

Felicity shook her head vehemently. "Emma can't stand him. She's afraid Leslie will ruin things between Liz and Walter."

"Leslie is a photographer," I continued. "He and Walter agree to do a book together. This involves spending a few days away from Trimmings. Leslie and Walter quarrel in a pub one night, and Leslie is never seen again. There's speculation: did Walter kill Leslie? Did Liz's stepmother kill Leslie?"

We went on to discuss the extraordinary turn of events, the cross-dressing aspect of the novel that Alan Grant uncovers, and why Marguerite Merriam is a vital element to the story.

Everyone had opinions they wanted to share. Eventually the conversation turned to the novel's themes as they related to the members' own lives and values. Most of the women thought it would be fun to masquerade as a man. Ron and the other two male teachers didn't think they'd have much fun dressing as a woman.

"Too restricting," Norman, a round, balding man in his forties claimed.

"You're so right," Corinne agreed. "Men are born with a sense of entitlement. Even in the twenty-first century. Do we have a woman president?" She turned to Joy. "A female head of the FBI? In some countries, women aren't allowed to drive a car, let alone run their own lives."

Marge spoke about a friend's son who was married and liked to dress in his wife's clothes. Why would someone do that? Viola wondered. This led to a lively discussion, which I had no desire to stop until I saw that Sadie's eyes were closing. I hoped she wasn't in pain.

"Getting back to the novel, would you say it ends on a positive note?"

"Absolutely!" Viola called out.

"All's well that end's well," Ron seconded.

We broke for coffee and cake, then continued our discussion for another half hour. *The wonderful thing about Tey's plots and characters,* I thought, as I devoured my third mini cannoli— Viola's contribution—*is that nothing's as it seemed. Leslie Searle's performance is very much like a magician's: detracting people while setting the stage for the real action. But Alan Grant's a magician of another sort. He realizes events and circumstances surrounding Leslie Searle don't ring true, so he chips away at facts, unearths others until he unravels Lee Searle's story.*

The meeting broke up shortly after. The new members thanked me and handed me my fee. Most everyone asked when

distracting

we'd be meeting again.

"I'm not sure," I answered each time. "I'll email you as soon as I've decided." I didn't know how much longer I'd be staying in Ryesdale. I had no doubt Al would let me continue to live in the house, but I was no longer his girlfriend and didn't feel comfortable paying him such a ridiculously low rent. The truth was, except for Joy and Mike, nothing was keeping me here. I sighed. Maybe this was the universe's way of telling me it was time to buy a home of my own.

Or time to move in with Brian. Not that he'd asked me, but we were heading in that direction.

"Good discussion," Joy said as she drove us home. "It got me thinking."

"Thanks. Thinking about what?"

"How hard it still is for women to be promoted to jobs designated as male positions."

"We've come a long way, baby. The president of my college is a woman."

"So? There should be plenty of women presidents of universities. At least fifty per cent." She gave me the eye. "Are there?"

"All right. I get your point."

"I was kind of an oddity in the Bureau, given the type of assignments I proved I could handle." Joy mused. "Even female criminals are in the minority. Don't get me wrong, I'm not wishing there were more of them, but not as many women commit crimes as men."

I laughed. "I'd say that's a good thing, wouldn't you?"

"Sure. Less criminals all around. But are there any female mob bosses? No, right? It's the twenty-first century. Somehow, it doesn't seem right."

We rode the rest of the way in silence. Joy turned into my driveway and yanked up the emergency brake. "So, any thoughts?"

"About what?" I asked.

She glared at me. "The murders, what else? Have you forgotten?"

"For the moment," I admitted.

"Well, I haven't," Joy said. "There's a murderer out there,

and he or she might be someone we know."

"I never got a chance to tell you about seeing Evan the other day," I said, and proceeded to do so.

Joy remained silent for minutes. "Stolen candlesticks," she mused.

"And someone in the gang photographed poor Evan stealing them. I told Brian. As far as I know, Evan's not in jail."

Joy nodded. "Which means the cops plan to use him to take down the gang of thieves."

I grimaced. "The poor guy's caught in the middle because he wanted to rescue his grandchild. But why did the gang pick on him?"

"Could be to get back at him for not paying the additional ten thousand dollars."

"I'd like to find out. It so unfair."

Joy glared at me. "Unfair or not, you're not planning on asking Evan."

"Of course not."

"And keep away from that warehouse. I hate to think of what those creeps would do if they found you snooping around."

"I've no intention of doing anything that dumb," I said frostily. I opened the car door and bid her good night.

CHAPTER THIRTY-ONE

The warehouse had turned into a lightning rod for me. After classes on Thursday, I drove to the pet warehouse to buy Puss a box of treats, which the fat cat certainly didn't need. Afterward, I circled around the parked cars, swinging as close to the other warehouse as I dared. The place looked deserted. The steel doors were closed, and since there were no windows facing the parking lot, I couldn't see if there were lights on inside. I nosed the car around the side, careful to avoid the range of what I now knew was a surveillance camera. No vehicles were in sight. Ferocious barking broke out from inside the building. Startled, I stepped on the accelerator and stopped just in time to avoid crashing into the cement retaining wall. The barking grew more frenzied. Judging by the commotion, I figured at least three large dogs were inside guarding the stolen goods.

I returned late the following afternoon, telling myself there had to be *some* activity eventually. Now it was dark enough so any light from inside would be visible through the small side window. The barking started up as soon as I approached, but I saw no light or sign of occupancy.

Why was I drawn to the warehouse? Why was so I intent on catching sight of some of the other gang members? Because both murder victims, Tim and Len Lyons, had tie-ins with local criminals. Which meant they probably had tie-ins with this gang of thieves. Hell, how many more criminals were there in

Ryesdale? I knew I was missing a link in the connection, but I had no idea who or what it might be.

Though I expected another lecture on the dangers of snooping, I couldn't resist stopping by Joy's house to report my lack of findings. I found her feeding Brandon his dinner. My news brought a gleam to her eyes.

"The cops know that's where the gang's storing their ill-gotten goods." She grinned. "And you've confirmed something else."

"What's that?"

"They only bring in the dogs when they've plenty to protect. It means one night very soon the gang will load up a truck and sell the stuff to out-of-state fences."

I felt a surge of excitement. "Is that what the cops are waiting for to make their bust?"

"They want to catch the entire gang in the act," Joy said. "Now I'm going to check out all robberies and burglaries in the vicinity for the past three months. I should have done it already."

"What will that prove?" I asked.

Instead of answering, she handed me Brandon's dish and sat me down beside his high chair. "Get him to eat as much as you can while I gather some vital information."

I grinned at her. "You're hacking into the police files."

Joy punched my arm. "Not hacking, Lexie. Checking up on a few facts. This will save us hours of poring through news articles."

Brandon gurgled and gave me a big smile, not the least bit upset that his mother had disappeared in the room beyond.

"You're a good boy," I crooned, offering him a spoonful of sweet potatoes.

He shook his head and clamped his little jaw shut. I decided to play a game I'd played with Jesse when he was a baby. I lifted the spoon higher than his head, to his left, then to his right as I sang a silly jingle. Brandon's eyes followed the action. I zoomed the spoon toward my mouth and pretended to eat it. Then I zoomed it toward his mouth, and he opened it obediently.

His plate was empty when Joy burst into the kitchen, her eyes gleaming with triumph. "I found the pattern!"

"You did? Tell me."

She sat down and placed the printout on the table. "There's been a robbery every two weeks in central Nassau County, as regular as clockwork. Not always the same day or the same time, but a pattern all the same."

I studied the sheet. Most of the robberies took place within a thirty mile radius of Ryesdale. "I've read about a few of these in the paper."

"Check out the last column," Joy ordered.

I laughed. "I can't make out all those abbreviations."

Joy took the sheet of paper from me and started listing what was stolen.

"They take a variety of items—jewelry, coin and stamp collections, crystal, figurines, paintings, pieces of sculpture, small antique pieces. Nothing large. Here it is! One pair of ornate sixteenth century silver candlesticks from Germany."

"That sounds like the pair I saw."

Joy thought a moment. "I bet they made Evan go along with them one night and steal the candlesticks to incriminate himself."

I thought a bit. "Corinne helped the Billingses bring Eloisa to the U. S. Do you think she's involved with this gang of thieves?"

Joy shook her head. "I don't see the connection, though anything's possible."

I rolled my eyes. "Come on, Joy. Look at her background. Her father was a Mafia boss."

Joy gave me a pitying look. "Corinne's female. Can you see a bunch of criminals like that goliath you described taking orders from a woman?"

"Maybe she murdered Tim and Len Lyons," I persisted.

Joy threw me a scornful look. "Anything else you want to pin on her?"

I shrugged.

Joy patted my arm. "I know you don't like Corinne, and you don't like the way she treats her sister. But she's the VP of a bank, for God's sake."

"A bank that was robbed."

"A coincidence. Banks are robbed all the time."

Brandon started to whimper. Always the good mother, Joy lifted him from his highchair and started crooning to him.

I stood to leave.

"Do you want to check out the warehouse tonight?" Joy asked. "Maybe catch some action going down?"

"I'd love to, though Brian told me to stay away."

Joy laughed. "Since when has that stopped you?"

I felt my face grow warm. "Never, I guess."

"You can tell him all about it tomorrow, after we check it out tonight."

We agreed I'd pick her up at ten o'clock, then I drove home and fed a hungry Puss his meal and a few of the treats I'd bought earlier in the week. I spent a few hours grading essays. When words began to dance before my eyes, I realized I was starving. Since I wasn't in the mood to prepare dinner, I decided to grab a light dinner at the local diner.

I drove into town, my mind ceaselessly churning. Did I really believe Corinne was Ryesdale's Villainess of the Year? God knew I wasn't fond of the woman. She was abrupt and hostile toward me every chance she got. I certainly didn't approve of how she treated poor Felicity. In fact, she seemed utterly contemptuous of her sister, ever since Felicity had declared her intention to move out and live on her own. I shuddered, remembering the picture of poor Felicity's Oscar, his neck twisted.

Did Corinne do that?

Or did Johnny Scarvino kill the poor creature and make it look like Corinne was the bad one?

Was Corinne the criminal boss behind the gang robbing communities all around Ryesdale? I had no proof, only the sense that Corinne was a nasty piece of goods even though she'd helped the Billingses bring Eloisa to the U.S. And look how well that had gone for Evan? Somehow, he ended up owing the thieves big time. Why?

Corinne was a woman, and a formidable one at that. She'd become VP of her bank, and from a comment Felicity let drop, was up for a promotion. She was making it in a man's world without having to pretend to *be* a man, like Lee Searle felt she had to in *To Love and Be Wise*.

Still, playing *donna* to a crew of gangsters was a far cry from succeeding in the financial world. This might be the twenty-first century, but it wasn't likely that hoodlums like The Giant would consent to taking orders from a woman. And why would Corinne, who was making good money as an officer in a reputable bank, want to risk it all to make more money than she could possibly spend?

The busy supper hour was over, and the diner was half empty. The hostess led me to a booth beside a window in the main dining room. I glanced through the menu and had no sooner put it down when my waitress, a middle-aged pleasant woman who knew me by sight, appeared at my side.

"A grilled chicken breast over a Greek salad and decaf coffee, please."

"You got it," she said with a smile, and hurried off to put my order in.

I unzipped my parka and headed for the ladies' room past the long counter in the adjoining room. I'd reached the cashier's station when I heard a familiar giggle. I retraced my steps and glanced down the row of booths I'd just passed. Sure enough, there was Felicity.

She didn't notice me because she was gazing adoringly into the eyes of the young man sitting across the table. He had his back to me so all I could see were broad shoulders and curly black hair, but they was enough to tell me he was one hot-looking guy. *How did Felicity manage to attract the likes of him?* I blinked away the unkind question and told myself I wasn't being fair. The girl was slow, but she was pretty and very sweet.

Felicity said something to her companion. He must have found it amusing, because he began to laugh, a genuine mirthful sound. He turned his face for a moment, allowing me see his profile. I covered my mouth in time to stop my gasp.

The man with Felicity was Johnny Scarvino!

I ran to the bathroom and scrubbed my hands while I tried to calm my agitation. How could that be Johnny Scarvino when Johnny Scarvino was dead! According to Brian, he'd been shot in a holdup.

Of course it wasn't Johnny Scarvino! Felicity would never spend time with the person she feared the most in the world. She wouldn't be sitting in a diner, laughing and talking as though he were a close friend.

Only it was Johnny Scarvino sitting with Felicity. I knew because I'd seen him the night of the baby shower.

I felt like Alice in Wonderland finding herself in one preposterous scene after another. My head began to spin. I leaned against the tiled wall in keep from falling. All my suppositions were wrong. I thought of Josephine Tey and the psychology of studying faces. Johnny Scarvino looked like a nice guy, so maybe he wasn't the villain.

Maybe Felicity was as fake as her name. What if the childlike, fragile person I knew and liked was nothing more than an act?

What if Felicity had killed her boyfriend and Tim?

What if she and Johnny Scarvino worked together?

I washed my face and hands and returned to my booth as the waitress was bringing over my salad. I forced myself to take a bite of chicken, then discovered I was ravenously hungry. I glanced at Felicity and Johnny across the room. They were conversing in low tones and she no longer looked happy. A few times their voices rose with emotion, drawing glances from the other diners. Finally, Felicity shook her head vehemently at what he was saying.

"No, I don't believe you!" she shouted, and ran out.

Johnny put money on the table and chased after her.

I wanted to help, but had no idea what I could do other than call Brian. Brian, who had told me Johnny was dead.

I finished eating and paid my check. I stepped outside, shuddering as a blast of cold wind hit me in the face. It was only early December. I dreaded to think of all the cold weather we were in for the next few months. As I backed out of my parking space, my headlights caught the couple in the car beside me. It was Felicity and Johnny. He was holding her in his arms as she sobbed her heart out.

CHAPTER THIRTY-TWO

At ten o'clock, Joy climbed into my car. She set down a large thermos of coffee, fastened her seatbelt, and rubbed her hands with glee. "All set! Let's find out what going down at the warehouse."

I drove slowly. "Where did you tell Mike you were going?"

"I told him the truth." Joy scrunched up her face. "Maybe I shouldn't have. He laughed and said I'd be home in fifteen minutes."

"I suppose we will be," I said as we passed the Roberts sisters' house. No lights were on. No car was in the driveway. "This isn't a stakeout, is it?"

"I guess not, at least not for long." Joy yawned. "I'm too tired to stay out late. Been up since six."

"I saw Felicity at the diner with Johnny Scarvino," I said as I turned right.

"Did you?" I heard the smile in Joy's voice. "Do tell."

I did. After a long minute, Joy sighed. "It sounds like he was telling her a few home truths, truths she didn't want to hear, judging by her tears."

I laughed, embarrassed. "At first she looked so happy. I was beginning to think everything I liked about her was all an act. What do you think he was telling her?"

"Could be about her sister. Or their father."

I pressed my lips together. "Brian told me Johnny Scarvino

was dead. Killed in a shootout."

"Interesting."

I stopped at a red light and faced Joy. "He lied to me."

"It sure sounds that way."

"Bastard," I muttered.

"And you're angry?" Joy asked. She sounded puzzled, as if she really didn't understand.

"I can't have a relationship with someone who lies to me," I said peevishly.

"I don't see the problem," Joy said reasonably.

"Thanks."

"No, really. Sounds to me Scarvino's part of an ongoing investigation, and they needed him out of the picture till today. Brian must have had strict orders from above to put out the word that Scarvino was dead."

I frowned. "Why would Brian be involved with New Jersey gangsters?"

Joy shrugged. "Cases cross over state lines all the time. Maybe this group of thieves has ties to New Jersey."

I remembered Brian's hesitation when I'd brought up Johnny's name.

"Makes no difference. He shouldn't have lied to me. He should have trusted me."

Joy burst out laughing. "Because you're now a member of the Nassau County Police Department?"

I gritted my teeth. "Thanks for seeing it from my perspective."

She didn't bother to answer. We rode in silence. When we were five or six blocks from the warehouse, Joy exclaimed. "Look at that!"

In the distance to the right of us the sky was lit up like the Fourth of July. "They've started without us," she mumbled.

I had to slow down because traffic was moving at a snail's pace. Because of the curve in the road, I could see the bright lights were coming from the warehouse parking lot. Ahead of us, several cop cars were parked helter-skelter, blocking the road. I opened my window and heard someone shouting orders above lots of yelling and cursing. A uniformed officer instructed us to pull over to the side of the road.

"Sorry. Police business. You'll have to turn around."

I opened my mouth to ask what was happening, when Joy delivered a sharp jab to my ribs. She smiled sweetly as the cop.

"Certainly, Officer. We don't want to get caught in the crossfire."

He nodded and watched me make a U-turn, then directed other cars to do the same.

I'd driven a block when Joy barked out, "Stop!"

The brakes squealed as I obeyed.

"Hang a left and park."

Again, I obeyed and stopped at the curb of the first house on our right. A few neighbors were walking toward the main road, asking each other what was happening.

"No crowd yet," Joy murmured. "It must have just gone down. We'll get out and cross through backyards."

Minutes later we'd worked our way to the back of the pet supply warehouse. I blinked at the bright lights shining on the parking lot and the thieves' warehouse, making everything as visible as it would be in the noonday sun. My eyes were drawn to the huge moving truck jutting out from the open doors of the warehouse. Several uniformed officers were overseeing the parade of handcuffed hoods being led into the paddy wagon.

"Recognize anyone?" Joy asked.

I shook my head. "It's difficult because they're all looking down. Yes! There's The Giant!"

He was escorted out of the warehouse, kicking and cursing. One of the cops prodded him into the wagon.

"Any sign of Corinne, dressed like one of the men?" Joy asked, grinning.

"Unfortunately, no." I scanned the faces of the police higher ups. "I don't see Brian here, either."

"He's a homicide detective. I wouldn't expect him to take part in this." Joy gestured with her chin. "See the truck? They were all set to move the stolen goods out of state. This bust was done right! They caught them in the act." Pride rang in her voice.

We continued watching until the last of the gang was loaded into the police wagon, then we walked along the edge of the road to my car.

"Did it work so well because they had someone undercover

working with the gang?" I asked.

Joy grinned. "I'd put my money on your Johnny Scarvino."

Amazed, I gaped at her. "Johnny? But he's one of them!"

She laughed. "'Cause his father was?"

I nodded.

"The force gets some of its finest officers from The Families."

"Hard to believe."

A blanket of gloom settled over me, and I said nothing else as I drove home. I was unhappy because what I'd expected hadn't taken place.

I told myself I should be glad the police had caught the thieves red-handed, putting an end to the burglaries in the area. They'd be brought to trial, and most of them would do time.

Instead, I was despondent because Corinne wasn't at the warehouse, along with The Giant and his cronies. Was I so fixated on her guilt, so certain she was a criminal because I found her obnoxious and wanted to see her punished? Was I flat-out miserable because my assumption was wrong? For all I knew, Johnnie Trevino had been their boss.

"Hey!"

I shot up with a jolt. We were back in Joy's driveway, where I'd driven on auto-pilot.

"Lexie, are you all right?" she asked, sounding concerned. "Want some coffee?"

I shook my head. "Tonight they caught some bad guys, but we still don't know who killed Tim and Len Lyons."

"We don't, but that doesn't take away from the big bust. And who knows? Maybe one of the guys in that crew will know something about the murders. If they do, they'll use it in exchange for a shorter sentence."

I forced a smile. "That sounds promising. *If* they know anything about it."

"They might. For all we know, Len was one of the gang, and Tim had his own connections with the underworld."

I hugged her good-night and drove home. Puss came to greet me as I entered the house from the garage, welcoming me with head butts as if I'd been gone for days instead of hours. Of course he had an ulterior motive. He gobbled down some of his new treats and begged for more. I obliged him, telling myself my obsession with the stolen goods warehouse wasn't a total waste. Puss got something for my troubles.

My cell phone rang. I ran to retrieve it from my pocketbook, which I'd left on the hall bench. I grinned when I heard Brian's voice.

"How are you?" he asked.

"Fine. I just got back from witnessing the big bust." All the excitement must have triggered something in my system because suddenly I was starving. I made a beeline for the kitchen and peered into the freezer.

Brian chuckled. "So I heard."

No ice cream. I checked out the pantry. No cookies. "You have spies everywhere," I complained.

"Not really. I'm down at the station doing paperwork. One of the guys called in to give us the lowdown. Mentioned he'd seen you and Joy on the scene."

"And we thought we'd kept a low profile."

"The guys didn't care, as long as you and the other looky-lous kept out of the way."

I opened my mouth to complain about his lumping Joy and me with the other rubberneckers, when the sound of two women shrieking at each other came from outside. I switched off the lights and ran to the kitchen window but couldn't see anyone.

"Gotta go," I said breathlessly.

"What's up, Lexie?" Brian demanded.

"Talk to you later," I said and disconnected. The land phone rang, but I ignored it.

Felicity and Corinne must have been going at it hammer and tongs in their backyard. Why outside? The temperature was in the low forties. I ran up to my bedroom and flung open the window, but couldn't make out more than the occasional phrase Corinne spit out like acid.

"...ungrateful bitch..." "You'll come crawling back....too late..."

"I can't stay here with you another minute," Felicity answered in her little girl's voice.

I didn't catch what nastiness Corinne spewed back, only Felicity's shocked response, "No, Corinne. You mustn't!"

Though I knew Corinne would vent her anger at me the moment I showed my face, I couldn't allow her to go on abusing her sister. I grabbed my parka, slipped out the front door, and edged along the bushes separating our backyards. I'd keep out of sight until I figured out the most diplomatic way to convince Corinne to lay off her sister.

Cajole? Threaten police intervention?

"I know it's the truth because Johnny told me." Felicity's voice rose defensively. "And I believe him!"

That earned her a roar of sardonic laughter from Corinne, followed by a string of curses. Felicity must have repeated what Johnny had told her in the diner, and Corinne let her have it with both barrels.

It wasn't a gun Corinne held on her sister, but a Bowie knife. She stood behind Felicity, her sister's hair wrapped around one hand, the other hand wielding the blade at her sister's throat. I gasped. From Jesse's brief obsession with knives and daggers when he was fifteen, I knew just how lethal a Bowie knife could be.

Thank God Corinne hadn't heard or noticed me inching closer. I had to stop her from killing Felicity, though how I was going to perform that feat remained a blank in my mind. Corinne's expression was somber. Tragic. Medea came to mind. The woman in pain who causes more pain. I expected to see helpless terror in Felicity's face. Instead, fury burned in her eyes.

"You killed Leo! The only man who ever loved me!"

Corinne let loose a jeering laugh that sent shivers up my spine. "Loved you! That *idiota* didn't love you! He figured if he latched on to the boss's sister, he'd get more than his share of the take. I did you a favor by getting rid of the scum."

Felicity turned her head until the blade cut into her skin. "Nooooo. Leo didn't work for you."

Again that derisive laughter. "Who else would hire that numbskull? Robbing people he knew. I would have let him go years ago, except his father worked for the family."

Felicity bowed her head. "I didn't know. He never said."

"Hah! I'm sure there was plenty he didn't tell you. For instance, your dumb Leo had a gambling problem. He owed me big time."

Corinne must have eased up on her grip, because Felicity sank to the ground. "He wanted out of all that."

"Never an option. Leo had to repay his debts."

Like a bullet, Felicity shot to her feet. She spun around and put her hands around Corinne's neck. "You shouldn't have killed Oscar, Cathy." There was madness in her voice. Why hadn't I ever noticed?

Caught by surprise, Corinne released the knife. I watched it fall to the ground.

"Oscar was ill, Frannie." Corinne's tone remained clipped. "I put the creature out of its misery."

Felicity scowled at her sister. "You enjoyed killing him. I saw in the photo." She pursed her lips. "I suppose you killed Tim, too."

Corinne shrugged. "Leo must have told him I was behind the robberies and the bank job. Tim made the mistake of trying to blackmail me." She snorted. "What a joke! Trying that on *me*!"

"Poor Sadie." Felicity's hands went limp. "You ruined her life"

"Sadie," Corinne dismissed her with a wave of her hand. "How long was she with Tim? A day? A week? She'll get over that by Christmas."

She crouched down to retrieve the knife. I considered running at Corinne and grabbing it from her. I had surprise on my side, but Corinne was a killer. She wouldn't hesitate to stick the blade between my ribs.

Too late. Corinne was standing again. She held the knife in her right hand behind her back. Felicity stared at Corinne, apparently unconcerned about the whereabouts of the knife. It dawned on me that both sisters were crazy, each in her own way. Was it their genes? Their upbringing? Finally, Felicity said what had been troubling her the most.

"Worst of all, you killed our parents! You deserve to go to prison for that!"

Corinne's laughter rang out. "John killed our parents. Have you forgotten the trial? Why we're living here in Ryesdale? John's in prison for the rest of his life."

"No, *you* killed Mommy and Daddy. You hated him for being so mean to us. Johnny told me."

"Johnny's dead."

"He isn't," Felicity insisted. "I saw him. He told me everything."

Corinne grabbed her sister's hair, twisting her around so that they were in the same position as when I came upon them.

"You're crazy, Frannie, you know that?" Corinne said in her sister's ear. "I told you, 'Don't listen to him. Be strong.' But you let Daddy get to you."

Felicity's sobs grew stronger. "I wanted him to love me, but he always pushed me away. He said we were useless because we're girls."

Corinne's voice turned harsh. "Our own mother was no better. She should have protected us from his anger. His cruelty. That's why I killed them. I did it for us!"

"You shouldn't have!" Felicity began to cry, sniffles and moans turning into wrenching sobs. "Mommy tried to help."

"She sent us away! To that cold place where everyone hated us."

I watched transfixed as Corinne let go of Felicity's hair and pulled her sister against her chest. She hugged Felicity, all the while never loosening her grip on the Bowie knife.

"I love you, Frannie, but you're out of control. I have to end it, once and for all."

She pulled back Felicity's head to draw the knife across her throat. I opened my mouth to scream, but nothing came out.

"No you don't, Frannie!"

A figure flew past me and tackled the two sisters to the ground. The struggle lasted less than a minute. Johnny Scarvino held Corinne in a tight grip, her hands behind her.

"Felicity, call the police," he ordered.

Felicity stared at him.

Johnny glared down at Corinne. "I knew you killed them and framed my father, but I had to hear it for myself." He tapped his chest. "I got it all down on tape."

I wanted to hold Felicity in my arms, but something primordial kept me from moving forward. "I'll call the police," I offered.

"Thanks, Lexie," Johnny said, sending me a beautiful smile.

He knew I was there all the time. I started for my house when

I heard a police siren coming closer. Then another. I grinned as a wave of relief sweep over me. Brian! He'd figured it out.

He was at my side a minute later, then he closed in on Felicity and Corinne or Catherine and Francisca. Johnny stepped back to let the police officers do their job.

CHAPTER THIRTY-THREE

"So tell me, Is it true you guys are planning to move in together?" Mike shouted above the soft rock and conversation buzz in the elegant Skyler Room of The Lion's Head Inn.

I didn't answer. Neither did Brian. Instead, he leaned over to nuzzle my neck.

"Well?" Mike persisted. His third vodka martini had made him oblivious to how close I was to taking a swing at his face. He had no business asking about something I'd agreed to but hadn't quite accepted in the deepest recesses of my soul.

Mike remained standing before us, grinning like a fool. Clearly, he wasn't walking away until he got a satisfactory answer.

"That's the plan," Brian answered, "soon as Lexie can wrap her mind around the idea." He planted a kiss on my nose. Despite my best intentions, I giggled. "Al's the most considerate landlord," Brian continued. "He told her to stay in the house as long as she likes." He tilted my head so he could kiss me full on the lips. "And I'm amenable to letting her take the rest of the year to make her decision."

Now I wanted to kick Brian in the shins for being so damn clever. So I was frightened. I was scared. He had no right to turn this into a joke. Though I knew he was serious about the deadline. Less than three weeks remained to the year, but who was counting?

"You guys will be happy. Like Joy and me." Mike zoomed in to hug us, and managed to drop his lemon peel on my shoe.

I pushed him away. "Mike, you're turning into a sloppy drunk. You're the host, remember?"

My words had no affect on him. He planted a resounding kiss on my cheek. "I'm the host. I can have as many martinis as I like."

I breathed a sigh of relief when he finally wandered off to ask, God knew what other personal questions, of his guests.

The song changed. Brian took my hand. "Care to dance?"

The dance floor was small, forcing us to hold each other close. He hummed as he wove me around Joy and Mike's guests, most of whom I knew.

I felt safe in Brian's arms, secure with a tingle of sexual anticipation. So why was I terrified of moving in with him?

"Don't fret, Lexie. We'll be fine together," he whispered.

"I know. I want to. I just—"

"Have cold feet. Had bad experiences. Need my space," Brian finished for me.

I laughed. "All of the above."

He stroked my cheek with the back of his hand. "I'll give you plenty of space," he said softly. "And you won't have to make dinner most nights."

I nodded. "I want us to live together. It's just taking some getting used to."

And that was it, I realized. I was terrified of making changes in my personal life for fear of making another wrong decision.

But Brian wasn't a wrong decision. He was decent through and through, and I loved him. I rested my head on his shoulder and smiled up at him.

We wandered over to the *hors d-oeuvres* table and helped ourselves to mini quiches and skewers of chicken satay. We managed to find an empty table. A minute later, Marge and Evan joined us. We chatted about Joy, who looked amazingly sexy in a slinky black dress, and the delicious food. Then Evan leaned over to kiss my cheek.

"I never thanked you for getting me to spill everything to this guy."

I patted his arm. "I knew you weren't at that thieves' den on your own volition."

Marge's face turned a stormy gray. "That Corinne, or whatever her name is, is as evil as Lucifer."

"She helped bring Eloisa to you," I said.

"And tried to force Evan to steal for her gang," Marge said. "Her greed has no limits."

Sadie sank into the empty chair and fanned herself with a paper napkin. "She's more monstrous than Simon in *Brat Farrar*—killing her parents, robbing the bank where she worked."

Joy came to stand behind me. "Come to think of it, she took on a male role like Lee Searle. Who would have thought."

I couldn't resist saying, "I told you, didn't I? You underestimated her."

"What's happening with poor Felicity?" Sadie asked.

"I'm afraid the whole episode's caused her to have a nervous breakdown. She's in a facility, getting the proper care," Joy said.

"And Johnny Scarvino's looking in on her," I said. "Odd how that worked out."

"They're working on releasing his father from prison," Brain said, "though he probably belongs there for all the other crimes he's committed."

I took the last bite of what remained on my plate and let the conversation swirl around me. Corinne was behind bars and the rest of us had resumed our lives. I was glad to be in the company of friends, all of whom were dear to me. Hard to believe I'd known them for four months and Brian for all of six months.

I giggled.

"What's so funny?" he wanted to know.

"Nothing." The trio was playing an old Cole Porter song. "Wanna dance?"

Brian stood. "I thought you'd never ask."

To my readers:

Writing the Golden Age of Mystery Book Club Mysteries gives me the opportunity to share some of my favorite mystery authors with my readers. Josephine Tey is one of the best, and I hope that reading *Murder the Tey Way* has inspired you to read some of her novels.

Marilyn Levinson

ABOUT THE AUTHOR

A former Spanish teacher, Marilyn Levinson writes mysteries, romantic suspense, and books for kids.

Marilyn loves traveling, reading, knitting, doing Sudoku, and visiting with her granddaughter, Olivia, on FaceTime. She is co-founder and past president of the Long Island chapter of Sisters in Crime.

Her website is: www.MarilynLevinson.com

If you've enjoyed reading *Murder the Tey Way*,
please consider writing a short review on your favorite online
retailer or Goodreads.

Made in the USA
Coppell, TX
19 October 2021